VESUVIUS

ALEX J. MCDONALD

www.alexjmcdonald.com

authorHOUSE®

AuthorHouse™
1663 Liberty Drive, Suite 200
Bloomington, IN 47403
www.authorhouse.com
Phone: 1-800-839-8640

First published by AuthorHouse 3/31/2009

ISBN: 978-1-4389-6852-0 (sc)
ISBN: 978-1-4389-6853-7 (hc)

Printed in the United States of America
Bloomington, Indiana

This book is printed on acid-free paper.

Dedicated to my brother-in-law
Michael Pearson
and his
wife, Betsy

For the battle they are fighting together and
Their unequivocal love
You are my Heroes

When seeking revenge; dig two graves

Confucious

CHAPTER 1

He rolled onto his side and scanned the room. When he tried to rise, bile rose in his throat. He waited-swallowing hard trying to choke it down then pushed up into a sitting position. The room tilted and he paused, waiting for the room to straighten up. When the dizziness passed he rose, carefully waiting for the room to fall from under him but it didn't. He took a few tentative steps and finally, confident he wouldn't fall on his face, crossed to the bedroom.

He stood at the bedroom door and waited for it, knowing the loneliness was there somewhere, sneaking up on him. The bed was neatly made as it always was, owing to not having been slept in for two years; the bed covers pulled taut, just the way she left them; her shoes still on the floor next to her side of the bed. He crossed the room hoping to sneak past but the sadness was there swirling around the floor like a fog, a tangible living thing, snaking around the base of the furniture, sliding up to engulf him once again. He tried to ignore it but it would not be denied. He realized it was not as strong lately; it seemed to have lost some of its power.

He made it to the bathroom and turned on the shower while the loneliness slithered under the door and hung in the corners, around the base of the toilet. The booze gave him some peace but it never lasted long enough. The pain dulled when he was occupied with work or other mental activities, but lay in wait for him to return unprepared so it could barge in on his mind, beating him up inside once again.

Ali showered then dried himself and glanced in the mirror; the bags under his eyes weren't too noticeable. He studied the gray in his mustache, the crooked nose, broken five times and felt old and tired. Ali dressed then went to the kitchen and poured himself a cup of hot, sweet Cuban coffee. Retrieving the morning paper from the front stoop, he sat at the dinner table and read the paper slowly, wondering if anything in it was really worth reading. It was full of death and crime and bullshit. He figured breakfast was a waste of time knowing his stomach probably would rebel against food anyway and was glad he drank vodka because the hangovers were less intense, at least he could function the next day. An old partner who was an alcoholic had taught him that. The same old partner ended up being forced to retire because he got caught drinking on duty and ended up homeless, sleeping in the bushes of a city park, covered with bug bites and open sores, smelling so bad he could not even stand himself. He eventually wandered, drunk, into the street and was hit by a fast moving car, lying dead, broken and bloody. Spending a lifetime as a spectator to the many ways humanity could mistreat each other would do that. It would be a few hours before Ali felt normal. He'd had a lot of practice the last two years.

Ali put his coffee cup in the sink and ran some water in it deciding he would wash it tonight with the rest of the dishes, maybe. He reached onto the top of the refrigerator and retrieved the pistol, clipping it to his belt. He picked up the leather clip and looked at the round gold badge with the seal of the state of Florida, police department and detective painted on it. He pinned the badge to the front of his belt and left the apartment.

Alejandro 'Ali' Castillo parked his Chevy in the back parking lot of the police station and trudged to the back door, stepping aside to let two uniformed officers pass. Inside the hallway, next to the door to the officer's locker room was a notice for a meeting of the newly forming Cuban-American officers Association. Alejandro didn't quite understand this need to have associations. In Miami, the police department had lots of organizations, Cuban-American officers association, Haitian-American officers Association, African-American officers and the Gay and Lesbian officers Association. Alejandro wondered why everyone wanted to be hyphenated Americans. Why couldn't they just be Americans? He especially didn't understand the Gay and Lesbian Associations. When did a sexual preference become special? Why not the child molesters and the people who had sex with animals? Maybe they should have an association. Alejandro figured if you made yourself different from the majority, you would be treated differently than the majority. Besides, there were only fifteen Cuban officers in the department, not a real big association. Didn't make sense, but then nothing had made sense to him since Maria died. He wasn't even sure why he got out of bed in the morning.

Alejandro poured himself a cup of coffee in the detective squad room and took one sip when the commander, Lieutenant Burt Davis, breezed into the squad room and frowned at Alejandro with a disapproving look.

"Don't get comfortable, got a body on Design Row. Get your ass over there and find out what's up. Crime Scene is there already. See Sergeant Smith." Davis said as he disappeared into his office.

Design Row was a street of shops where the rich and politically powerful spent their time. Interspersed among the shops of expensive clothiers were restaurants with menus without prices. If you had to ask how much the cost, you shouldn't be there was the philosophy. The body was in the alley behind one of those restaurants. Ali could see the feet protruding from behind a green dumpster. He was met by a patrol sergeant in uniform, sweating in the morning sun. The weather should turn cool in a few weeks, bringing a sigh of relief from the poor slobs who had to wear polyester uniforms and thirty pounds of gear around their waists.

"Morning, Ali," Sgt. Smith shook his hand. "Nice way to start the day, huh?"

"Not hardly," Ali replied. "What's the story?"

"Patrol unit got the call from the Haitian cleanup guy, came in early to straighten up for the lunch crowd. Found the body when he took out the garbage. Victim's a white male, possibly thirties. Hard to tell though, the killer messed him up pretty bad. Can't see much of the face, it's pretty mutilated." Sergeant Smith flipped his notebook closed.

"Good thing the power crowd didn't find him first. The chief would have gotten an early morning call from one of the politically powerful." Ali smiled grimly.

"Probably will anyway. You know how it goes. Demands for extra patrols, screaming about the crime rate and all that," Smith agreed.

"Well, let's go spoil my day." Ali grimaced as he walked toward the dumpster.

The body lay on its back. The face, or what was supposed to be the face, pointed into the morning sun. The skin was chalk white and shiny, like most dead bodies after the blood stopped flowing. The corpse was fully clothed, in fairly expensive clothes at that. Ali squatted next to the body and took an inventory, noticing the backs of the hands were a deep purple color. The face was criss-crossed with deep cuts, showing the white of the bone underneath. The cuts were clean, no blood, apparently done after the heart stopped - post mortem. The skin between the cuts was also purple, more lividity. Ali remembered the first dead body he had seen with lividity. He thought the victim had been severely beaten. The lividity meant the body had lain face down for a while with the arms down by its sides, probably somewhere else. It had been dumped here.

Ali noticed a blood stain on the shirt, upper chest. Not enough blood. Something was wrong with this picture. He slipped on a pair of rubber gloves and rolled the body onto its side. There was a small stain in the center of the back of the shirt. He rolled the body onto its back again and unbuttoned the shirt. The hole in the chest was ragged and shaped almost like a triangle. Exit wound. He motioned to a crime scene technician and together they worked the shirt down and rolled the body onto its side again. A bullet hole in the center of the back, perfectly round with charred edges. Point blank. Ali straightened up and looked at the crime scene technician.

"This guy was shirtless when he was shot. The cuts on the face were postmortem mutilation. The gun was placed against the skin so he knew the person who shot him then he was dressed and dumped here," Ali said, thinking out loud. The crime scene tech nodded.

"Pretty strange," the tech answered.

"I don't know why but I get a weird feeling about this one. Make sure we get good close-ups of all the wounds before they move him I don't want to lose the appearance of them. Did we check his pockets yet?"

"Yea, I got his wallet right here," the tech answered, handing it to him.

"Nothing's missing. Money and credit cards still inside. ID's there too."

Ali took the wallet and thumbed through it. He looked at the driver's license picture and a handsome blond man, whose face had almost pretty features with a Scandinavian looking nose and forehead, stared back at him. The victim could have been any one of the male actors on the numerous television shows. Ali suddenly wondered if it had been this way with Maria. Some cop looking at her driver's license because he couldn't tell what she looked like, trapped in the tangled, twisted metal of what had been her car. He pushed the thought from his mind but it took effort. It didn't want to leave.

Ali copied the address from the driver's license. He would have to wait for the medical examiner to positively identify the body.

Glancing down at it he realized no one who knew the victim would ever recognize him now. He checked the wallet again and found a VIP card for the Parrot Cage, a local gay bar. So the victim was gay. Ali wondered if he had been the victim of a lover's quarrel. Gay lover's quarrels got pretty violent, mutilation not an uncommon occurrence. Ali sighed. At least it was a place to start.

Ali followed the walkway through a jungle of tropical plants, onto a patio of gray and red brick giving it the feeling of an old, Spanish style home. He peered through the frosted glass of the front doors; past a large Egret etched in the glass then pushed the button for the doorbell and could hear a ring somewhere in the depths of the house. Finally, a white indistinct blob materialized behind the frosted glass and the front door opened, revealing a kindly looking black woman dressed in a white nurse's uniform. He introduced himself, holding out his hand, hoping she wouldn't notice his discomfort and wondered if the cop that came to tell him about Maria had felt this way. This was a part of the job every cop hated, one never knew what to say or how to comfort the next of kin and still ask questions without seeming callous. He gently explained why he had come and she put her hand to her mouth with a gasp when he told her of the body. He could sense her shock and sadness, having been in her place himself. She asked him to wait and disappeared into the interior of the house, leaving him to admire the furnishings. There were satin covered couches of various sizes and colors. The paintings on the walls were obviously expensive and Ali recognized some of them although he didn't know the names of the pictures or the painters. The furnishings had a subtle oriental flair. The floors were light gray tile. It was open and airy; giving the feeling it was larger than it was.

The nurse returned and motioned him to follow her through the house then led him through a tiled hallway, his footsteps echoing on the floor. The trek ended in a bedroom, dominated by a large bed, a figure in the bed was gaunt and pale and an oxygen tube snaked across the man's face pumping oxygen into his nose. His skin was gray and peppered with dark splotches and his eyes were sunken in dark sockets and his breathing was labored. A metal table next to the bed was littered with medicine bottles. The sight of him made Ali take an unconscious step back, almost afraid to get too close as if he might become that ghastly figure in the bed.

"It's all right Detective. I'm not contagious, although I am dying." the figure in the bed rasped in a barely audible whisper. "Please, do come in."

Ali stepped into the room and stood at the foot of the bed. He cleared his throat and glanced uncomfortably around the room.

"I'm sorry to disturb you." Ali began.

The man in the bed raised a hand, cutting him off.

"Vera explained to me why you're here. You have news about Michael. My name is Daniel Murray. Michael Peterson and I were married, not legally of course, partners most people would say. Society has a difficult time understanding people like us." Murray smiled sadly. Ali nodded.

"We found a body. Murdered I'm afraid. We won't be able to identify the victim positively for awhile but the identification on the body was Michael Peterson's."

"And your most likely suspect is whoever knew him best, am I correct?" Murray asked. "It's okay detective, I'm an attorney so I know how these things go. Right now you're wondering why I am not reacting more strongly, right?" He smoothed the covers on top of him with a quivering, blue veined hand, the hands of a skeleton.

"I'm dying Detective Castillo, probably very soon. I am in the end stage of AIDS. I will be dead in a few weeks, maybe even days so the thought of death doesn't shock me and I'm too tired to react. I have been waiting for death for some time now. I can't cry or scream and yell like the loved ones of most of your victims, I don't have the strength. See these dark circles on me? Those are Kaposi's sarcoma, cancer. It's one of the symptoms. My body is being invaded by all kinds of diseases. One of them will take me very soon now." Tears welled up in Murray's eyes. "I loved Michael. We've had a monogamous relationship for five years now. Five years and I can't even cry for him and as you can see Detective, I certainly couldn't have killed him."

Ali tried hard not to be revolted. He feared he would catch something just from breathing the air despite what the scientists said.

"When did you last see Mr. Peterson?"

"Last evening, he went out around eight, I think. I took my medicine. It puts me out of my pain and out of consciousness," Murray answered.

"Do you know where he went?" Ali asked.

"The Parrot Cage probably. Michael liked the place. He had been going out in the evening more often recently. He needed to get away from this, I suppose. Watching me die took its toll on him." Murray replied, weakly waving his hands around the room.

"I'm sorry for your loss. If I have any more questions, I'll be in touch," Ali took one last look around the room and at the pathetic man in the bed.

"I doubt seriously I'll be here when you return," Murray replied. He reached toward a tube near his side and pushed a button on a plastic square enclosing the tube. "Morphine," He smiled sadly.

Ali met up with the nurse in the hallway and she silently led him to the door. At the front foyer he turned to her.

"I'll be in touch," he said to the nurse.

"We won't be here. Mr. Murray has days at most." She closed the door behind him.

Ali was stuck in traffic and had time to think. Queers, he would never understand it. Ali had grown up with a macho father and a very feminine mother, even had done his share of picking on the effeminate kid in high school. They didn't know for sure if the kid was queer but it was enough he had feminine traits. The thought of two men or two women having sex together was nauseating. Alejandro had been a boxer since grade school, when his father enrolled him in the YMCA boxing club, learning to move and dodge the punches of his opponents, and to hit back. He had won the Golden Gloves in high school. His father called him Ali, short for Alejandro. Over the years, the nickname had become synonymous with the famous boxer. His world was one of macho tough guys who had no tolerance for the other types. Now, all you heard about was perverts, the Priests who had sex with altar boys, teachers having sex with male students. The world had gone totally nuts and Ali longed for the old way when things made more sense.

He thought about Murray and his apparently genuine feelings for the dead guy, if he was in fact, Michael Peterson. He remembered the day Maria died; how she left in the morning to go to work leaving Alejandro sleeping after a late night callout. He didn't even know she had left until he was awakened by a loud pounding on the door, blinking at the uniformed cop in the morning sunlight and struggling to figure out what the hell he was talking about. *Accident? Maria? What was going on?* He looked out in the parking lot and realized her car was gone. Suddenly, the words pushed through the fog of interrupted sleep, and his world crashed in on him. He heard the cop telling him he would drive him to the hospital and Ali dressed quickly, numbly, not even sure what clothes he put on. The drive to the hospital was a lost memory, Ali did not notice anything outside the windows because he was praying and hoping that this was a mistake, it had to be; this could not be happening, he just saw her this morning sleeping peacefully when he crawled groggily into bed.

The emergency room was crowded with people including Lt. Davis, the department chaplain and Maria's co-workers from this very hospital which was where they met. Her friends hugged him and said something to him but he could not remember their names but knew they just seemed familiar. His mind raced as one's does in these times. *She will be okay its probably just a few bumps and bruises. What if she's not? What if she dies, what am I gonna do? Why dosen't somebody tell me something? Where the hell is the doctor?* He felt as if his heart would explode. His stomach roiled and he felt lightheaded. The people around him moved as if in slow motion. Whispered conversations he could hear but not comprehend. He prayed, *Please God let her be alright.* Time seemed to race and stand still all at the same moment. LT. Davis sat next to him on the hard, uncomfortable, fake leather couch and put his hand on Ali's shoulder. Ali knew it was there but could not feel it. He was numb most of the time afterwards. Everything seemed surreal. Ali remembered the day and the exact moment they had met. He had come to the hospital to get some x-rays on a case and Maria worked in the Radiology department as a transcriptionist. She had greeted him with the prettiest smile he had ever seen and he was instantly smitten. They chatted for awhile and Ali broke one of his cardinal rules, never date someone he met on the job. They spent every day together since that first date and both felt as if it was kismet and they were meant to be together. *Now God is going to take her from me? He would not do that something so cruel; she is going to be alright! Where is the damn doctor, what is taking so long?* Suddenly, a doctor appeared down the hallway and approached and it was that moment when time stops, that split second when hope and despair have equal standing. Your heart stops beating and you can't breathe as if taking a breath will bring bad news. That one split second in time where nothing happens and everything happens at the same time. Your mind races and stands still simultaneously, your heart hopes beyond hope that everything will be okay but fear and dread battle for control. The doctor is saying that he is sorry, that they did everything they could but she is gone. You feel as if a giant hand has slammed into your chest and your body and mind collapse into themselves and you can't stand up. The people around you are sobbing and holding each other but you can't feel anything but disbelief and numbness and anger and sorrow and rage all at the same time. You ask to see her, as if needing to be convinced that this is not a mistake or a nightmare you will suddenly wake up from.

"Give us a few minutes. You don't want to see her like this," the doctor says. *Like what? What did they do to her, why can't I see her?* Then the doctor walked away leaving Ali to stand stock still, afraid to move because then this will all be real and it can't be real, this isn't happening. Then the doctor reappeared and led Ali and Lt. Davis and the chaplain down the hall to a treatment room cluttered with medical equipment and monitors, their screens all dark as if standing reverent vigil. On the gurney in the center of the room was a body covered up to the neck with a clean white sheet. There was no blood. *How can there be no blood?* Ali could see her face at the end of the sheet when he entered but he could not see her clearly from this angle. *Maybe it's not her maybe they were wrong.* Then he walked stiff legged to the table. He thought it was her but she looked so different with dark lacerations and bruises against the white skin. *Is it her? No it isn't her but it looks like her but it can't be her God please this isn't her* but he knew it was and the world stopped. The rest of it was a daze. He wanted to walk outside and scream at the top of his lungs at God and damn him for this. He wanted to punch the walls but the strength to do so escaped him.

The funeral was a fog, but two weeks later he surfaced and the pain grabbed hold of him and wouldn't let go. When it hit, he had screamed and cried until he gasped for air and shook violently. He punched the walls, harder than he ever hit an opponent in the ring, breaking his hand in the process. He finally collapsed, exhausted. The pain was only a constant emptiness now. The house was an empty, mute statue with no warmth, no happiness. God, I need a drink he thought.

Ali changed directions and headed to the Parrot Cage. He knew it would be closed at this hour but he wanted to see if any cars were left in the parking lot from the night before. Like Michael

Peterson's car. He suddenly realized he had forgotten to ask what kind of car Peterson drove. Shit! He would have to call and find out. He was forgetting details like that lately.

The parking lot of the Parrot Cage was empty. Luckily, it was a small bar, unlike the bigger gay bars in the city. One in particular was huge, next to a shopping center and on weekend nights, the customer's cars filled the parking lot of the bar and the shopping center. Ali hoped Peterson hadn't gone there from the Parrot Cage. Hopefully, someone would remember Peterson being here. If Peterson went to the other one, no one would remember him in the throngs of customers. Ali headed toward the morgue.

Ali pushed the metal door open to exam room number three. The coroner was standing at a sink, her back to him. The body of Michael Peterson lay naked on a metal table in the center of the room, a towel covering his genitals. The body had been cleaned and prepped for examination. Ali cleared his throat.

"Hey Ali, Howya' doing?" The coroner asked, turning to face him.

"Okay Sarah, how about you?" Ali smiled.

Dr. Sarah Barrett was a thirty something brunette, who ran five miles every day. She always had a bright-eyed look, even in the middle of all this gore. Ali approached the body on the table and looked down into the face of Michael Peterson. He had learned to keep from going crazy by considering a dead body as a curiosity. What had the priest said at Maria's funeral that the body was merely a vessel? Appropriate.

"What have you found so far?" Ali asked.

"Well, you were right about the wound. Gunpowder speckling shows it was point blank. The one in the back was the entry; the one in the chest was exit. Caliber looks like a forty-five. We'll know more later and you were also right about the shirt being put back on after death. No bullet hole in the back of the shirt. The angle of the wound appears to indicate the victim was bent over in front of the shooter, with his shirt off."

"Did he have his pants on do you think?" Ali asked.

Barrett raised her eyebrows questioningly.

"Just humor me, okay?" Ali said.

Barrett retrieved the pants from a biohazard bag on a nearby table and held them up to the light.

"Judging from the lack of bloodstains on the front, I would think his pants were off." She pointed to the front of the pants. "Why?"

"I'm just trying to cover all the bases. Do me a favor, check for any signs of sexual activity but do it later, after I leave. This guy was gay, and I wonder if he had a lover's quarrel with somebody. What about the mutilation to the face?"

"That is kind of interesting. There were a total of four slashes, a very sharp knife with a thin blade. The cuts go down the center, across the middle and then one across at each angle. Kind of shaped like an asterisk. The cuts were post-mortem. Either the mutilation was for kicks or to slow down identification," Barrett said.

"Did we positively ID this guy yet?" Ali asked.

"We rolled the prints first thing. I'm just waiting for comparisons to give positive a match," Barrett replied.

"Okay. Call me when you have everything," Ali said.

"See ya" Barrett replied, leaning over the body again. She looks like she's praying Ali thought as he left.

Ali stopped at the reception desk and used the phone. He waited until it rang seven times and was just about to give up when Murray's nurse answered.

"Murray residence."

"Hi. This is Detective Castillo. May I speak to Mister Murray?" Ali asked her.

"I'm sorry Detective. Mister Murray isn't able to talk right now."

"Oh. Well maybe you can answer a question for me. What kind of car did Mister Peterson drive?" Ali asked.

"A Ford Taurus, station wagon. Light blue." the nurse answered. Ali noticed she sounded pleased she remembered.

"Do you know the license number?" Ali asked hopefully.

"No, sorry I don't," The nurse answered. Ali thanked her and hung up. No matter, he could get the tag number from DMV.

Ali returned to the office and checked with the DMV. He received the tag number to Peterson's car. Next, he called dispatch and put out the description of the car for road patrol. Hopefully, some street cop would find it.

Ali returned to the Parrot Cage. *Early afternoon, should be somebody there by now.* It was not uncommon for the owner of a bar to spend the afternoon cleaning for the next night's business. He spotted a black Mercedes in the parking lot and figured someone was there. The Parrot Cage was on the point of a curved back street, just off the beach. The breeze from the ocean swirled around the corner and blew strongly down the street as tourists strolled past at the end of the street, enjoying the ocean view.

Ali parked around the back and walked to the front door. He peeked through the glass door and spotted a tall thin man behind the bar. He tapped on the glass and the man walked to the window, peeked through and yelled from behind the door, "We're closed!" Ali held his badge to the glass.

"Police, I need to ask you some questions," Ali replied.

A key turned in the lock and swung the door open. Ali held up his badge for a better look and stepped inside. The place smelled of stale beer and old cigarette smoke. It was an old bar, with wooden floors and walls. The bar along the back wall was ornately carved along the top.

The man wore a flowery print shirt and very tight khaki colored pants, his shirt was unbuttoned down to mid chest revealing numerous gold chains. He had jet black hair, slicked back into a ponytail and a carefully trimmed mustache which was pencil thin and followed the line of his upper lip. He wore a diamond stud earring in his right ear and what appeared to be an expensive ring on every finger, diamond bands on both thumbs.

"What can I do for you officer?" the man asked, suspicion and a little disdain crept in his tone.

"I'm investigating a homicide. The victim was last known to be headed to this place," Ali replied.

"Oh, dear God!" the man exclaimed, holding his hand to his mouth. "Please, come in." He ushered Ali to a table and sat across from him.

"Are you the owner here?" Ali asked.

"Yes. Bradley Fontaine," the man replied. He held out his hand and Ali shook it. Fontaine shook hands without grasping Ali's hand the rings biting into Ali's palm. He fought the urge to wipe his hand on his pant leg. Ali's father had taught him to shake hands firmly. It showed strength.

"I'm Detective Castillo," Ali replied.

"Forgive my initial reaction, Detective. It's just that gay people are always harassed by the police. I assumed you were here to check my liquor license or something," Fontaine smiled.

Yeah, and all white cops beat up black people for fun, Ali thought. He was really tired of hearing how cops mistreated members of special groups; like cops sat in roll call and debated whether to beat a black man, Spanish, or gay man that day. Every cop Ali had ever known treated everybody with the respect but if you acted like an asshole, you got treated like one, race, creed nor color entered into it. Ali couldn't care less if Fontaine slept with sheep.

"Are you acquainted with Michael Peterson?" Ali asked.

"Michael? Of course, he's a nice man. He and Daniel, his lover, came here frequently. They even met here, I seem to recall. Poor Daniel, I hear he doesn't have long. Have you met Daniel?" Fontaine wiped at an invisible speck on the table.

"I've spoken to Mr. Murray, yes," Ali answered. "Do you know if Mr. Peterson was here last night or in the last few days?"

"Is this about Michael? Is he involved in something?" Fontaine asked.

"Mr. Peterson was murdered," Ali answered, watching for any reaction. What he saw surprised him. Fontaine's eyes welled with tears. He quickly grabbed a napkin off the table and wiped his eyes.

"Why don't they leave us in peace?" Fontaine sighed.

"They who?" Ali asked.

"Society, they are forever assaulting us, harassing us. Why can't they live and let live?" Fontaine replied. "Do you know why I named this place the Parrot Cage? It is symbolic of the gay in today's society. A beautiful bird trapped in a cage of social unacceptance."

Here we go, Ali thought. He tried to adjust his expression to show caring. "Back to my question, was Mister Peterson here last night?" Ali asked. Before Fontaine could reply, a door opened somewhere behind the bar and a husky man with shoulder length, blond hair appeared. He was shirtless but wore a black leather vest and black leather pants. An earring six inches long dangled from one ear.

"My bartender, Greg." Fontaine solved the mystery. "Greg?" Fontaine yelled to the bartender, "Was Michael Peterson here last night?"

"Yeah, he's been here a lot lately." The bartender replied.

"Did he leave with anyone?" Ali asked.

"No. He danced with a few people, but I saw him leave alone," Greg replied approaching the table. "Michael has been here a lot since Daniel got ill. I think he's probably looking for someone to care about him. Watching a lover die is horrible." Ali fought the emotion welling up inside him. He didn't feel sorry for Peterson or Murray. At least they had some hope for awhile. Maria was gone in a flash and he couldn't even say 'I love you' one last time.

"Has Peterson been spending time with anyone in particular?" Ali asked both of them. Fontaine shook his head.

"He's left with a few different people. But no one more than once."

"No one that might have gotten jealous or angry over Peterson seeing someone else?" Ali asked.

"No, sorry" the bartender, replied.

Ali left his card and asked them to call him if they remembered anything. He checked the parking lot for Peterson's car again, still no light blue Taurus. He had hoped someone would drive up in it and he could pounce on him and make the arrest and this would be over. Well, it looks like Peterson left in his own car. Ali wondered if he took someone with him. He thought about the conversation. Peterson had a few different lovers recently. He wondered if Murray knew. Gays seemed like such pathetic, needy creatures to Ali.

Ali turned on the television and settled on the sleeper sofa with his sandwich and a beer, watching the television without really seeing it. He was numb as usual. If he thought about things, feelings came with the thoughts and, the feelings were too painful. The loneliness hung in the room. He finished his sandwich and drank another beer, then another and one after that and felt himself getting foggy. Good, that would keep him from feeling. He staggered to the bathroom and undressed, looking at himself in the mirror, noticing the soft, loose belly. His once hard, muscular body looked like soft rubber. He felt the fear inside. Forty years old felt like a hundred. He had worked out all of his life, now suddenly he was middle-aged and out of shape. Forty had sneaked up on him and made him useless. He was not sure what happened. It seemed that one minute he was a young, tough man who could run for miles and spar in the ring for ten rounds and still go home feeling fine then one day he stopped and he was forty and out of shape. It was said that women had a change of life but no one ever mentioned the change for men. Maria had noticed the change but she never said anything to him about it, never mentioned the added weight and the lack of enthusiasm for things he had once been on fire about. He thought of friends his age that had gotten cancer or heart disease and died and wondered how much time he had left. Better to go quick like Peterson.

He knew he should get back in shape, but every time he thought about it he felt too tired and he hated himself for that. Now, he felt like he couldn't get the strength to scratch his head. Two more beers and he felt groggy. Maybe he could sleep without the bad dreams tonight. It wasn't likely but it was worth a try. He fell asleep hating himself. And the dreams came again.

Ali hadn't even finished his first cup of coffee when his day turned to shit. He sensed a presence and looked up to see two men approaching. They stopped at the front of his desk and the shorter one gave him a condescending look. He was dressed in a very expensive charcoal color suit which could not even begin to hide the rolls of soft fat underneath. He clutched a hand-tooled leather briefcase. The other man was tall and slim, dressed in a peach pullover and slacks, his graying hair neatly styled.

The one in the expensive suit asked, "Detective Castillo?"

Ali nodded in reply.

"I'm Irving Abramowitz, the attorney for CAD. You know what CAD is?"

Ali did but shook his head anyway.

"CAD stands for Coalition Against Discrimination. I am their attorney. This gentleman is Rodney James. He is the president of CAD," Abramowitz finished.

"What can I do for you?" Ali asked, knowing the answer would not make him happy. CAD was a politically active group which created a monumental pain in the ass for police departments.

"We're here to discuss the Peterson situation." Abramowitz smiled an oily grin.

"What about it?" Ali countered, watching Rodney James for a reaction. He could see the contempt in his eyes.

"We would like to know what you're doing on this case," The attorney answered.

"Are you a member of the family of Mister Peterson?"

"No. We 're a concerned party," James interjected

"Sorry gentlemen I will not discuss an ongoing investigation with anyone but immediate family of the victim. Since you are not family, this investigation is none of your business unless of course you have information to further my investigation." Ali leaned back in his chair.

"So this is a typical case of a queer getting killed and the police could care less." James stated coldly.

"No. This is a case of it being none of your business." Ali felt the back of his neck getting warm.

"This is par for the course. If the cops aren't beating up gays, they look the other way when someone else does," James replied.

"Look pal. I investigate every case to the best of my ability, no matter who the victim is. I don't like it when somebody dies on my watch so don't come in here spewing your bullshit. Now get out of my office." Ali fought to keep his anger in check. He felt like punching Mr. Peach Ensemble James in the face.

"We're wasting our time here," Abramowitz rose to leave. "Just remember, Detective, we'll be watching. This is a hate crime and it will be treated as such or we'll demand to know why."

"Fine, just stay out of my way," Ali spat at Abramowitz's departing figure. That was all he needed, politics jumping into his investigation. He could envision this case turning into a pain in the ass.

Ali called the medical examiner's office and was told there was no evidence of sexual activity on Michael Peterson's body. Ali considered that. If he wasn't having sex, then he must have known the killer or was forced into the bent over position. Ali didn't like the possibilities that presented.

CHAPTER

It got better every time. The rush seemed to swell inside him making him feel bigger than life. The satisfaction was so strong it threatened to draw him inside, making them one. He decided this was how God must have felt after he created the earth. Power was the sweetest drug of all. He knew he should wait for awhile but he couldn't control himself. The joy of the act was too strong.

He hefted the gun in his hand and reveled in the feel of it. He pointed it at a spot on the wall and clicked the trigger, dreaming of the next one. Hunting them was easy. They weren't hard to find, just go to where they hung out and wait. They almost came to you, begging to die.

He remembered hunting as a boy with his father sitting on a platform high in the tree and waiting for the deer to wander by then, boom. He hated every minute of it. It seemed so unfair to kill such a beautiful thing. He cried all the night before but he could never let his father see his tears. He would call him names and slap his face, which he often did anyway. He remembered the look of disgust on his father's face when he cried in front of him the first time; the sting of his father's hand stunning him, making the earth beneath him reel and fall away. He couldn't win his father's approval no matter what he did and he tried so hard. He had played sports because he feared his father's displeasure. So what if he was gentle and sensitive and prone to cry, so what. His father would stand over him and call him a girl and yell at him to shut up and stop crying then the hand would slam into his head and make him cry harder, bringing another slap and more demands to stop. He passionately hated the man and had been ecstatic when he died in that car. He remembered the State trooper coming to the house to tell him and his mother that his father was dead. His mother however had been inconsolable

His mother was the one who insisted he join the scouts in order to have another male figure in his life. If only she had seen what he learned from the assistant scoutmaster who sneaked into his tent and coaxed him into doing that thing. He was frightened at first but learned to accept it. He was still disgusted with it but he didn't fear it anymore always silently praying he would have the chance to kill him someday, but the chance never came, so he satisfied himself with the others.

He checked himself in the mirror, the blond hair was now jet black, the dye having done its job. He brushed it into his eyebrows. No one would recognize him now. The blue eyes were gone, replaced with brown eyes, the contact lenses were invisible. He smiled to himself and went into the bedroom. He selected a pair of carefully pressed, tight fitting jeans and wiggled into them completing the outfit with a light gray shirt and four gold chains. He packed his tools into the small green duffle bag and left the house, whistling to himself.

The bar was crowded, forcing him to squeeze through the crowd at the door. The crush thinned out once he was inside. The air conditioner struggled to cool the room but failed. He pressed his way to the bar and someone caressed his buttocks as he pushed through the crowd. He glanced around but couldn't spot the culprit. Whoever it was didn't know how lucky he was, he would live another day. A slim redhead slipped up beside him as he sipped his drink. They exchanged smiles as the redhead asked him to dance. He nodded and slid from the stool. They regrouped at the dance floor and the redhead encircled his waist with his arms. The dance was slow and the redhead snuggled against his shoulder. He smiled. *This was the one.*

The killer impatiently stretched his legs against the floor of the car and watched the front door of the bar. The redhead should have come out by now. He had been given the slip of paper with the address on it at least fifteen minutes ago. Suddenly, he saw him exiting the front door and hugging the doorman. He reached onto the seat beside him and retrieved an empty liter size bottle. He placed the spout of the bottle over the barrel of the gun and held it in place. He wound duct tape around until the gun was attached to the bottle. He watched the redhead as he loaded the pistol. He stepped out of the car as the redhead crossed the parking lot, fishing his car keys from his pocket as he went.

He followed, slithering between the parked cars. The redhead stopped at the door of a blue Jaguar and inserted the key in the lock. His heart raced with excitement. He glanced around quickly as he stepped up behind the redhead, pointed the gun at the back of the head and pulled the trigger. The gun made a muffled poof sound as the redhead's face and back of the head exploded. The dead man lurched against the door of the Jaguar and dropped like a stone, face down. The face destroyed.

He walked quickly to his car and got in. As he exited the parking lot he smiled. This was good.

He was still smiling when he reached home. He unlocked the front door and stepped inside. He slipped the pistol from under his jacket and ran his hand down its cold hard length. He loved the feel of it. It was power and ego combined. He felt as if the gun was a living thing that did his bidding.

He put the gun on the nightstand and undressed deciding he would take a shower, then sleep. He felt unstoppable.

Ali answered the phone on the second ring. He whispered into the receiver, trying to force his voice to work. He switched on the light and copied the address, blinking in the harsh light. His mouth was caked with dried saliva and he couldn't swallow. He had passed out early tonight. Good thing too or he would still be drunk.

Ali fumbled for his clothes, trying to find them with his eyes closed since the light blinded him and made his head pound. He shuffled to the kitchen sink and poured a glass of water. Taking a sip he swirled the water around in his mouth then spit it out then gulped the rest of it and cleared his throat.

Ali sipped *cafe con leche* as he drove, his head starting to clear. He parked next to a marked police car and surveyed the scene.

The body lay next to a Jaguar, covered with a yellow blanket. Lined up along the crime scene tape were rows of men, some holding hands, others with their arms around each other, all watching the body under the blanket as if it might rise up. Another gay man was dead. Ali suddenly had an uneasy feeling. He found the supervisor in charge.

"What can you tell me Sarge?" Ali asked, not really wanting to hear it.

"White male, came out of the bar and apparently was shot in the back of the head as he was opening his car door," the Sergeant replied.

"Anybody see the shooter?" Ali asked.

"Nope and nobody heard anything either. The doorman, if you can call him that, saw a car leaving. Two patrons left the bar a few minutes after the victim and found him between the cars."

"Nobody heard the shot?" Ali glanced toward the bar, gauging the distance from the door to the body and guessing it to be around fifty or sixty feet. "It seems like the door person should have heard the shot."

"Maybe the music was too loud," the Sergeant shrugged, "Doorman's over there." He pointed toward a leather-clad figure in the crowd talking to a uniformed patrolman. Ali shuffled over and stood listening to the conversation.

"I really didn't see anything. He walked toward his car and I stepped back into the doorway. I just happened to see a car leaving the parking lot. I notice cars leaving sometimes," the doorman explained.

"What kind of car?" the uniformed officer asked.

"Blue, light blue, a station wagon. Small, like a Taurus," The doorman replied. Ali's head lurched. A Taurus, light blue?

"Are you sure?" Ali asked.

"Yes. My mother has a Taurus. Why?" the doorman asked.

"Never mind," Ali answered, turning away. *Son-of-a-bitch. Was it Peterson's car? Dammit.* This was not turning out well.

Ali bent over and lifted the yellow blanket, looking into the dead face. It was destroyed, but not from slashes the bullet had done that. He pulled on rubber gloves and parted the hair on the back of the head. The bullet hole was similar to Peterson's, a gunshot point blank. *Shit.* He examined the face. *Only a large caliber weapon makes that big of an exit wound, another forty-five?*

Ali recovered the sheet and checked the ground around the body looking for any empty casings. He searched under the car and the surrounding area, nothing. That meant it was a revolver an automatic would have ejected the spent shell. Only one company ever made a forty- five- caliber revolver and they didn't make them anymore. Not for about eight years, he guessed. The gun might not be too hard to trace. He made a mental note to contact the manufacturer and see how many they sold in the area.

Ali leaned against his car and let the crime scene techs do their job. Two murders, one probable suspect. Someone who liked to kill gay men or a spurned lover, maybe someone who slept with both victims? He decided to call Murray and press him a little harder. Even though Murray was sick, Ali needed some answers.

Ali glanced toward the east and saw streaks of pink and yellow; the start of another day dealing with the dead and the dying. A uniformed cop approached and handed Ali a piece of notepad paper with the name and address of the victim were written on it. Henry Bascomb. Ali wondered who Henry Bascomb was and what he had done to deserve to die like this. Not that anyone deserved to die like this.

Ali pushed over the back door to the police station and almost ran into two bicycle cops wearing shorts. He turned to let them pass. *Cops wearing shorts? What the hell had happened to this job?* Real cops didn't wear shorts when Ali started. He would be glad when he could retire.

Ali entered the Detective Bureau and spotted the Lieutenant standing in his office door. He beckoned to Ali and turned away. Ali followed and dropped into a chair in front of the desk, his head pounded from lack of sleep and an early evening coma. The Lieutenant frowned at him and Ali suspected the boss knew about the drinking. The Lieutenant also knew why, but he decided long ago if it didn't affect the job, he wouldn't interfere hoping Ali would work out of it in time.

"Talk to me Ali."

"Looks like the same killer, large caliber gun, gay victim. The doorman saw what he thinks was a light blue Taurus leaving the area. Might be Peterson's car, then again, maybe not," Ali replied.

"Just what I didn't need to hear, I have been on the phone for the last hour with the gay activists trying to calm their fears and now you tell me we may have another victim of the same guy. This is going to get ugly," he sighed.

"Why don't you tell the gay activists to go find the guy for us, or leave us alone to do our jobs?"

"You know the answer to that one. Find this scumbag Ali and do it fast," the Lieutenant answered.

"Do my best," Ali replied rising to leave.

"Do better than your best. Please," The Lieutenant replied. Ali considered giving a smart reply but decided against it. The boss knew he did his job one hundred percent.

Ali dialed the number to Murray's home. The phone rang so many times he started to hang up when he heard the nurse answer.

"This is Detective Castillo. I need to speak to Mr. Murray please?" Ali asked. He waited for a reply and thought he heard a sob on the other end of the line. Finally, the nurse answered in a small quiet voice.

"I'm sorry Detective. Mr. Murray died early this morning. "

"Oh." Ali was stunned and saddened. He never knew what to say at these times knowing from personal experience the words were empty and hollow even if the intention was good. "I'm sorry. If there is anything you need, please call."

"Thank you," the nurse replied and the line went dead.

Ali wondered where he should go from here. He dug in his top desk drawer and finally found the bottle of aspirin. There were only three left and he figured he needed at least four or five. He realized he had been using the aspirin a lot lately. He shuffled to the water fountain and popped the aspirin in his mouth, leaning over and gulping water to wash them down. They caught in his throat like dry little terds. He coughed and one came back out. He cursed to himself and tossed it back in. It took three more swallows of water to get it down.

Ali returned to his desk to find the intercom light on his phone blinking. He picked it up and cleared his throat to clear the aspirin residue.

"Ali?" He heard the Medical Examiner's voice.

"Yeah, I'm here," Ali croaked.

"You okay?" She asked.

"Yeah, fine. Whaddaya got?" Ali asked.

"I started the exam on this mornings offering. Mr. Bascomb?"

"What'd you find?" Ali queried.

"Well, I just started the prelim and noticed something unusual and thought I should call right away," The M.E. replied. She continued when Ali didn't reply. "I found some small particles of plastic speckled around the wound, the kind consistent with a plastic bottle. It looks like your killer used a plastic bottle as a homemade silencer. Did anybody hear a shot?"

"Nope and that would explain why. That is very interesting, anything else?" Ali asked.

"Like I said, I just got started. I'll let you know if I find anything else. I also rechecked Peterson's body. Guess what? I found the same type of plastic in his wound, looks like a homemade silencer was used there too. Sounds like the same killer."

"Thanks doc." Ali answered and hung up.

Ali pushed open the door to the Teletype room and smiled at the dispatch operator whose name he couldn't remember. He handed her the message he had written to be sent to all police agencies to find out if any other jurisdictions had similar types of homicides. It was a shot in the dark but anything would help. At this stage he really was at a loss as to where to go with the case. He headed back to his desk and called the only manufacturer that built a forty-five-caliber revolver. He was informed the company made over seven thousand of the guns. There would be seven thousand people to call and those seven thousand probably sold the guns to seven thousand others. This was a waste of time.

Ali parked in front of the apartment building and glanced at his notebook. The doorman from the shooting scene had given this address. He wandered down the plush carpeted hallways with ornate light fixtures scanning the apartment numbers. Finally, Ali found the correct door and knocked. The door opened at the third knock and Ali recognized the doorman from last night. His hair was wrapped in a towel his eyes still droopy from sleep. He was dressed in a fluffy green bathrobe and had large fuzzy slippers on his feet. The robe was slightly open, revealing chest. Ali thought he didn't look like a gay man. He looked like a weightlifter.

"It's very early, Detective," The man said, turning to lead Ali into the apartment.

"Sorry. But I need to get started on this case, the pressure is getting bigger," Ali replied.

"Ah yes, of course, the gay political faction trying to show they are doing something for us poor misunderstood queers," the doorman replied, He poured himself a glass of orange juice and offered a glass to Ali, who declined.

"What can you tell me about what happened last night?" Ali asked.

"Not much. I was working the door and didn't know anything had happened until somebody ran up and said there was a body in the parking lot. I went over and saw that poor man lying in a pool of blood and called the police. That's about it," the doorman sipped his orange juice.

"You didn't notice anything unusual? Anybody you didn't recognize? Did you hear the gunshot?" Ali stopped and waited.

"Detective, it was very crowded last night. I was standing at the door, the music was loud. As far as seeing anyone new? It's hard to do that. Every day someone realizes his true orientation and decides to come to a place like that to explore their desires. There are lots of new faces every night. Sorry." The doorman eased into a chair and pulled the robe across his knees.

"Okay, if you think of anything, here's my number," Ali replied, handing over his business card.

Ali returned to the scene and walked around the parking lot. Yellow strips of plastic crime scene tape fluttering in the wind. He never failed to be amazed at the serenity of crime scenes the next day. The crime scene tape and a spot of blood marked the violence and confusion of the end of a person's life. Afterwards, it was as if it never happened. Ali stood and looked toward the door of the bar, mentally calculating the distance. The doorman probably couldn't see or hear anything from this distance. Ali sighed and climbed into his car. He glanced at his watch. In a few more hours he could go home and have a drink. He never drank on duty but lately found he was thinking about it while working. He realized he needed to stop. Maybe tomorrow.

Lieutenant Davis fidgeted in his chair. He hated to see the chief get talked to like this. By that asshole of a mayor and his do-boy City Manager who were a matching pair of dickheads. Davis could barely avoid looking around the fancy office, it would be perceived as boredom or disrespect and these two demanded respect. They never learned that one did not demand respect, it had to be earned. The chief had earned Davis' respect, thirty years as a cop in this department had earned him that. The Chief had worked in every division, had been in three shootouts and survived on the streets, a real cop not some pussy that had spent little time in the real world and climbed the ladder from behind a desk.

"Chief, if you don't understand the situation properly, let me lay it out for you. The gay community is a large influential voting block in this city and I am up for re-election next year. I don't need any bad press that will screw that up. I want his bastard caught and I want it done immediately. I know you have faith in this Detective Castillo but I also know his history. I hear he has a drinking problem. I should order you to form a task force to find this killer but I will give you a little leeway. I have however, contacted the FBI and requested their assistance. They are sending an agent who is a profiler to assist," the mayor ran out of gas and sat back in his chair.

"Mr. Mayor, Ali Castillo is one of the best homicide cops I know, he will find this killer. We don't need help from the Feds," the police Chief replied, his face turning a slight shade of red.

"That was not a request for your input Chief, it was an order. You are on very shaky ground with this administration and the citizens of this city as it is. The crime rate has gone up thirty percent since last year and the voters are not happy," the mayor answered, his voice rising in anger.

"The crime rate has risen thirty percent because this administration has put this city into a financial bind. I have fifty seven less cops than last year, I can't hire more because of the lack of money and the officers of this city have already worked a week without pay to try to help this city recover and you blame us for the crime rate?" The Chief appeared to be about to jump out of his chair and slug the mayor, which is what he secretly wanted to do. He had one year left on his job contract and he was gone. His youngest daughter would graduate from the University of Miami this next quarter and then he and his wife could haul ass out of this place and move to his house in Boone North Carolina where he could sit on his deck and watch the leaves change in the fall. He hated having the mayor dictate how cops should do their jobs. Police work was the most unique profession in the world. It was dictated by the vagaries of crime which was generally committed by someone who decided on the spur of the moment to rip off someone else and the cops were supposed to be clairvoyant and know it was going to happen and stop it while at the same time handling the fifty other calls for service from the public, which were not really police matters but the public demanded service just the same. Nobody re-elected the cops, they did their jobs because it was what they did and who they were all the while being second guessed by someone who knew nothing about police work but was a private citizen who was lucky enough to get the most votes from the twenty percent of the public who bothered to vote at all.

"Be careful Chief, I am your boss and don't you forget it," the City manager interjected. How could I forget, the Chief thought, you remind every day.

"I understand," the Chief answered rising from his chair. Davis joined him and they left office together.

"This sucks," Davis said as they waited for the elevator.

"I know but we have no choice. Make sure Ali knows we're on his side and this is not a reflection on his ability," the Chief replied. That was one of the traits Davis liked about the Chief, he cared about his people. He was a squat, balding man with thick arms and beefy hands. He had a USMC tattoo on his left forearm. He wore a uniform everyday, four stars resting on the shoulders of his uniform shirt. The cops on the street liked him too. It was not unusual for a cop to be on a traffic stop at two in the morning and see the Chief arrive to back the cop up. That was how respect was earned. He had been the Chief for fifteen years, which was a feat in itself since most police chiefs in the country lasted an average of four years.

Ali groaned when he returned to the office and saw Lieutenant Davis beckoning him from his office door. He entered and was surprised to see a woman sitting in the chair across from Davis' desk. Davis pointed Ali to a chair and he sat, wondering what the hell was going on now. She was probably some reporter wanting to harangue him about not solving the case yet.

"Detective Ali Castillo, Jamie Stevens," Davis said indicating the woman sitting beside Ali. "Agent Stevens is from the FBI VICAP unit. The chief asked her to help with this case. She will be working with you."

Ali turned and held out his hand. Fucking feds, he thought, just what I need. Stevens returned his handshake and he noticed it had strength. Not like a woman's handshake. He sized her up in a glance, like a cop sizes up everyone. She was dressed in a business suit, her light brown hair was short but attractive. She had very shapely legs, which were crossed at the knee. He realized her blouse was gapped open slightly between the buttons and he could see the lower curve of her breast in the gap. He looked away quickly, feeling guilty. Jesus! Now he was looking at other women. He felt like he was cheating on Maria. He suddenly felt flush.

"Glad to have you," Ali lied.

"Thank you," Stevens smiled back at him.

"Well, I'll leave you two to get acquainted, but first I need to speak to Ali alone," Davis said, dismissing Stevens. She rose and turned to leave and Ali noticed she had a very trim, firm body.

"Look," Davis said when they were alone, "I know you don't like this. But it's the Chief's orders. Make it work Okay?"

"Yeah, whatever," Ali sighed and rose. "But she's not fucking up my case."

Ali returned to his desk and pointed to the empty desk across from him.

"You can use that one." He said to Stevens.

"Ali. I know you are pissed that I was pushed on you like this, but I promise to do what you think is right in this case. I'm here to assist and provide backup and psychological profiles. I hope we can work together like partners, deal?" Stevens asked, sitting down at the desk.

"Okay." Ali mumbled. *Just what I need, a Fed for a partner.* He handed over the file on the case and leaned back in his chair. "I thought the FBI profilers worked out of an office in DC and just sent their reports to the locals."

"Ever since nine eleven, the Bureau has been trying to change their image and work more closely with local departments. The profiling unit is stretched thin since a lot of agents are assigned to Homeland Security to try to outthink terrorists, so here I am. It's a new procedure to send us to the local agency to work the cases with the local cops."

Ali didn't think it would work but it wasn't his decision. He leaned back to give her time to absorb the information in the files. Finally Stevens glanced up at him.

"A plastic bottle for a silencer? This guy is careful. That tells me he probably has done this before maybe, even got caught once. I think we'll probably find he has a record. I would guess an aggravated battery charge or maybe attempted murder."

"What else can you tell me about him?" Ali leaned forward, interested.

"Traditionally, serial killers are white males. That's pretty much a given, except for the guy that killed those kids in Atlanta. He has a problem with his own sexuality and he's struggling with the fact that he is gay, or bisexual. The mutilation to the face indicates hatred or anger. He likely was introduced to homosexual sex in his formative years. Around twelve or thirteen I would guess. Probably by an authority figure or someone he trusted. "

"You mean he was molested. I've heard of molested children growing up to be killers but not killers of just gay men?" Ali was unconvinced.

"Many times they try to get even with the person who started them on this path but since that person is unavailable they find substitutes." Jamie replied. "Unfortunately, this guy thinks that whoever he is getting even with made him the way he is, which is not the case. Men don't make other men gay. It's not like they want to be gay. When I was getting my degree I had to do an internship in a hospital that did sex reassignment surgery. Some of the requirements before the surgery were blood studies, chromosome studies and psychological review and assessments. The interesting thing was that every one of the subjects had dominant female genes. One of them even had male genitalia externally and female sex organs inside that didn't function. The belief was that he was twins, one male and one female, that never separated in the womb. Do you really believe that a man would wake up one day and decide to become gay? Especially the way society treats them, ostracized, brutalized and discriminated against. You would have to be crazy to want to live that way."

"Maybe they are crazy. I have to admit that the thought of two men makes my skin crawl and I want to throw up. But that doesn't mean I think they should be brutalized. Nobody deserves that." Ali answered. "Guess that means I'm a homophobe."

"Why do you think you feel that way?" Jamie asked, amazed that he was opening up to her like this.

"Probably my macho upbringing, I was raised by a very typical macho, latin father. He was very religious and we went to mass every time it was held. The bible was crammed down my throat my whole life. Doesn't the bible say that man should not lie down with animals or other men or something like that?" Ali asked.

"The bible also preaches that all of us are god's children. I think that the bible teaches acceptance more than anything else. That is a very powerful word. Just think if we all practiced acceptance how the world would change. Most wars start over religion, everybody thinking that theirs is the only right religion. Think how the world would be if the Israeli's and the Arabs accepted each other's right to be different and have different beliefs? The Middle East would be peaceful. Or if blacks and whites accepted each others right to be different and have different beliefs. Think about what would happen if any two groups of people who are in conflict accepted each other's right to be different and not change to suit the others beliefs. This world would be a very different place." Jamie finished and waited for the argument she knew would come because she had heard it so many times.

"So we should accept every other person's right to be different. Like a killer's right to believe killing his victims is his right and we should just accept it?" Ali asked.

"That's not what I'm saying. Society needs laws and restrictions for the society to function. There have to be rules to protect society from the evil that exists but in some ancient societies, having sex with children and other men or even having concubines was an accepted norm. Society changed and laws were made to stop those behaviors. Society and its evolution create laws and say what is accepted and what is not. But sometimes the ones who demand certain laws are doing so to force their personal prejudices and beliefs on all of us. Look at the Jim Crowe laws of the past, where it was illegal for a black man to be in a certain area of the community at a certain time or be subject to arrest. That has changed because our constitution says all men have inalienable rights and finally someone pointed out that the Jim Crowe laws violated that and the law was repealed." Jamie finished.

"What I'm tired of is hearing that I don't have the right to think the way I want to or I'm an evil bastard who should be drawn and quartered," Ali answered. "I don't mean me personally but you get what I'm saying."

"There's that acceptance thing again. If everyone just accepted each others right to think and feel the way they do things would be less stressful. The problem is that people like our killer act on their basal instincts. You don't have to like others beliefs just don't beat the hell out of them and let them be the way they are."

CHAPTER 3

Patrolman Jeff Rice was what the supervisors called aggressive. The street people called him an asshole. Rice loved to find stolen cars. They were an obsession with him, especially the ones that fled. Rice loved a good chase. The ones he found, like this one, dumped and left in a field were boring, nothing but paperwork and Rice was anxious to get back to the hunt. He glanced at his watch again, wondering where the crime scene tech was. At least this stolen was wanted in connection with a homicide. Rice might get an "atta-boy" letter in his file, and he loved that most. Rice paced and looked at Peterson's stolen car and fumed. Why didn't the tech hurry up and get there.

The tech arrived and Rice ignored her. He called on his radio for a wrecker and sat in his car. The tech finished fingerprinting the car and walked up to Rice's open car door.

"I'm finished. Can you ask the wrecker to take it to our storage room and I can do more processing there?" The tech asked. Rice nodded.

He watched her walk away and thought, nice ass. The tech's only thought of Rice was one word, asshole.

CHAPTER 4

Ali glanced at Jamie Stevens and frowned. How much did he want to tell her? Well she was part of this now so she was in all the way.

"Patrol found Peterson's car dumped in a field. The lab is processing some prints now. Let's go see what they find." Ali stated flatly. Stevens rose with him and they left for the lab.

"Found some good prints. The computer should have them matched in a minute if the scumbag has ever been arrested," the print specialist said, facing the glowing computer screen. Ali lounged against a desk. His head still hurt but not as much. The aspirin were beginning to work. Stevens sat next to the print man and watched the screen, saying nothing.

Then the computer stopped and Ali could see it had found a match.

"Gotcha!" The print man smiled and hit the print button. The printer fed out a picture and criminal history. Ali grabbed the printout and looked at it, the face of a black man stared back at him. He handed the printout to Stevens. Ali wanted to tell her the profile was wrong. He wanted to tell her the theories were all screwed up but he held his tongue. He wondered why he was angry with her. Was it because of the fact she was a fed and local cops didn't trust

Feds, or was it because he was mad at himself for being attracted to her? He didn't know and couldn't dwell on it. He had a bad guy to catch.

"Okay everybody. You have the printout and you know who we're after. He is a suspect, I repeat, a suspect. We need this guy to talk to us. But you have to defend yourselves so if he gets stupid do what you have to do to go home tonight but please try to bring him back in one piece." Ali glanced around at the cops around him hoping they got the message.

The Patrol Sergeant stood and addressed the cops, giving them their assignments. They trooped down to the garage and piled into police cars. Ali and Stevens climbed into Ali's unmarked car. She had been quiet for the last hour.

"Is something wrong?" Ali asked.

"Just wondering what I did to piss you off. It seemed to be immediate. It usually takes me at least a day to piss somebody off." Stevens replied.

"Really?" Ali chuckled. "I'm sorry I just get focused sometimes and tend to come off that way." He lied.

"Are you sure that's all it is. Or is it because I'm a female federal agent? What irritates you the most, the female part or the federal agent part?" She asked.

"Neither. I'll try to do better, okay?" Ali answered. He wished he could tell her the truth. She had the kind of eyes you could talk to. He wanted to tell her about his pain and the cause of it but he couldn't.

"How involved can I get in this arrest?" She asked, changing the subject.

"You're a cop. You're a part of this investigation, do what a cop would do." Ali replied.

"Okay I'm just trying to find the ground rules."

Ali parked his car on the grass swale behind the marked police cars. The uniform cops quickly walked down the sidewalk to the suspect's residence, three houses down. Ali and Stevens followed closely. The uniforms scattered to the four corners of the house. The Patrol Sergeant headed to the rear of the house and Ali stationed himself at one corner, in the gap between the suspect's house and the next one.

One of the uniformed officers banged hard on the front door and yelled, "POLICE!" Suddenly, there was a crashing of glass from the rear of the house and Ali saw a flash of the suspect running from the rear of the house and vaulting the fence. He heard the Sergeant yelling for the suspect to freeze. Ali spun and sprinted down the sidewalk, his body fighting the sudden exertion. He saw the suspect sprint across the street in front of him. A uniformed cop streaked past him, followed closely behind by Jamie Stevens. Ali thought he was running hard but tired quickly, his heart pounding in his chest, sweat already streaming down his face. The suspect cut diagonally across the street and disappeared between the houses, Jamie and the uniform close behind. Ali willed his legs to run faster but seemed to be running in place. He slowed and then stopped. He bent over and placed his hands on his knees, gasping for breath. His head pounded and he thought he would vomit. Ali forced himself to stand upright and the world swam before his eyes. He staggered a few steps, found his feet and began to walk. He could hear yelling behind the houses and walked toward it. He was angry with himself. What the hell happened to me he wondered. He felt very old and realized he hated being forty-three years old and hated being in the shape he was in.

The uniformed cop and Jamie Stevens rounded the corner of a house, the handcuffed prisoner between them. Ali stopped and watched as they passed him, headed for a patrol car. He felt useless. Stevens was barely breathing hard. Shit! He knew he had made a great first impression.

The uniformed cop deposited the protesting suspect in a patrol car and slammed the door. The prisoner was loudly proclaiming his innocence.

"I din do nuffin' M'fuckahs.What you chasing me fo?"

The Patrol Sergeant sheepishly approached Ali.

"Sorry Ali. I let him get past me. Had my head up my ass I guess." Ali patted him gently on the shoulder.

"Don't sweat it. At least we got him," Ali answered. *And without any help from me.*

At the Homicide office, Ali had the suspect escorted to the interrogation room then went to the men's room. He filled his cupped hands with water and immersed his face in it. He held his face in it for a few seconds then dumped the water in the sink. He dried his face and stood in the middle of the room, sadness washed over him and he wished he could just go home and curl up.

Stevens met him in the hallway scrutinizing his face carefully, noticing the pale skin and the puffiness around the eyes. Davis was right, she thought, the man drinks too much. She also noticed the crooked nose and there was something about his eyes she didn't want to notice. They had a gentle sadness in them but there was strength too. She felt a twinge of interest. Damn. The eyes got her every time.

"You okay?" Stevens asked him.

"Yeah, fine." Ali answered sadly. He led the way into the interrogation room.

Otis Washington slumped in a chair with a defiant look and glared at Ali as he entered. Ali sat in a chair across the table and stared back. Stevens stood in the corner and watched.

"Tell me what the fuck dis bout, Crackah." Washington demanded.

"Murder," Ali replied. He watched Washington's mind chew on the word for a few seconds, fear creeping into his eyes. He looked away for an instant then glared again, regaining his bravado.

"Man what the fuck you talkin bout. I ain't murdered nobody," Washington spat.

"The man whose car you were driving was stolen during a murder. You were in it, give a better explanation," Ali said.

"Wha' m'fuckin car?" Washington asked, seeing a glimmer of hope for his survival.

"The Taurus wagon. Your prints were on it. It was left in a field. Tell me about it."

"I din' steal no wagon. I seen it in the field, when the white dude left it. I was fixin' to ride but I seen the POlice comin' and I dipped." Washington sat up in his chair.

"You saw the dude who left the car there?" Ali asked.

"Yeah, I can even give ya'll a sketch if'n y'all wants."

"That would be very helpful." Ali smiled at him.

"That'd get me out this bullshit?" Washington asked hopefully.

"Maybe," Ali replied.

Ali knew he should be doing something. But didn't know what? He had a sketch of the man whom Washington had seen dumping the car but not much else. He unlocked the door to his apartment and tossed the keys on the coffee table immediately flipping on the television for sound to cover the quiet. The quiet was always the worst. He went to the bedroom and stripped, putting on a pair of tan slacks and boat shoes. The boat shoes reminded him of his father. His father had been a fisherman and wore handmade sandals everyday of his life while on the boat. Now there were shoes specifically for boating. Jesus!

Ali poured himself a drink and flopped on the couch. The news was on and a reporter was discussing his case saying how the police were not able to develop any leads then Abramowitz came on and began a verbal attack on the police. He said the police were not working to solve the case because it involved gay victims and the police were prejudiced against gays. Ali grabbed a pillow and tossed it at the television. He switched it off and sat gulping his drink. He felt it burn its way down to his stomach. The quiet in the room began to rise until it became deafening and Ali had to flee. He grabbed his keys and left the apartment.

Ali gulped from the bottle he had purchased at the convenience store. He glanced to the east and saw slight flashes of lightning in the distance. The cemetery was dark, the perimeter surrounded by a tall wrought iron fence with a huge lock on the gate. Ali wondered when they started locking up cemeteries. That seemed like a sad comment on modern society; families unable to visit their loved ones whenever they wanted. The front gate of the cemetery was guarded by a small concrete guardhouse. The lights were on in the guardhouse and Ali could see the gray haired guard seated inside reading a book. Ali recognized the guard and knew he would never be permitted entry this time of the night because this guard took his job very seriously. No matter, Ali knew how to get in; he had done it many times before. He followed the wrought iron fence around the perimeter to the back farthest from the guardhouse. There was a bar missing from the fence here, that the neighborhood kids probably used to sneak in and smoke pot among the headstones. Ali slipped through the gap and walked through the cemetery. Large oak trees were interspersed through the cemetery, in among the headstones like dark silent sentries standing watch over the graves. At the base of the trees were stone benches for the families to sit and rest. A streetlight shone through the leaves of an oak making the foliage look like a halo. Ali could smell the sweet fragrance of freshly mown grass and some of the wet blades stuck to his shoes. A faint breeze whispered through the treetops giving a peaceful calm feeling to the place. Ali decided it gave the dead peace in their eternal sleep. He could hear the whish of passing cars on the road in front of the cemetery. He tripped and fell, coming face to face with the gray headstone bearing Maria's name.

The gravestone was made of light gray granite with small gray flecks. A carved angel perched on top of the stone, its arms outstretched toward heaven. He pushed himself upright and leaned against the cool stone. He thought of Maria and her warmth when she hugged him tightly but now all he had was cold gray stone. He tried to tell her how much he missed her and how he needed her now, but sobs choked down the words. He began to cry uncontrollably, howling at the wind that had suddenly stiffened. Rain began to pound his back as he slammed his hand onto the wet earth, screaming her name. He didn't know how long he had been screaming when he collapsed, exhausted on the wet grass. His clothes were soaked through and he was suddenly cold. He heard the whirr of the security guards golf car as it passed on the concrete path that dissected the cemetery.

Bright light suddenly blinded him and he held his hand in front of his face to shade his eyes unsuccessfully trying to push himself upright when a voice spoke loudly to him.

"What the fuck you doing, buddy?" The voice growled. Ali rolled onto his back and looked at the sky.

"I don't know," he answered the voice.

"Castillo. Is that you?" The voice asked. Ali thought he recognized the voice but couldn't see past the flashlight. Ali tried to sit upright but the world swam before his eyes causing him to slump onto his side. The flashlight swung away from his eyes and he recognized the police Sergeant towering over him. The Sergeant noticed the empty bottle beside Ali and then glanced at the headstone, recognizing the name. He had been on the scene of Maria's accident. The Sergeant sighed and reached a hand down to Ali.

"C'mon hotshot, let's get you home in one piece." He said, pulling Ali to his feet.

Ali lay on his back on the living room floor and watched the room spin. He felt like vomiting but couldn't. He had already done that numerous times. In the first few days after Maria's death he had been completely numb, unfeeling and unseeing, staring at the walls, not seeing anything. Then the anguish came. It snuck on him slowly, replacing the numbness with unbelievable anguish. Ali started drinking to numb it then felt guilty about being so weak and that led to more drinking to chase away the guilt. He had always been strong, taught by his father, the strongest man he had ever known, to handle problems. He remembered his father's forearms more than anything. His father fled Cuba to escape Castro, having been a vocal supporter of Bautista's government. His father knew that he and his family would be killed by Castro and his people so he left his homeland and fled to South Florida, America and freedom. Ali's family settled in Ft. Lauderdale not Miami like most exiles. Ali's father felt it important to assimilate into American society not into another community where only Spanish was spoken and the community was made up of people like them. Unfortunately, there was not much work in America for a displaced Cuban who spoke little English so his father took a job in a beer distribution warehouse loading trucks for twelve hours a day. The work was hard but the long hours of lifting and loading kegs and cases of beer was suited to him. Ali's grandfather had owned a farm in Cuba and Ali's father grew up with a shovel or hoe in his hands. The work built his body into hard sinew and his forearms took the brunt of the work, building them into thick trunks of muscle but his father loved the sea and anytime he could escape the farm for a few hours he could be found at the boat docks looking longingly at the boats moored there. As soon as he was old enough he had left the farm and gone to Havana, getting a job on a fishing boat. He worked hard and saved his money and was able to buy a small boat. He fished the waters between Cuba and Florida and knew them well and when the revolution came he snuck his pregnant wife into the boat and fled to Florida. Ali's brother was born soon after their arrival and Ali a year later. Ali's father said he would never return to Cuba under Castro.

Ali had been large as a child and the other boys picked fight with him to prove they could take the big dummy as they referred to him. Ali hated to fight and stayed inside most of the time eating. He gained a lot of weight and that just caused more harassment and teasing. Ali's father took him to a boxing academy near their home when he was ten. Ali hesitated at the door, terrified to go in, but his father's firm hand in the middle of his back propelled him inside. Ali immediately fell in love with the gym. The smell of old leather and the noise appealed to him more than he would have ever believed discovering he loved the exertion and the feeling of accomplishment. Ali worked harder than any of the other kids and was immediately noticed by the coaches who took extra time with him and guided him to win the Junior Golden Gloves championship when he was fourteen. His father's job at the beer warehouse didn't allow much extra money to pay for training so Ali worked at the gym in exchange for training time mopping the ring, emptying spit buckets and cleaning the bathrooms.

Ali remembered all this, lying there on the floor. How the hell did I ever get to this, he wondered? Life had been so good and the best was the day he met Maria, immediately drawn to her wide, dark eyes. He discovered that their histories were similar, both displaced Cubans. Ali was thirty years old at the time, a little old to be falling in love his friends said. But he had always known the perfect woman would find him, someone he felt he was meant to be with. Not that he was celibate he had dated lots of women. Some of them had even thought he was the one for them, but Ali didn't share their enthusiasm. The relationships were nice but Ali never got THAT feeling. The one that makes your heart race and you count the hours until you can see that person again. He felt it almost immediately with Maria and she later told him she felt the same. They dated for only six months before they moved in together and Ali had never been so happy, so content. Marriage was a foregone conclusion and happened a year later. For ten years they had been together, feeling like one was the other part of the other. Friends told them they were disgusting to be so happy for so long. Most of their friend's marriages had evolved into a sort of comfortable togetherness but Ali and Maria had always been like young lovers. They held hands when together and both of them felt they were not just lovers but best friends. Then that fateful morning, Ali's half of his whole was ripped from him. There was something horribly wrong with every minute of every day. He had nothing to look forward to, nothing to hope for. Ali knew what his father would say. He would tell Ali to get back up, like he had done so many times in the boxing ring and get back in the fight, but Ali felt like he had no fight left and that was unacceptable to him. He felt differently now, after the visit to the cemetery. Grief was a funny thing. Initially it overwhelmed you and knocked you down, making you numb and unable to focus, like you were watching your life through a television screen, an observer not really connected to anything you saw totally unfeeling. Then it morphed into an incredible agony, crushing you making it seem as if you couldn't breathe. For some it stayed that way until it won, causing them to take their own lives. If it didn't kill you it became a pain that eased with time without notice until one day you realized the pain was dull and you could function again and sometimes it became an epiphany and you discovered where you had been and got angry, determined to win over it. Ali had arrived at that point. He knew it was time to get back up and get back into the fight but wasn't sure he could. His body had failed him like never before and he hated it. Dammit he thought; get your ass back up. He wasn't sure he could but knew he had to try, even if it killed him. He thought of his father and how he had valiantly tried to survive. He had developed Parkinson's disease and ended up in a wheelchair unable to do anything for himself having to sit and watch television and usually dozing off within an hour of waking in the morning. It had torn Ali apart, watching the man whom he thought was the toughest guy in the world reduced to having someone wipe his butt. The indignity of it had been the worst. His father had always been a proud man who never asked for help. A month before he died, Ali had visited and asked his father how he was doing and was devastated when his father whispered to him, looking him directly in the eye ' I want out of this prison I'm in'. Ali knew what he had meant by that. His body had become an inescapable prison and his father wanted to die.

The day his father died, Ali had gotten the call at the office and raced to his father's side. When he entered the room, his father had taken one last breath and sighed and was gone. Ali had sobbed, seated next to the bed, holding his father's hand. He told him he loved him and would always make him proud. Then he moved on, unable to grieve because having already grieved the loss of the man he knew, for three years. Ali felt that the death of a father was the most profound occurrence in a man's life.

It was like the passing of a torch and the loss of a counselor and friend. He and his father had a rocky relationship growing up; Ali felt his father was always too hard on him, trying to make him the best he could be and Ali resented it sometimes. But over the years he and his father had come to understand each other and learn to respect each other. Ali understood his fathers wanting him to do the best he could and his father had come to respect him for what he had accomplished. Ali still missed him every day, not consciously, but there was always a sense of a part missing.

CHAPTER 5

R uth Lefebre was not her real name she was born Jane Jones. What a horrible name, unless you were the alter ego of some female superhero. She had legally changed her name when she decided to go into real estate. It was not uncommon for agents to change their names, it impressed the high end clientele and she thought Lefebre was classy, elegant and just mysterious enough to be interesting.

Most of her clients thought it phony as hell, but Ruth didn't care. She specialized in the very expensive homes on the Intracoastal Waterway and as long as the money was good the clients could kiss her ass. She also had decided the new agent she had hired had a phony name too. Who was really named James Brand? As long as the real estate license was good she couldn't care less.

Lefebre sat at her desk and watched the new agent enter the office and walk to his desk and she sighed. He had a gorgeous body and Lefebre hadn't gotten laid since her fourth ex-husband left, three years ago, after she caught him banging the next-door neighbor. She wouldn't have cared if he hadn't done it on her kitchen table and she hadn't walked in on them. She kicked his ass out the next day and sold the table.

She watched Brand and thought what a waste. She had made some subtle advances but he seemed oblivious. She figured he was gay since he handled most of the gay clientele which worked for both of them, since the gay men were mostly professional and had money to spend. And they knew what they liked and were willing to pay for it. She made money and didn't care that Brand was probably playing mattress tag with the buyers.

"Good morning James." Lefebre smiled at him and he returned it. God, she thought, no one has teeth that perfect.

"Good morning, boss lady. You look magnificent this morning." His gushing greeting caused Lefebre to blush slightly.

"What's on your plate today?" Lefebre asked.

"I'm showing the Mason house to that couple, you know the interior designers." Brand answered, pouring himself a cup of coffee. Lefebre smiled. The Mason house was beautiful. It was waterfront and very expensive, bound to bring her a large fee.

"Well, do your best, I would really like to unload that one."

"Don't I always?"

Brand sat at his desk and thought to himself. Yes I always do. That's why I survive. Like the real James Brand whom police would never find. He was in hundreds of pieces in the Everglades, fed to the alligators, fish and turtles. He had been chosen after careful and meticulous research. No family, no one to report him missing and no one to look for him. Taking over his life and identity had been easy once he got a social security card getting a drivers license had been a snap. The fools at the drivers license office hadn't even asked why he needed a duplicate driver's license or how the first one had been lost. No fingerprints requested, simple. The real estate license was already issued so no one even asked for fingerprints on that either. That was what he was really good at, research and careful planning. That was the reason the cops would never catch him, he was too smart for them, the idiots, like that fat dumb Sheriff in Bryant County.

Everyone had bought his story about his parents. He had played the part so well that the Sheriff had never questioned the story of how his step-father had killed his mother and then himself. He planned that one carefully too. Made sure no one saw him leave the house but made sure the neighbor saw him return to find them dead, and his act of being emotionally destroyed when he found the bodies had fooled them all. Of course, living in rural South Carolina helped. He had hollered hello to the neighbor lady when he stopped at the mailbox at the end of the dirt road leading to his house and got the mail. He had timed it perfectly. The Sheriff had even returned the forty-five revolver, he used, after the coroner's inquest. That gun had been put to good use many times since then.

He remembered the surprised look on his step-father's face when he walked into the house and saw his wife, her head blown apart, lying on the kitchen floor. His step-father had been too stunned to even react when Brand stepped out of the pantry and put the gun to his temple and pulled the trigger. It was her own damn fault. She should have never married that bastard after his real father died in that truck crash. She should have found a good man not another pig.

The coroners report read exactly what he had planned. His mother was shot from five feet away, and the wound to his step-father was a contact wound, right against his head, indicating self inflicted. Perfect. The grieving son had received the life insurance money and even got the gun back. He went to live with his aunt until he was old enough to live on his own. As soon as he turned eighteen he left Bryant County and never looked back. It was all a matter of careful planning just like now. He had planned today for months, chosen the victim's carefully and spent months building the room in his house. He had loved sneaking up behind the others and blowing their brains out, but the real dream, the one he harbored for years was to keep them for a while and make them suffer, mentally and physically. Then, end it for them when they thought it would never end. Today it would come true. He was so excited he could hardly contain himself, but concentrated on the plan. As long as he did that he could never go wrong.

Brand glanced at his watch and willed time to hurry. He was meeting the clients in two hours.

Brand stood in the driveway of the massive house and leaned against his car repeatedly glancing at his watch. They were fifteen minutes late. He scanned the front of the house and admired the large double mahogany doors. They were at least ten feet high. On either side of the doors were large stained glass windows that reached all the way to the roof. If the windows had been clear one could see the inside of the house from the street. The curving driveway was paved with sandstone colored blocks.

A burgundy BMW drove up the circular driveway and stopped behind Brand's Cadillac. The passenger emerged first. He had blond, permed curly hair and a neatly trimmed pencil thin mustache. He was dressed in a plum colored silk shirt which was unbuttoned halfway down his chest, four ornate gold chains hung around his neck. He was heavy set with love handles hanging over the edge of yellow slacks and his skin was pasty white like bread dough. He gave a limp-wrist wave at Brand. The driver emerged, a tall thin man with a tennis player body, not very muscular but well tanned like he spent quite a bit of time in the sun. His hair was short and neatly trimmed and he wore dark slacks and a white pullover, which accented his tan.

"I am so sorry we're late," the blond one said. "We got tied up with a client and just could not get away" He emphasized the 'could not'.

"No problem," Brand smiled and gestured toward the front door of the house. "Right this way to the house of your dreams."

Brand unlocked the key box on the front doors and removed the key. He unlocked the mahogany door and swung it back, stepped back and with a flourish toward the interior said, "ta da!"

The blond walked through the door and exclaimed, "Oh my God, it's magnificent."

The dark haired one stepped inside and stood silently scanning the room. He walked into the center of the great room and smiled.

The interior of the house was more impressive than the outside. The floors were light blue marble. To the left of the foyer was a staircase of marble that swept to the second floor. The rear wall of the great room was glass from floor to ceiling and beyond the glass was a swimming pool with a fountain in the center, beyond that was the Intracoastal Waterway. To the right of the great room was an open kitchen with black marble counter tops. The cupboard doors were black faux marble with gold handles.

The blond walked up to the dark haired one and flung his arms around his neck, kissing him on the cheek. The two of them separated and went opposite directions through the house. They returned shortly and glanced at each other. Then the blond gave Brand a big smile and said "we'll take it."

"Great," Brand beamed. "I'll get the paperwork from my car." He turned and walked outside, retrieving a briefcase from the backseat of his car. Brand returned inside and set his briefcase on a kitchen counter. He pulled a stack of paperwork from his briefcase and set it on the counter.

"Now comes the fun part," Brand said, beckoning them to join him.

An hour and a half later the paperwork was finished and Brand placed it in his briefcase, snapped the locks shut and leaned against the counter.

"Now to celebrate I would like to take the two of you to dinner, my treat. How about, Le Cordon around seven?" He said.

"That would be very nice," The dark one replied with a smile.

"Great. See you then." Brand replied, picking up his briefcase. "Now I assume you two would like to check out the house some more. Lock up when you leave."

Brand handed the blond the keys and walked to his car. This is going perfectly, he thought. He realized his heart was pounding and his palms were sweaty. At last, the dream becomes real. These two were going to be perfect. He would wipe that smug look off that dark haired bastards face.

Brand sipped his wine and watched the two lovers gushing at each other about the new house. They had spent the last twenty minutes describing how they would decorate it. Brand felt like vomiting. He wanted to kill them both right here at the table but knew it wasn't possible. That would spoil the whole plan. He would wait until the right time.

The three of them finished dinner and drinks. They were walking toward their cars when Brand gave the blond a wink.

"Why don't you two follow me to my house for a nightcap?" He asked. The blond nodded at his partner who agreed. Brand gave them the address and walked to his car. The lovers followed him home in their burgundy BMW and parked in the drive. They had their arms around each other as they followed him into the living room. Brand made them drinks and they settled on the couch to make small talk. It took about ten minutes for the Rohypnol to take effect. The blond nodded off first and the dark haired one was not far behind. It happened so fast Brand was afraid he had given them too much but relaxed when he heard them breathing deeply and evenly. He changed to jeans and a t-shirt before moving them into the special room, knowing it would be a difficult and sweaty job. Brand finally got them settled into their new room and went to bed almost too excited to sleep.

Brand woke early and dressed in casual clothes. Ruth wouldn't expect him at the office today. He had left a message on her machine that he was taking the day off to celebrate the sale of the Mason house. Brand poured himself a cup of coffee and unlocked the door to the room. It was solid wood, with insulation sandwiched in the middle to dampen any sound. Brand stepped into the room and looked at the two them seated against the wall. Both were secured to the wall with two inch thick chains and they were gagged with duct tape. The room was stark, with clean tile walls. Behind the tiles the walls were solid concrete with six inches of studio grade insulation, covered with drywall. The fluorescent overhead lights gave a glaring effect.

The blond thrashed against his bonds, the brunette lay still and silent, tears welling in his eyes. How pathetic, Brand thought.

"Struggle all you want you'll never get loose and if you did, there is no way out of this room. And, oh by the way, this room is completely soundproof. No one can hear you scream." Brand said to the blond, who lay still, panting from the exertion. "Kinda looks like every room you've ever seen in a hostage movie, doesn't it? That's where I got the idea. I really like it don't you?" He walked to the dark haired one and kicked him in the chest causing him to gurgle out a scream through the tape over his mouth. Brand smiled grimly at the blond. "You'll leave when I decide and not before and I haven't decided your fate. Now you boys behave yourselves."

Brand closed the door and went to the living room to watch the news. He hoped they would say something about him today. Otherwise, this wasn't half as much fun. The phone on the coffee table rang and he slowly lifted it.

"Yes?" Brand said to the receiver.

"Are you having fun?" Brand knew the voice as well as his own.

"Yes I am and you?"

"Not as much as you are I'm sure. Just remember, when the fun's over make it public. Okay?" The voice said with a slight irritation.

"Don't sweat it. I know what you want." Brand replied. The phone clicked dead in his ear.

CHAPTER 6

A li opened his eyes and found himself staring at the bottom of the toilet. The cool tile on the side of his face felt so good, he didn't want to move besides he knew the room would flop over as soon as he sat up. He couldn't remember getting to the bathroom. He struggled to focus and finally remembered crawling there, vomiting violently one last time before he passed out. He struggled to remember the night before. He remembered the promise he had made to himself. He had never woken up on the bathroom floor before and realized he had reached the bottom. He struggled to sit upright and finally succeeded, fighting the nausea, using the toilet to hoist himself up. He looked down at his clothes. The mud had dried to sand and he was standing in a pile of it that had fallen off his clothes. He stripped and climbed into the shower, letting the water cascade over his head. He soaped himself and scrubbed roughly, feeling the sensation on his skin. It reminded him that he was still alive. Ali wasn't sure if that was good news or bad news.

Ali stood naked at the stove and stirred the scrambled eggs in the fry pan figuring the eggs would be the only thing his stomach would tolerate. When the eggs were finished he set the pan on the sink and ate standing up, still naked. He laughed at the sight. *Look how low you've sunk standing at your sink and naked, eating eggs from the pan with a spoon.* His father would have beaten his ass if he could see him. Ali's father never ate anywhere but at the dinner table. His shirt was always buttoned and he always scolded Ali for not sitting up straight. He used to say a man is judged by how he carries himself. Ali wondered what that judgment would be right now.

Jamie Stevens cheerfully met Ali in the parking lot. Ali assumed she had been up for hours. Probably went for a ten mile run this morning before breakfast or some shit like that. She looked good he had to admit. Damn, why did she have to stir something in him? Ali wished he didn't have any feelings for anything. It was better that way.

"We've got a problem," Stevens said as she fell into step with Ali. What more could go wrong, Ali wondered.

"Two gay men are missing." Stevens continued, looking into his face for a reaction. Ali seemed to deflate.

"When?" He asked.

"Last night. Last time they were seen was looking at a house they wanted to buy."

"Last night? How can they be missing so soon? It takes twenty four hours for a missing person report on an adult." Ali stopped and looked into her face.

"I put out an alert for any missing person reports on gay men. The patrol unit that took the report figured it was within the profile."

"Great. Well, maybe they stayed out all night to celebrate and decided to get a motel room. They'll turn up." Ali turned and continued walking.

"Not likely. Their administrative assistant said they never go anywhere but home. They're a monogamous couple and are home-bodies. She went to their house and the cats hadn't been fed. This is completely out of character for them. They also didn't call their business or show up this morning." Stevens said.

"Look. It's only nine o'clock. Let's give them some time." Ali replied.

"The assistant says they are always at the store at seven that's why she went to the house. She has a key and said the beds haven't been slept in and there was no coffee or any breakfast made."

"Shit." Ali muttered as they entered the Homicide office.

Ali checked in with Lieutenant Davis and got a ten minute ass chewing about the missing gay men and what the hell was he doing on the case. Afterward, Ali met Stevens at his desk and grabbed the car keys and the missing person report. He beckoned with his head for Stevens to follow him and silently led the way to the police parking garage. Ali said nothing on the ride, he was busy mulling over the case. He needed a break and needed it soon.

"Can I help you?" The woman behind the reception desk asked as Ali and Jamie approached. Ali showed his badge.

"We're here about your missing bosses." Ali told the receptionist. The receptionist developed a sudden panicked look as if the police being involved meant there was really something amiss. The receptionist dialed her phone and whispered 'The police are here into the receiver.' She replaced the receiver and looked at them each slowly. "Someone will be with you in a minute."

Ali glanced around the lobby. The floors were marble tiled, *Probably fake*, Ali thought. The walls had large paintings with lots of bright colors but no shapes Ali recognized. *Why have pictures that have nothing on them?* In the corner of the lobby stood a flowered Chinese vase with tall, wispy peacock feathers, protruding from it. The room had a cold feeling to it. Ali always thought interior decorators had too much talent and no warmth. A side door opened and a middle aged woman dressed in faded jeans,t-shirt and ragged old tennis shoes approached, holding out her hand. Her gray hair was pulled into a ponytail. Ali wondered how much contact she had with the clientele, dressed like that. Probably not much, he decided.

"Kristie Jones," the woman said. "I'm the coordinator here."

Ali introduced himself and Stevens and they followed her through the door. Jones led them into another room, which was filled with an assortment of large pillows, furniture, and all of the assorted decorations the firm used to bilk unsuspecting customers out of their money, believing this junk to be the latest thing in interior design. It looked like a work room, with long wooden tables where the designs were made and stored. The tables were cluttered with items in different stages of completion.

Jones passed through another door and into a hallway. She opened a door to an office and walked behind the desk.

"Please, sit down." Jones beckoned to two chairs.

"This is all very upsetting." Jones said, settling into her chair. "The boys have never been missing like this."

"By the boys, you mean, your bosses, Daniel Carnes and Jonah Martins?" Ali asked.

"Yes, sorry. I have known them since they started and I have been like a mother to them. I helped them along when they started in the business so I refer to them as my boys." Jones answered, smiling.

"And how long has that been?" Stevens asked.

"Twelve years. They were real green when they started, college degrees but no business sense. Now, they're the top interior designers in town."

"How long have they been a couple?" Ali asked.

"Since college, they were together in school and then started this business together. They are so good together."

"And why do you think there's anything wrong with them not showing up today? Couldn't they have just decided to take off for a couple days together? Maybe met someone they wanted to be with?" Ali asked.

"No. First, detective I resent the implication. YOU are obviously one of those closed minded homophobes that considers gay men to be promiscuous perverts. Second they wouldn't just take off a couple days, as you put it, because one of their biggest clients is due to meet with them today and finalize the decoration of his house. The contract is worth over a million dollars they wouldn't just decide to miss that."

"My question has nothing to do with them being gay I would have asked the same question if they were a female, male couple." Ali replied. "What was their last activity, if you know, and where would they have been last seen?"

"They had a meeting with a realtor to look at houses. They were in the process of upgrading." Jones answered. Ali figured upgrading meant they had made enough money to move to a fancy house to prove to their upscale clients that they were in fact the hottest designers in town.

"Do you know what realtor?" Ali asked.

"I figured you would ask so I dug out the card." Jones replied, handing a business card across the desk. Ali glanced at the card to make sure it had the address on it and tucked it into his pocket.

"Will there be anything else?" Jones asked, rising from her seat.

"Not right now." Ali answered. "But we'll be in touch."

Ali rose to leave then stopped. "I'll need their address book, to check with friends who might have seen them."

Jones reached into the top drawer of the desk and removed an ornate leather bound address book and handed it to Ali.

"Thanks. I'll get this back to you." Ali said.

"You just find my boys detective." Jones replied.

"Well, that was interesting," Jamie said when they were back in Ali's car.

"How so?" Ali asked.

"Well it's interesting to know the 'boys' as she referred to them have been together since college," she answered.

"Why?" Ali asked.

"It rules out the possibility of a stranger and it rules in the possibility that you really are a homophobe," Stevens replied.

Ali frowned at her.

"Jesus Ali, I was only kidding. My, you are more grumpy than usual this morning." Stevens pouted. "I thought we had gotten past the fact that I am a fed that's interfering with your case and had become friends, somewhat."

"Sorry," Ali answered. "Bad night. Well, Miss Fed, where do you think we should go from here?"

"My guess would be to talk to the friends of the missing men." Stevens smiled, realizing that she had not overstepped any boundaries.

"Let's talk to this realtor first. They were the last to see these guys, maybe they have a clue where they went." Ali said, holding up the business card.

"Good plan."

Ali parked in the front of the real estate office and led the way to the front glass doors. He held the door open for Stevens and followed her inside. The office was small and had two desks, one on each side of the office. The front sitting room was occupied by two large chairs and a felt covered love seat. Ali hated felt seats; they always made his ass sweat. Piled on a small table between the chairs, were magazines and real estate brochures. The bookshelves behind the desks were piled with files and important looking listing books. The office appeared to be cluttered and gave the impression of being a very busy place. Ali wondered if it really was a busy place or set up that way so that prospective clients would think they had come to the right people to sell their overpriced houses. The front office was empty. Ali called out if anyone was there and they heard a door open somewhere in the back, behind a partition. Ruth Lefebre appeared through a break in the partition, wiping her hands with a paper towel.

"Hello folks, can I help you?" Lefebre asked with a wide salesperson smile reminding Ali of a shark smiling at its prey just before it ripped it to shreds. Ali had always hated pushy salespeople. *Probably figures we're fresh meat to be ripped from the bones.*

"Detective Castillo, Homicide, and this is Special Agent Jamie Stevens, FBI," Ali said, holding up his badge. LeFebre frowned at the badge.

"Police, Homicide?" Lefebre asked. "Is there a problem?"

"We're investigating the disappearance of two of your clients, Daniel Carnes and Jonah Martin." Ali answered.

"My god," Lefebre slumped into a chair, clasping her hand over her mouth.

"We understand you were the last to see them." Stevens said, examining Lefebre's face for signs of deception.

"No sorry. My associate was handling that sale," Lefebre replied. Stevens glanced at Ali, the look saying Lefebre was telling the truth.

"Is your associate here?" Ali eased into a chair across from Lefebre.

"James? No, he took the day off today. He'll be here tomorrow." Lefebre replied.

"I'll need his full name," Ali said, taking out his notepad.

"James Brand. That's his license there above his desk," Lefebre pointed at the wall above the empty desk. Ali stood and examined the license and the picture attached to it, writing in his notepad. He sat back down and asked for Brand's address and the address of the house he had shown the missing men. Lefebre gave the information willingly. When they were finished Ali stood. He handed Lefebre his card and asked her to have Brand call when he returned.

"Certainly, dear god, how sad. I hope you find them safe." Lefebre said, taking the card.

As Ali drove, Jamie studied him with a sidelong glance. He seemed different today, pensive, but less burdened as if he had come to a decision about something or had let something go. She remembered the evening before, having spent it with a glass of wine and thinking about him, couldn't help but think of him, no matter how hard she tried.

He made her feel something she hadn't felt in a very long time; of being safe and protected, which was a funny thought for an independent woman like herself. She carried a gun and could fight and shoot with the best of them but sometimes she needed a strength she couldn't find within herself. The way he moved was graceful but there was a hint of danger, as if he was a powerful animal, just waiting to pounce. She also felt she could trust him, in a way she hadn't trusted a man for a long time or maybe never really had.

Jamie's last relationship had ended badly. She found out her lover had been untruthful and unfortunately unfaithful. She caught him and that was that. She dumped him immediately then blamed herself for not giving enough and not feeling strongly enough feeling that she had failed and didn't know how. It had taken her a long time to realize it wasn't her fault but it happened because it was supposed to happen. But she believed she could never trust a man again. Betrayal was a bitter pill to swallow but she finally choked it down.

But this man was different. Something about him made her feel as if she had been wrong about men. She knew about him losing his wife and she knew about the drinking. Maybe it was her maternal instincts or her innate need to help him. Her psychology professor had seen that in her, her need to heal others. She even told Jamie that she believed it was the biggest reason she studied psychology and joined the FBI. Professor Cortello said she had an unconscious need to heal the most injured, the most twisted minds that society had to offer. Jamie didn't agree. She believed that deep down she just had a need to love and be loved.

Jamie studied Ali's large hands and remembered how she had thought of those hands last night fantasizing about those hands on her, touching her and shielding her from harm. She imagined that with more time, she could have something with Ali, something special. Any man, who had loved as deeply as he had once, surely could love like that again.

They arrived at the office around noon to find Lt. Davis standing in his office, glaring at the television in the corner, with his hands on his hips, a deep scowl on his face. The noon news show was on the television and Davis pointed at the screen. Rodney James was standing in front of a phalanx of microphones, flanked by lawyer Abramowitz. James was decrying the fact that gay men were being 'hunted down and killed like dogs' and as usual the police were doing nothing and obviously didn't care. James then alluded to the police needing to look at themselves and went on and on about the belief that the police were homophobic and were known to mistreat the gay community and maybe the killer was a cop. He then named Ali by name and accused him of dragging his feet. James demanded federal intervention. A reporter asked James if he was aware that there was an FBI agent assigned to the investigation. James took a scoffing tone and said "They assigned a woman. Obviously the FBI sent her there as window dressing and not a real investigator."

Jamie snorted behind Ali.

"Window dressing, talk about prejudice and stereotyping. He obviously doesn't know anything about me." Jamie sneered.

"Don't listen to that bullshit, comes with the territory." Ali replied.

Abramowitz stepped to the microphone. He equated the gays to the victims of the Holocaust then ranted about the police not caring about Jews, blacks or gays and how the white boy fraternity in the police department only cared about the rich white taxpayers. He continued about how those groups paid taxes too and deserved the same service. Abramowitz stepped back and the news conference ended. The news anchor appeared and began a story about a train accident in Arizona.

Davis clicked off the television with the remote. He turned to Ali and Stevens and made a wry face.

"Get this son of a bitch" Davis growled. He walked behind his desk and sat down. Ali started to say something and Davis waved them toward the door.

Ali found a stack of police reports on all the recent hate crimes against gays he had requested on his desk. He handed half of the stack to Jamie and sat down.

"Let's go through these first and find the most promising candidates." Ali opened the first report and began to read, across from him Jamie started on her stack.

CHAPTER 7

Jonah Martins could not see anything. His mouth was dry and his lips were cracked from dehydration. He tried to lick them but couldn't reach them because of the gag in his mouth. He tried to move his hands for the hundredth time but the metal bit into his skin and it burned like acid. He hadn't been able to feel his hands for hours and now they felt like concrete clubs at the ends of his wrists. The pins and needles feeling in his hands has ceased long ago. His shoulders were frozen into position and the muscles burned. He was able to shift his position slightly and get the feeling back in his shoulders. He tried again to pull his feet toward him and remembered they were secured to the floor. He choked back a moan and sat still. He could hear breathing near him and knew, or sensed that Daniel was near him somewhere in the same room. Jonah couldn't speak to him. He wanted to comfort him and tell him everything would be okay but he knew different. He had heard about the gay men who had been killed and he believed they were going to die, he just didn't know when. Why was Brand doing this to them? At least he believed it was Brand. The last memory he had was of having dinner to celebrate the house purchase and then having drinks at Brand's house. He was sure they were still there in Brand's house.

The floor underneath him was cold on his naked buttocks. He assumed Daniel was naked also. He hadn't heard anything from Daniel in an interminably long time, the sobbing had stopped long ago. He only knew Daniel was still alive from the breathing. It was slow and even so Jonah assumed Daniel had passed out or gone to sleep. Jonah lay still and tried not to think or feel.

James Brand unlocked the door to the room and swung the door wide but neither Martins nor Carnes stirred. He closed the door quietly. Brand stood over Carnes and studied him the soft fat lopped over his waist and looked like a fish's belly in this light. Disgusting Brand thought. He spent hours every day exercising to look good and this pig looked like this? He deserved to die. Brand's heart raced and his muscles tensed. His breathing quickened and his knees felt weak. He was going to enjoy this immensely.

Brand unhooked Carnes hands from the wall and dragged him forward pushing him face down on the floor, hooking his hands to the ring in the floor. Carnes eyelids fluttered and he looked into Brand's face but his eyes were unseeing. This won't do, Brand thought, it was no good for him if they didn't feel it. Brand left and returned with a pitcher of ice water and dumped it onto Carnes head whose body jerked. He swung his head side to side and looked at Brand again with clear eyes, wide with terror.

"Much better," Brand jeered. "This is going to be fun. Well maybe not for you but I'm gonna enjoy it."

Brand turned to Jonah. He knelt down and put his face so close Jonah could feel his breath on his cheek.

"Listen carefully. You're gonna hear your boyfriend moan like never before." Brand whispered. He turned to Daniel and began.

Jonah heard it all, the blows thudding against skin, the muffled screams. His body wracked with sobs but there were no tears since his body was empty of fluid. He tried to scream and beg Brand to stop but only grunts came out. He tried to struggle against the restraints but only thrashed around slightly, he was bound too tight. He prayed to God but got no answer. His heart pounded in his chest and his body shook uncontrollably. After what seemed like an eternity the screaming stopped. He could hear Brand breathing from exertion. He was suddenly freezing cold.

Jonah lay perfectly still, straining to hear movement waiting for the blows to hit him, holding his breath but nothing happened. He could hear feet shuffling then he heard the door open. Jonah heard Brand's voice say 'it's time'. The door swished closed and Jonah heard footsteps whispering toward him across the cold tile floor. He held his breath, waiting, his heart pounding in his ears.

Jonah heard a clicking noise, two clicks then nothing. Suddenly an explosion deafened him, causing him to leap against the restraints. He could not hear anything then slowly he heard a hissing noise and his ears started to ring. He heard a sound and realized it was his voice screaming against the gag. He thrashed and kicked as best he could to no avail, he was still tied just as tightly so he froze and tried to listen to the room against the ringing in his ears but he could only hear muffled sounds. He thought he heard the door open and close then nothing, but a hissing in his ears. He began to pray.

CHAPTER 8

Ali parked in front of the house and turned off the engine. He and Stevens watched the house for a few minutes and studied it. It was a one story old Florida style house still sporting jalousie windows. The yard was overgrown and filled with weeds. Adjacent to the front door stood a gray plastic garbage can, overflowing with empty beer cans. This was an old neighborhood, which had withstood the years poorly at best. The paint on many of the houses was faded and bare in spots and old cars crouched in the driveways up and down the street. In the window of the house, Ali could see the curtains move slightly then close. Somebody was home.

Ali led the way to the door, carefully picking his way around sandspurs sprouting up from the cracks in the walkway. He raised his hand to knock when the door swung inward with a jerk causing Ali to take an instinctive step backward and nearly trip over a crack in the front stoop. The man in the door wore an old faded Harley Davidson t-shirt and ragged blue jean cutoff shorts. His hair was a wild mop and his scraggly beard clung to his face.

"Who the fuck are you and what do you want." The man snarled menacingly.

"Police," Ali said, holding up his badge. "Michael Dipetro?"

"Yeah, so?" Dipetro stood blocking the door.

"Got some questions, may we come in?" Ali asked, shifting his weight to the balls of his feet, preparing to deflect any punches that might be thrown.

"No you can't. Speak your peace." Dipetro answered eyeing Stevens standing behind Ali.

"Okay. Mr. Dipetro. You were arrested and pled guilty to battery with a hate crime enhancement is that right?" Ali asked.

"So what?" Dipetro replied. "I punched a faggot in a bar when he made a pass at me."

"Would you care to elaborate?" Ali asked.

"I was in a bar. Went to the bathroom and some queer grabbed my ass, so I decked him." Dipetro said.

"Why was it deemed a hate crime?" Ali wondered aloud.

" 'Cause when I hit him I called him a 'fuckin' Faggot' and when the cops came he cried like a bitch that it was a hate crime and they charged it that way. Anything else?" Dipetro started to close the door.

"Thanks for your time," Ali said as the door slammed in his face. He turned and followed Jamie down the walk toward the car.

"That wasn't very helpful," Jamie said over the roof of the car as she waited for Ali to unlock her door. Ali just grunted in reply.

Ali drove while Jamie counted down the list they had made. There were five possible contacts on the page. She and Ali had spent the morning narrowing down the list from the police reports. It seemed there were a lot of crimes listed or charged as hate crimes that really weren't because the police officers on the street were afraid to not properly classify the crimes as hate crimes for fear of being wrong or second guessed by the prosecutors or the media or the special interest groups like CAD that made noise on television.

Ali looked at Jamie and sighed.

"This is a waste of time," he said. "I guess you were right. We are spinning our wheels because we don't know what else to do." Jamie had reviewed the cases and believed that none of the people on the list fit her profile but Ali insisted they try. Now, he knew he was wasting his time. He made a decision.

"Let's find Peterson's house keeper. There has to be something that connects these victims. Anything would be helpful." He suggested.

"Sounds like a good idea." Jamie answered.

Ali found the house with no trouble. The real trouble had begun when he called the nursing agency and tried to get the nurse's address. The woman who answered the phone had grilled him for ten minutes to prove he was a cop and his reasons were legitimate. She explained away her actions by saying that it was not unusual for family members to try and find nurses they accused of stealing from the elderly patients. Ali finally convinced her and got the address.

The nurse opened the door in answer to Ali's knock and recognized him immediately. She smiled sadly and stood side to let them in. Ali introduced Jamie as the nurse led them to a sitting room in the back of the house. The room had large windows all the way around it, giving a view of an immaculately manicured backyard with numerous orange and grapefruit trees. Ali suspected the room had once been a screen porch that had been converted. That was common in Florida.

The nurse pointed them to chairs on the porch and sat down across from them eyeing Ali warily, waiting for the reason for their visit.

"Mrs. Winston. I really want to express my sympathy for Mr. Murray's death. I know you were close to him and his death must have been hard." Ali said gently.

"Yes it was very hard, but we had time to accept it was going to happen I just hate that he had to suffer over the death of Mr. Peterson like that. I think that really sped things along. He stopped trying to survive and went more quickly than expected," the nurse looked down at her hands clasped in her lap and appeared about to cry.

"We really have just a few quick questions. Did Mr. Peterson or Mr. Murray do anything unusual in the weeks before Peterson was killed?" Ali asked.

"What do you mean unusual?" Winston looked puzzled.

"Any thing you can think of, any change in routine, meet with people they didn't usually have contact with?" Jamie prodded.

"No not really. Mr. Peterson went to work every day and came home except for those evening meetings with that realtor." Winston replied.

"What realtor?" Ali asked.

"Well, Mr. Peterson talked to a realtor about putting the house up for sale after Mister Murray died. He said it would be too painful to live in the house without him." Winston answered.

"Mrs. Winston, this is very important," Ali said leaning toward her, "We have two men who are missing and we need to find them fast. I think the same person has them that killed Mr. Peterson. Do you know the name of this realtor?"

Winston rose from her chair. "I have Mr. Peterson's address book here. I was sending thank you notes to those that attended the funerals." She went into the house and Ali glanced excitedly at Jamie.

"Think it's the link?" Ali asked Jamie.

"Maybe," Jamie replied.

Winston returned holding a business card, which she handed to Ali. He glanced at it and wordlessly handed it to Jamie. She looked at it and silently read the name. Ruth Lefebre.

Ali led the way into the real estate office and headed to the back where Ruth Lefebre was talking on the phone, seated at her desk. She glanced up with a shocked look as Ali punched the hang up button on the phone, cutting off her call.

"What do you think you're doing, detective?" Lefebre demanded.

"We need to talk right now." Ali answered sitting across the desk from her. He tossed the business card on her desk.

"Another of my victims has a connection to you and I need to know what it is right now." Ali said. "The victim's name is Michael Peterson and he had your business card. His housekeeper says he was looking for a house, so who handled his business, you or Brand?"

Lefebre scowled at Ali and opened a file drawer next to her desk. She flipped through the folders and finally extracted one, dropping it on the desk in front of Ali. He opened it and turned toward Stevens.

"Brand," Ali said to Stevens. He turned to Lefebre and asked, "Is Brand here, or is he off today.

"He took a few days off, I told you that before," Lefebre answered.

"We need his address, right now," Ali demanded. Lefebre pulled a notepad to her and wrote the address on it. She passed it to Ali and sat back in her chair with a frown on her face, wanting to ask but not daring. Ali answered the question for her.

"We don't know what Brand's involvement is but it would be good if you don't call him and tell him we want to talk to him. We'll find him and ask our questions then you can ask him about this." Ali rose to leave. He turned toward Lefebre. "If you do warn him I promise you will go to jail for obstructing justice, are we clear?"

Lefebre nodded.

CHAPTER 9

Bobby Joe Miller wished he could get into the restroom to bathe, but he would have to wait until dark when all the little mommies with their kids had left the park for the day otherwise the cops would get called and he would get arrested for some bullshit charge, again. He glanced at the dirt caked on his hands and arms. It seemed he could never get completely clean anymore. He also wished he could wash his clothes but again he had to wait until the day time crowd had left the Laundromat for the day. Not that he noticed the stench anymore. His sense of smell seemed to have died a slow death when he wasn't looking. He was sure he smelled awful because when he was near other people they always gave him that frown and moved away from him or maybe it was just the fact that he was another homeless scumbag and decent people didn't want to be around him. He couldn't count the number of times that mothers had grabbed their child and hurried away when he approached like he was some ogre that was going to grab the kid and scurry down a sewer drain to devour the child and suck his bones clean.

Bobby Joe's life wasn't always this way. He had a decent job back home in Tennessee in the local bank and was entrusted with millions of dollars of other people's money and virtually their financial lives until he started to think those strange thoughts.

He wasn't sure when it started but he seemed to remember it was after the car accident. He got hit by a local drunk who didn't seem to care that his driving privilege had been taken away. Bobby Joe was minding his own business, driving home one evening when the other car came out of nowhere and hit his car broadside, causing Bobby Joe's head to slam into the doorpost. He was in a coma for a week and when he woke up he was different. He started to hear things other people didn't. He slowly got worse until one day he wandered away from home and never returned, living for a time in the woods. The eastern Tennessee Mountains got real cold in the winter months and Bobby Joe wandered south to Florida with another homeless guy he met who promised that life on the streets was better in warmer climes. Bobby Joe had to admit he was right about that part. Even in winter, South Florida was tolerable sleeping in the open at night. A light blanket of plastic trash bag was enough to keep the chill off and you didn't wake up covered in a blanket of snow.

Bobby Joe wondered for a time what had become of his wife and kids, but couldn't seem to remember their names. He could see their faces as plain as his own when he closed his eyes and he still had the faded wrinkled photograph in his wallet. That was the only thing in his old wallet, having lost all of his identification long ago.

Bobby Joe huddled in the bushes behind the fast food restaurant and waited. The kitchen help usually took out the garbage this time of the morning and Bobby Joe wanted to be the first to get something to eat. The hamburgers were usually fresh in the early afternoon when the lunch crowd had thinned out and the leftovers got thrown out. If you waited until the place closed, the meat was usually pretty smelly by then but the cops didn't get called if the place was closed and nobody saw you digging in the dumpster for scraps. Bobby Joe would chance it he just had to be quick. He had learned to move fast so that as soon as the cook was back inside the rear door Bobby Joe was moving. Grab the leftovers quick and back into the bushes before anybody noticed. He was close enough to faintly smell the stench of rotting garbage coming from the dumpster but it didn't bother him much. Many nights he had slept next to a dumpster. The city was nice enough to make a rule that the dumpster had to be encircled by a fence to hide it from decent people who should not have to look at something so disgusting, which made it a perfect place to sleep secluded and fairly safe from prying eyes. On cold nights the dumpster was warm from heat generated by the rotting contents but you had to get there early to claim it before somebody else did otherwise you might have to fight for it and could easily end up stabbed or worse. When you slept behind the dumpster, you had to find just the right spot to curl up because if you didn't, you ended up wet from the constant stream of liquid seeping from the bottom of it. God only knows what that shit was, but it was green and looked like toxic waste and smelled worse and was tough to wash that out of your clothes, especially when you only got to wash them every few weeks.

The back door of the hamburger joint opened and Bobby Joe got ready. The young black kid walked toward the dumpster, carrying a black plastic garbage bag. He heaved it over the top of the dumpster and turned back toward the back door. Bobby Joe prayed that the bag hadn't ripped open when it landed. Many times the bag tore open and Bobby Joe's efforts were futile. He would end up grabbing what he could get, scraping mold from the bread and eating around the rotting ground beef trying to find the edible parts. The fresh ones were best even if they were cold.

As soon as the door closed Bobby Joe was moving. He reached over the top of the dumpster and grabbed the bag. He pulled it down and ripped the top open. The hamburgers were still wrapped in wax paper. Damn! Two of them were still warm. This was turning into a good day after all. Bobby Joe stuffed the warm burgers into his jacket pockets to be eaten first. He grabbed a few more and stuffed them into his old backpack. He tied up the hole he had torn in the bag and placed it carefully back into the dumpster. He didn't want it to tear, so his street friends wouldn't have to dig for the good ones. He was lucky to get here first but you had to have consideration for others. Bobby Joe ducked back into the bushes and headed for his nest at the old abandoned building where he spent the day, napping and hiding from the hot sun. Tonight he would go to his other nest up under the bridge near the river.

Bobby Joe climbed into the hole where a window had been in the back side of the old office building. Before his eyes were able to adjust to the darkness, an arm grabbed him around the neck and dragged him to the ground, a gruff voice growled into his face, the breath thick with smell of alcohol. He looked up into the dirty face, mostly covered with a scraggly beard. The face grinned with a mouth filled with brown stained teeth. Sasquatch, that bastard. Bobby Joe tried not to be afraid but he was, everybody was afraid of this asshole. They all called him Sasquatch because of his size and because he was just plain mean. None of the street people knew his name and nobody wanted to. He preyed on the others, never finding his own food but taking it from others through fear and intimidation.

"What'd you bring me today?" Sasquatch growled at Bobby Joe. He started to grab for Bobby Joe's pockets but Bobby Joe quickly handed him some of the other hamburgers he had gotten from the dumpster. Sasquatch grabbed them and walked away, leaving Bobby Joe grateful to not have been beaten and all his food taken. Sasquatch had killed a friend of Bobby Joe's, choking him to death in the night because of some imagined snub when the victim stood up to Sasquatch's demands.

Bobby Joe moved deeper into the gloom of the building and settled into a safe corner to eat the warm burgers he had found. The first bite hurt his teeth but he ignored it after that, the food taking away the emptiness in his belly. Bobby Joe had noticed his teeth hurt lately and a few of them were loose. He figured it was just part of his lot in life.

His belly full, Bobby Joe settled into a corner. When one lived on the street, one learned to sleep in a corner where no one could get behind you. Bobby Joe tucked his backpack under his head for a pillow and settled in for the day. He wanted to sleep but didn't dare with Sasquatch lurking around. He heard a rustling noise and his heart raced, fearing that Sasquatch was back for more food. An old white haired woman, wearing a dirty long skirt and stained t-shirt appeared out of the gloom.

Crazy Mary they called her. She talked to herself all the time, saying things that made no sense and were not connected together.

"The beast is gone, you're safe," Mary whispered to Bobby Joe. Good. Sasquatch was out of his hair for the day. Bobby Joe went to sleep.

CHAPTER 1O

Ali parked down the street from Brand's address. He checked the address on the piece of paper in his hand. He looked down the street to the correct house.

"Should be the fourth one down on the right," he said to Jamie, pointing with his chin.

"I don't see any cars in the driveway," Jamie answered. "Could be in the garage though."

"Let's look but let's do it carefully." Ali replied opening his door and sliding out of the car. He led the way to the house. It was a one story and appeared to have been built in the late sixties. The design was old Florida but the jalousie windows had been replaced with modern single hung style. The driveway was laid with gray and sandstone color paving stones. The shades in the windows were closed and it appeared there were shades and blinds in the windows, making it impossible to see in. Ali walked around the front of the house, carefully watching the windows for any movement. Jamie went the opposite direction headed for the back of the house. Ali peeked in the windows of the garage. Empty. He joined Jamie in the rear of the house. In the back of the house was what appeared to be an windowless addition to the building. Ali thought that was a little unusual. They returned to the front door and Jamie rang the bell. No reply. Ali looked at Jamie and shrugged.

"Let's call Mr. Brand and see if he'll come in for a chat."

Jamie nodded in agreement and they headed back to the car.

Ali hung up the phone and looked at Jamie, hunched over her computer keyboard typing rapidly. He felt a twinge of desire. *Dammit. Why can't I stop thinking about her?* He imagined what it would be like to hold her in his arms, feel her warmth against him, to feel something again, anything. He pushed the thought from his mind.

"Brand will be here in an hour," he said to her, causing her to look up at him.

"How do you want to go at him?" Jamie asked.

"Slow and easy for now, after all he isn't a suspect, yet, we just play it by ear and see what develops," Ali answered.

Ali met Brand at the door of the homicide office and led him to an interview room. They used to call them interrogation rooms but that was no longer politically correct. As Brand settled into a chair Ali noticed he did it with a controlled arrogance as if he were the king settling into his throne. Ali asked if he could get him a drink or anything. Brand refused and Ali sat across from him, putting the table between them to create a psychological barrier. Ali knew Jamie was watching from behind a one way mirror and apparently Brand did too as he glanced toward the mirror and a small smile tickled the edge of his mouth. He has been in an interrogation room before, Ali thought.

"So, what can I do for you?" Brand asked, apparently trying to take control of the interview immediately. Interrogations are a mind game and Ali was not going to let Brand have the upper hand. He held his hand up to Brand, signaling him to wait. Ali studied the file in front of him, pretending to read it. He waited until Brand started to glance around the room getting distracted.

"You showed and sold a house to Johan Martins and Daniel Carnes is that correct?" Ali asked suddenly, catching Brand off guard. "Tell me about that."

"They were clients like any other. I showed them a house they liked and they bought it," Brand answered after a short hesitation, mentally trying to regroup.

"Did you have any other contact with them after the paperwork was signed? Celebrate or anything?" Ali asked.

"I took them out to dinner to celebrate. I frequently do that with clients," Brand answered.

"That's very nice of you, must get expensive though," Ali replied.

"Lots of realtors do that Detective. After all, when you sell a very expensive house the commission is very lucrative. It helps to treat clients well and increases the word of mouth clients. You do that for one, they tell their friends and their friends bring their business," Brand gave him a condescending smile.

"Michael Peterson. You know him?" Ali asked, switching subjects to keep Brand from pre-forming answers to questions he thought Ali was going to ask.

"I'm not sure. Why?" Brand asked. He seemed very comfortable with the conversation, too comfortable.

"He had your card and our information is that he was looking for a house. Somewhere to live after his partner, who was dying of AIDS, passed away," Ali answered.

"Oh yes. I remember now, very sad man. Had a lot on his mind and was grieving. Yes, I showed him a few properties."

"He didn't like what you showed him or he wasn't ready to buy yet," Ali queried.

"Neither. He never called me back,"

"Where did you take Martins and Carnes for dinner?" Ali asked, switching gears again.

"Le Cordon, the maitre'd knows me there and I confess he gives me a small break on the cost, so it isn't so difficult to take clients there and it helps bring him repeat business so everybody wins. The food is excellent there, you should try it." Brand answered.

"I don't care for French food, gives me gas. What happened after dinner?" Ali asked.

"We went our separate ways. I went home and I don't know where they went." Brand answered.

"Anybody see you come home?"

"I have no idea." Brand replied.

"You specialize in gay clients. Why?"

"They have very good taste and they have sufficient funds and like nice things. Like expensive houses. It's lucrative for me," Brand gave him a little smile.

"Are you gay?" Ali asked quickly like a sudden thrust.

"No! Will there be anything else Detective?" Brand shot back. A dark frown had crossed his face when he answered and Ali saw him realize it and quickly replace it with a pleasant smile. Too late, Ali thought.

"That will be it for now Mr. Brand," Ali said pleasantly to disguise the fact that he noticed the reaction. "Thank you for coming in we'll be in touch if we need anything else."

After Brand left Ali met Jamie in the office.

"Well?" He asked her.

"You definitely struck a chord with the gay question. There was a lot of anger but he tried hard to hide it. I liked your technique, kept him off balance. He definitely has some issues. I would say he is definitely a suspect or at least a person of interest. We need to focus on him a little harder," Jamie answered. Before Ali could reply his phone rang. He answered and listened then hung up.

"The M.E. wants us. They're doing the autopsies on Peterson and Bascomb."

Ali and Jamie pushed open the door to the autopsy room. The bodies of Peterson and Bascomb lay on their backs on shiny steel tables. Bascomb's chest gaped open from a Y shaped incision. The Medical Examiner was bent over Peterson's body on the adjacent Table. She glanced up as they approached.

"Hey guys. Sorry it took so long to get these done but I figured I would do them together so I could compare findings right away" the Medical Examiner said, pulling thick blue rubber gloves off her hands.

"There is something weird here. I don't know what to make of it," the M.E. frowned. Ali and Jamie approached the bodies on the tables.

"What's strange?" Jamie asked.

"Well, look at this," the ME said pointing at Peterson's chest. "There are bruises on this man that appear to have been by a shoe. And some that look like he was beaten. Not severely, but beaten just the same. How long was he missing before they found him?"

"We're not sure but maybe overnight," Ali answered.

"Well that would be consistent with the lividity. You were right Ali he was definitely dumped where he was found and he laid face down for a while, maybe ten or twelve hours, the lividity is not real pronounced," The ME mused. "They were definitely killed with the same gun, forty-five caliber. We don't have the projectiles so I can't do ballistics but I 'm sure it was the same gun. It looks like Peterson was kneeling in front of the victim when the fatal shot was fired judging by the track of the bullet wound and he was naked, either forced or voluntarily. My guess would be voluntarily as his clothes were not torn as if they were forced off. I don't know if he took them off because somebody was pointing that big ass gun at him though. My guess would be that he was coerced to go somewhere and then held and beaten for awhile. We examined his clothes under the microscope and found no epithelials other than his so it doesn't look like he had his clothes on when he was beaten. There was also no blood."

"So what's weird?" Ali asked.

"Well," the ME said, "The fact that there's no blood isn't unusual in and of itself since the bullet stopped the heart immediately so there would not be any blood when the facial cuts were made. But we checked Peterson's car and found only a small amount of blood, his, in the car that shows he was killed elsewhere and driven to the dump site in his car. My guess is he was held somewhere, beaten and shot. You need to find me that site and I can prove it. Question is where? The weird part is that Bascomb wasn't beaten. The killer just walked up and shot him in the head but Bascomb looks like he was stalked or maybe picked at random. That's what's weird. The M.O.'s are inconsistent."

"Are you telling me there are two killers?" Ali asked with surprise.

"Or maybe just two different motivations," Jamie interjected.

"That's right," The ME answered, "Same gun, same type of silencer but different reasons? Unless the killer realized after shooting Peterson that the gun would destroy the face if it was a head shot."

"Would there be a lot of blood where Peterson was killed?" Ali asked.

"There would be some. Probably not a large amount since, like I said, the bullet stopped the heart immediately," the ME answered. "By the way, we got positive ID on Bascomb from dental records, using what was left of the lower jaw and also confirmed it by fingerprints. Bascomb's attorney is waiting for you in my office. Apparently he has no next of kin so the attorney is handling his affairs and wants to claim the body."

Ali and Jamie entered the ME's private office and were greeted by a well dressed older man in a very expensive suit. He rose to shake Ali's hand and Ali noticed that his fingernails were well manicured and appeared to have a clear polish on them. He also noticed the Rolex.

"Michael Riley, detectives, Mr. Bascomb's attorney," Riley said by way of introduction.

"Mr. Riley, how long have you been Mr. Bascomb's attorney?" Ali asked when they had all been seated.

"Ten years. I handle all of Mr. Bascomb's affairs." Riley replied.

"Mr. Bascomb has no next of kin?" Jamie asked.

"No. Mr. Bascomb was never married and his parents passed fifteen years ago. He has no siblings," Riley replied.

"No cousins, aunts, uncles, no one?" Ali asked.

"No. His parents were also only children," Riley replied. He did not seem willing to reveal a lot of information. Like most lawyers, they ask but don't tell.

"I have to ask a question and I mean no offense but it is important. Was Mr. Bascomb gay?" Ali asked.

"I don't think Mr. Bascomb's sexual preferences are any of your business, detective," Riley sniffed.

"I can't reveal any information but we think there may be a connection to Mr. Bascomb's sexual preference and his death," Jamie said.

"Yes. He was gay. From what I understand, he was gunned down in front of a gay bar. So I assume you already knew the answer." Riley snapped.

"Sorry but we had to confirm it. What did Mr. Bascomb do for a living?" Ali said.

"He was an investment banker, why?" Riley asked.

"Did he have any involvement in real estate? Was he looking to buy or sell a house?" Ali asked.

"No he didn't. If he did I would know," Riley answered. He rose indicating the interview was over. "If it's all right I would like to tend to my client's arrangements. I assume the body will be released soon?"

"The ME can answer that question, thank you for your time." Ali shook his hand.

Ali and Jamie returned to the office. Ali plopped into his chair. There were two men out there going through who knew what and he was no closer to finding them and finding them was top priority, preferably before they were slaughtered like the two in the morgue.

"What was it the ME said about Peterson?" Ali asked Jamie.

"Which part?" Jamie replied.

"About him being held somewhere, before he was killed," Ali answered.

"What about it?" Jamie asked, puzzled. Where was he going with this?

"Remember at Brand's house. The back part had no windows and it looked new. No windows means prying eyes couldn't see in and not much sound would get out." Ali mused. He sat up and slid his computer keyboard to him. He brought up the city building department website and clicked on the search function for building permits. He typed in Brand's address and punched the enter button. In a few seconds the computer told him the website was down and under repair. Damn. Ali grabbed the phone and dialed the building department. The clerk who answered the phone informed him she couldn't do a search because the computer was down but should be back up by tomorrow. She also informed him, in no uncertain terms that the department closed in five minutes it was after all two minutes to five o'clock. Ali hung up and glanced at his watch. He had lost track of time. He realized he was hungry.

"I'm gonna grab some dinner, you hungry?" He asked Jamie.

"Yeah, are you quitting for the day?" She asked.

"Yeah, I can't think of anywhere else to go from here." Ali answered.

"I hate to quit with those two still missing but maybe if we eat we'll get a new perspective. What if we took the sketch of the guy who dumped Peterson's car to the Parrot cage and asked around? It might stir somebody's memory." Jamie said.

"Lemme clear it with Davis." Ali rose and headed for the Lieutenant's office. He would have to approve any overtime. It didn't take much convincing. Davis told Ali he and Jamie could work twenty four hours a day if it would help catch the killer.

Overtime wasn't a problem when the case was a political and public relations hot potato like this one.

Ali asked the hostess for a table in the back of the restaurant, preferably one where he could sit with his back to the wall. It was a cop thing; he was never comfortable with his back to the room. The waitress led them to a secluded table and seated them. She left after telling them their server would be with them shortly. Ali opened his menu and chose a steak and salad while Jamie ordered a grilled chicken salad. After the waitress left, Ali decided to pick Jamie's brain.

"Well, tell me about our killer. Don't most serial killers leave notes or clues for the police to taunt them?" He asked.

"Only in the movies. John Wayne Gacy killed thirty three men and boys and the police had no clue until one victim was raped and then let go. Gacy never taunted anyone or gave any clues to his killings. Gacy was very careful and buried his victims in his basement. He even poured lime on the bodies to try and destroy the evidence. Ted Bundy never taunted the police either. Jeffrey Dahmer killed and partially devoured his victims. One of his victims escaped and flagged down a police car but Dahmer told them he and the victim were lovers and had a domestic. They returned the victim to the house and left him there and Dahmer later killed him. All of these killers crimes had sexual overtones and involved sexual assault or perversion. Our guy has sexual overtones only by the fact that the victims are all gay. There have been no sexual assaults. This guy's in a rage against a certain segment of society that he feels wronged him in some way. That's indicated by the mutilations to the face. He can't stand to see them left whole. He wants them disgraced and humiliated like he feels they did to him. I would suspect, like I said before, that he was sexually abused and instead of realizing the abuser was a child molester, he has fixated on the sex aspect. The abuser was definitely male, someone he respected, like a teacher, youth counselor something like that. He thinks that because the sex was with the same sex, male, he thinks it made him gay or at least bisexual. Gacy was reportedly bisexual. Our killer is very polished and likable. Most serial killers are the guy next door, even pillars of the community. They are charming and very good at deception. Look at Dahmer. He convinced two cops that the victim who escaped was a lover despite the victim telling them he had been kidnapped, raped and others had been murdered, very smooth. Serial killers are the ones who hide in plain sight as it were. No one suspects them until they're caught." The conversation made Ali glad there were no other diners nearby. The conversation would have turned their stomachs.

CHAPTER 11

Bobby Joe Miller opened his eyes and glanced around in the gloom, something was moving on his arm. He looked down and saw a large cockroach crawling up his arm. He flicked it off and shuddered, God how he hated those damn things. The bugs were the one thing he couldn't quite get used to living on the streets. They were always crawling on him. Bobby Joe sat up and peeked around, looking for Sasquatch, fearing that bastard would choke him to death in his sleep and take what little food and clothes he had. He saw nothing and struggled to his feet. Bobby Joe gathered up his backpack and the sheet of cardboard he had lain on to keep from having to lay on bare dirt.

Bobby Joe stopped at the door and glanced carefully around, making sure no one was waiting in ambush before stepping out of the vacant building. Living on the street made a man like a wild animal. The world of the streets was a predatory world. It was a matter of daily survival. A man could be beaten nearly to death for something as trivial as a toothbrush or a stale sandwich. The homeless stuck together to a certain point but if one had something another wanted if was every man for himself and the law of the jungle prevailed. Survival was nature's strongest instinct, the second strongest being sex.

Bobby Joe saw no danger and stepped from the building, turning left towards the hamburger stand and it's dumpster hoping there would be some non rancid food he could grab to survive another day.

Bobby Joe found three fairly fresh sandwiches in the dumpster. As he was putting them in his backpack for later he saw another street dweller coming and scurried off into the bushes to keep from getting beaten. The dumpsters would get busy soon and there was sure to be a battle for the scraps. Bobby Joe was lucky he got there early. He headed down the sidewalk of the main thoroughfare as sun was beginning to dip into the west, the sky a mixture of red, pink, blue and gray as dusk slithered across the streets. The streetlights were beginning to come on and the cars gathered at the traffic lights had their headlights on. Night was going to be here soon and Bobby Joe needed to get to his hiding place under the bridge before it got too dark. Otherwise he was fair game for the others and the cops.

He passed a city park and saw a group of homeless men and women gathered on the picnic tables and heard them arguing loudly over a bottle of wine one of them had begged from somewhere. Bobby Joe figured somebody would call the cops soon. He avoided the parks because after dark the parks were closed and the cops would arrest you for trespassing. He had been foolish enough to get caught there twice and spent two nights in the county jail. The jail wasn't bad because you got to bathe and they gave you clean clothes but the law of the jungle was even stronger in the jail and there was no where to go and no place to hide if someone took a dislike to you. Bobby Joe had suffered a pretty bad beating the last time and he did not ever intend to go back. That was why he liked the bridge. The cops pretty much left you alone as long as you were out of sight and no one called them to complain about you.

Bobby Joe scurried up the embankment under the bridge and into the crawlspace at the very top. He settled his backpack and spread out his cardboard sheet then dug the hamburgers out of his backpack and began to eat slowly, savoring the taste. He always savored his food because he never knew when he would eat again. He hoped his buddy Chuck would show up with a bottle because he really needed a drink. Chuck sold newspapers on the corner and always had just enough money to get a bottle and Chuck always shared with Bobby Joe.

Bobby Joe finished his hamburgers and settled back into his nest. He heard the gears of the drawbridge start to hum and grind as the bottom of the bridge began to drop slowly down to let a boat through. Bobby Joe watched as a large yacht glided under the bridge, all white and clean and shiny and beautiful with all the lights lit up. He watched it clear the bridge and listened to the gears begin to grind as the bridge lowered. That was the other thing he liked about the bridge. He loved watching the boats and it was peaceful here.

Bobby Joe saw a dark figure appear and begin to climb up the embankment toward him. He tensed and squinted into the dark, gripping his pocketknife to defend himself if he needed to.

"Bobby Joe. It's me Chuck," the figure said and Bobby Joe relaxed. Chuck struggled into the small space and plopped beside him.

"I got some beer. It was all I could get." Chuck said, holding up a six pack of Budweiser. Bobby Joe didn't care. It was wet, cold and had alcohol, everything he needed. Bobby Joe pulled a can loose from the group and popped the top. He put the can to his lips and drank, letting the cold sharp liquid fill his mouth. He held it in his mouth enjoying the taste before swallowing. God that was good.

Bobby Joe and Chuck shared the six-pack as Chuck recounted his day on the corner selling papers. He complained about the rich fat bastard in the Cadillac who almost ran him down and the cop who harassed him for not having his orange safety vest on.

They finished the beer and shook hands and Bobby Joe thanked him for the beer, promising to get something for them to drink tomorrow night. Chuck slithered and slid down the dirt embankment headed for his sleeping place. Bobby Joe knew he slept behind the bank nearby, hidden in the big Florida Holly tree in the corner of the parking lot.

Bobby Joe settled in for the night. He had a clear view of the area under the bridge and the parking lot next to the bridge. He could see for a hundreds of feet in three directions giving him a clear view of anyone approaching. He listened to the hum of the cars overhead crossing the metal span of the bridge and drifted off to sleep.

Bobby Joe started awake and glanced around. Not sure what woke him up. He heard a car door slam somewhere and looked down into the parking lot. He saw a burgundy BMW parked in the corner of the lot. That was what had wakened him. It was usually so quiet here that he decided he must have been awakened when the car drove in. He watched as a large man walked around the car and appeared to be wiping it down with a cloth. Strange time to be waxing your car, Bobby Joe thought. Besides he was trying to sleep.

"Hey Asshole, wax your car somewhere else!' Bobby Joe yelled.

The man whirled around and peered around trying to find where the voice had come from. Suddenly, he turned and trotted away out of Bobby Joe's view. Bobby Joe chuckled to himself. Chickenshit will probably come back during daylight to get his car. He drifted back to sleep.

Bobby Joe woke up two hours later. When you lived on the street you didn't need an alarm clock and you never slept past sunup. The wise man got moving before the sun came up because if you slept too long you were easy prey. Bobby Joe looked down and realized the BMW was still there. He gathered up his belongings and slipped and slid down the embankment. He walked to the BMW, glancing around to make sure no one was watching then 'ed the car and peered in the windows. Holy shit! The keys are in it. He could use this car. Beats walking and sleeping in the dirt he decided. He checked the doors and they were unlocked. Bobby Joe piled his things in the backseat and slipped into the driver's seat. He took a deep breath through his nose; the smell of the leather was magical. He sank into the seat. God this leather is comfortable. He turned the key and listened to the engine purr. Man, this is nice.

Bobby Joe dropped the car into reverse and backed out of the parking space. He dropped the car into drive and drove from the parking lot. He turned on the radio and found a station he liked, man this is living, he thought. He decided to cruise around for awhile since the streets were pretty empty. He knew he would have to hide this car during the day to avoid the cops. He figured he could use this car for at least three days before the cops found it. But for now he was going to enjoy it.

CHAPTER 12

Ali parked the unmarked car half a block from the Parrot Cage. He figured a police car, even an unmarked one might scare away the patrons and he wanted to try and talk to as many as he could. A pair of men passed as Ali locked the car doors. They were wearing leather chaps with thongs underwear, making their buttocks hang out the back of the chaps. Their outfits were completed by leather vests. Maybe this isn't such a good idea Ali thought. He caught Jamie looking at him over the roof of the car and shrugged with resignation. Jamie met him at the front of the car and chuckled.

"Well, at least you didn't vomit in front of them." Jamie grinned at him. Ali didn't think it was funny. He was disgusted but tried to shove it out of his mind. They were stopped at the door by a very large tattooed man with huge arms and Ali instinctively sized him up, deciding he was all strength and not much speed. In the ring he would get his butt whipped unless he got a hold of you and then he would probably break your back. Ali held up his badge and asked for Bradley Fontaine. The doorman disappeared inside and returned shortly with Fontaine in tow.

"Hello detective. Come to see how the other half lives?" Fontaine smiled at them.

"We'd like to talk to some of your customers if we could," Ali replied.

"As long as you don't chase them away," Fontaine answered.

"Since you're here, have you seen this guy?" Ali asked, holding up the artists sketch provided by Otis Washington. Fontaine peered at it and shrugged.

"Could be a thousand people." Fontaine said. He turned and led the way into the bar.

The bar was as Ali remembered it, dark and smoky, clouds of cigarette smoke seemed multi-colored from the light of multiple televisions positioned around the ceiling. The television screens were large and flat, the newest models. The images on the screens were graphic videos of gay sex, homosexual and lesbian. Each screen showed a different video. Now Ali felt like vomiting. Couples danced in the gloom. They were all men dancing with men or women dancing with women. Ali glanced at Jamie and smiled inwardly. Now, who's uncomfortable he thought. Ali nudged Jamie and leaned over and hollered in her ear to be heard over the pounding rock music blaring from huge speakers.

"Let's split up and show the picture around."

Jamie nodded and moved away from him. Ali approached a couple dancing and tapped the taller one on the shoulder who turned and frowned at him as if he thought Ali was trying to cut in. Ali held up his badge and yelled that he wanted to ask the man a question. The man shook his head and pointed to his left ear indicating he couldn't hear Ali over the music.

This won't work, Ali thought. He looked around and spotted Fontaine standing at the bar sipping a drink. Ali pushed his way through the crowd.

"Having any luck detective?" Fontaine asked. Ali glanced at the drink in Fontaine's hand. It looked like straight scotch on the rocks. God Ali wanted a drink. He felt his mouth starting to water. He choked down the spittle and leaned toward Fontaine.

"The music's too loud. Nobody can hear me!" He hollered. "Can you ask the DJ to turn it down for a few minutes?"

Fontaine gave him a disgusted look and pushed away from the bar threading his way to the DJ booth. Ali watched as he spoke into the DJ's ear. Suddenly the music stopped and the dancing couples separated.

"Hey, what the fuck?" One of the dancers yelled. Fontaine leaned into the microphone.

"Sorry boys and girls. But we have some guests. That gruff looking man at the bar in the off the rack suit is a cop. He's investigating the recent murders of our friends and needs to talk to you. The music will resume shortly."

Every head in the room turned toward Ali. He and Jamie made their way through the crowd holding up the sketch asking if anyone had seen the person depicted in the sketch. They were met with empty looks and shaking heads.

"Are you investigating the guy who got shot in the head in the parking lot too?" A frail man with a wispy mustache asked.

"Yes we are." Ali answered.

"I was there that night. Can we talk outside?" The man asked.

"Sure." Ali answered. The frail man headed toward the door and Ali waved at Jamie over the man's head.

Once on the sidewalk the frail man glanced around nervously.

"I didn't see the shooting, but I did see someone walking away right after I heard the noise," the frail man said.

"This guy?" Ali asked holding up the sketch.

"No. The man I saw was large, heavy set but not fat, very dark hair," the man answered. He glanced from Ali to Jamie. Ali thought he looked like he was going to wet his pants.

"Can you identify him?" Ali asked hopefully.

"No I only saw him from the back and I'm not sure he did the shooting. I just saw him walking away from the area. He looked like he was in a hurry."

"Okay lemme get your information. I'll need to get a statement from you later." Ali said, pulling his notepad from his pocket.

Ali stared out the window as he drove. *I need to get into Brand's house. Time is running out for the missing men, maybe they are already dead.*

"You handled your disgust well." Jamie said, interrupting his thoughts.

"Gee thanks. I thought it was oozing out of my pores." Ali answered.

"We need to speed things up you know. Those missing men may still be alive." Jamie said.

Ali parked next to Jamie's car in the parking lot and shut off the engine. They sat silently for a few seconds. Ali felt like he was ending a date. He wanted to lean over and kiss her but fought the urge. The silence stretched until Jamie broke it.

"I'll see you in the morning." Jamie said and opened the door. Ali smiled sadly and nodded as Jamie closed the door and walked away from him toward her car. She could feel his eyes on her. *Damn, she thought why didn't I do something? I know he felt the same way. I sensed it but I didn't dare make the first move.* She wished she had. Maybe this wasn't the time or the place but she had really wanted him to kiss her. Damn.

Ali waited until Jamie had entered her car and closed the door. When he heard the engine start he dropped the car in drive and eased away feeling guilty for wanting her. He wished life was simpler and he didn't miss Maria so much. *I really need to get on with my life* he thought. *Really, really need to get on with my life.* He glanced at his watch and checked the time. It was eleven pm. He decided he would start tomorrow getting back into shape. He had planned to start today but the trip to the Parrot Cage changed that.

Ali thought about Jamie during the drive home. Why did she have such an effect on him? He had not been attracted to any woman since Maria died. He wondered if there was something wrong with him. Shouldn't he be loyal to Maria? But didn't he have a right to live? Goddam I need a drink he thought. His mouth watered and he hurried to put his key in the lock.

Ali slipped off his jacket and tossed it on the couch then looked around the room for it because he knew it was there. IT was always there, waiting for him. Waiting to pounce on him and make him pay. The guilt and the pain were like a living thing that would not let him alone, would not let him walk past it. He hated himself for not being there that morning. He was asleep for Christ sake, asleep when Maria needed him most, while the life drained out of her. He was dreaming while she fought for breath, for life itself. Asleep! Some husband you are, it usually taunted him. But right now it hid itself from him, the room silent and mute. Maria's things sat silently staring back at him.

This was even worse Ali decided as he poured himself a drink and sat in a chair at the kitchen table scanning the room waiting for it to emerge. He contemplated the glass in his hand. He knew he needed to stop, wanted to stop. His mind told him the booze was killing him, that he was stronger than this. He had faced larger stronger opponents in the ring and emerged victorious, not unscathed but victorious. He unconsciously rubbed the scar on his eyebrow as he drained the glass. He poured another, drank it and poured a third. The heat in his belly warmed him and suddenly he didn't care if it came or not, he could face it now. But it never appeared. Ali staggered to the couch and fell onto it and was asleep almost immediately.

CHAPTER 13

James Brand opened the door and glared down at the still figure chained to the floor. There was no movement. He walked over and kicked the nearest leg causing the figure to lurch awake. Jonah Martins unconsciously tried to curl into the fetal position but couldn't because of the chains. He strained to see through the blindfold but all he saw was darkness. He could sense Brand circling around him, could hear his bare feet swishing on the tile floor, turning his head to follow the sound. There was still a slight buzzing in his ears from the recent gunshot. He tensed, waiting to be struck but nothing happened.

"Don't worry you pussy I'm not going to hit you, yet. You'll know when I'm going to because I'll tell you. Right now I want to tell you a story. It's a story about your little lover boy. At this very moment, he's floating in a nasty polluted canal being eaten by the fish and the crabs and any other hungry fucking creature that comes along and I'm sure they will, attracted by all that blood draining from the gaping hole in him that my gun made. Yeah they're gonna find him and eat his eyes out and swim into his mouth and chew on his tongue and his balls and that dick you love so much, you piece of garbage." Brand was shouting now. Martins whimpered from the image he had in his brain.

"Why are you doing this James?" Martins whispered, his throat bone dry from lack of water.

"Because I love it and its fun and you deserve it!" Brand screamed into Martins ear, spittle flying from his mouth and spraying Martins cheek. "You people fucked up my life and this is what you get for it."

Brand left the room, slamming the door behind him. God that was good he thought. He showered and flopped on the leather couch in the living room. He retrieved the remote and flipped on the television, settling on the news. He got bored quickly and turned on the DVD player, smiling at the graphic sexual image on the screen. He began to stroke himself. He felt like a god and gods were invincible. The cops would never figure out who he was. He gritted his teeth and began to move his hand faster. Yeah he was invincible. He flashed to the image of his parents lying on the kitchen floor, the blood draining from them and pooling on the linoleum as he reached the crescendo.

Brand pushed himself from the couch and cleaned himself with a hand towel. He was drained but calm and satisfied. He poured a scotch in a crystal goblet from the bar in the corner and considered what to do with Martins. He would kill him of course but how and when was the question. He considered skinning him alive with a sharp knife. That would be fun. No, he would wait for the right time. He wanted to make him suffer and suffer for a long time. Better to let him think about Carnes and let him hurt and hurt and hurt some more before giving him his sweet release. Brand contemplated death. Was it a sweet release or was it an end to everything and there was nothing beyond. If that Baptist preacher that screamed and cajoled and vilified the congregation when he was growing up was right, then he was gonna burn in hells hot fire. Well, he guessed he would see what he would see, but not anytime soon. He planned to have a lot more fun before that happened, a lot more fun.

Brand quietly opened the door to the room and peeked around it. Martins lay motionless but breathing. Brand walked through the house turning out the lights and went to bed.

Brand lay in bed thinking. He tried to remember how it all began. He joined the scouts because his step-father wanted him to have some manly interests and Brand found he liked being in the scouts. He enjoyed being outdoors in the woods, he always had. He remembered taking long walks near his house and watching the squirrels chasing each other around the old oak near the far fence at the bottom of the neighbor's field. Brand especially liked the camping trips. The first had been near the river. The boys fished and swam in the river, laughing and pushing each other under water only to burst to the surface screaming with glee. Brand remembered the smell of the tent canvas. It was even stronger when it rained and the tents were wet. It was combination of canvas, mildew and hay from the tents being stored in the scoutmaster's barn. He loved to lie in his sleeping bag and listen to the rain tapping on the tent.

He couldn't remember exactly how the other thing started. He recalled being caught masturbating one night by the assistant scoutmaster when he was twelve and had just discovered that he had an erection and wondered what to do with it. He had heard about sex, all the boys knew about it and he decided to see what the fuss was all about. Well, he found out all right. It was the most amazing feeling he had experienced in his young life except the first time he kissed a girl on the lips. The flashlight blinded him in the dark and he was terrified but the assistant scoutmaster talked to him gently, telling him it was a natural thing for a boy his age. Then he showed him more sensations he could never have imagined.

The assistant scoutmaster was a burly, hulking man of eighteen with a constant slouch and thick arms and legs. A scar ran from the base of his nose to the top of his upper lip and one front tooth was chipped. Brand remembered the feel of the man's mouth on him and how that chipped tooth had scratched him when he was most sensitive and he was not the only one. Before Brand knew it, all the boys were participating, waiting for the sound of loud snoring from the head scoutmaster's tent before they began their explorations. The assistant scoutmaster told them it was a natural way for boys to learn about sex and was harmless, a boy's passage from boyhood to manhood. The only other time Brand had explored his sexual desires was the time he and the girl from the next farm got naked in an old barn and examined each others bodies. He was too young to get an erection and had just touched and looked.

Brand had never really considered himself to be weird or strange. He fantasized about women, especially his best friend's aunt. She was a big breasted woman and she was the one he had fantasized about when he satisfied himself. He and his buddies looked at the naked women in the magazines his best friend had spirited away from his father's secret stash in the bedroom closet, joking and dreaming of what they would like to do with those women in the magazines. But Brand also had another need. He didn't want to because it disgusted and nauseated him especially when it led him to pick up men in public bathrooms. He loathed and hated the man who made the need exist within him. He had never felt any desire for young men just the ones his own age. Remembering all of this caused the rage to build within him and he feared it, hated himself for it and wished he had the nerve to put that damn gun in his own mouth and pull the trigger. But he was seldom overwhelmed by it. He had his share of female companions and he loved the feeling of being with a woman, so he knew he was not a fag. Dammit he wasn't one of those prissy feminine assholes who spent their time cruising the gay bars looking for love. No, he was a man's man and no one could tell him different. He was a powerful beautiful creature who had control of it and no one would ever stop him. Finally, he dozed off and slept.

CHAPTER 14

Bobby Joe decided he was in love with this car. The radio was the best he had ever heard and Garth Brooks never sounded so sweet. He leaned back in the heated seat and rocked his head to Garth, feeling better than he had in a long time in fact couldn't remember when he had felt this good. He stopped at a red light and spotted a police car on the opposite corner. Shit! He prayed the cop didn't see him. Suddenly the blue lights on top of the police car came on and the police car made a hard right and accelerated down the street away from him. Whew, Bobby Joe breathed a sigh of relief. I better park and hide out somewhere. He realized he stuck out like a sore thumb in the light traffic this late at night so he turned into a parking garage and drove to the top floor. He found an empty space between two minivans and parked. Thank God for moms with minivans. They made good places to hide a car. Bobby Joe parked and climbed into the back seat rolling down the windows slightly to let the breeze blow through the car. This high off the ground the breeze was pretty stiff and it wasn't as hot as it was under the bridge where he usually slept. Bobby Joe opened his last beer and sipped it slowly, savoring the sweetness.

He finished the beer and settled down for the night, mentally reminding himself that he couldn't sleep too late. Somebody leaving for work in the morning would see him sleeping in the car and call the cops, which would not be a good thing.

CHAPTER 15

The ringing phone caused Ali to lurch to a seated position. The room spun for a second as Ali glanced at the alarm clock on the nightstand. Five thirty a.m.? Who the hell was calling him this early? Ali fumbled the phone to his ear.

"Hello," Ali whispered with sleep into the receiver.

"Hey sleepy, you need to wake up. They found a body that might be one of our missing guys. We need to get there." Jamie Stevens' voice said in Ali's ear.

"Where?" Ali asked clearing his throat. His voice was stronger now.

"In the Intracoastal, floating." Jamie answered, "Davis has paged you three times, and he's pissed."

Ali vaguely remembered fumbling for the pager in the dark and turning it off. Damn!

"I'll pick you up at the station in half an hour," Ali told Jamie and hung up. He swung his feet over the edge of the bed and nearly fell to the floor. Damn I'm still drunk he realized. He stumbled to the shower and washed quickly then turned on the cold water to try to clear his head but all it did was give him a chill. He dressed quickly and made himself a cup of coffee in the microwave then poured it into a covered travel mug to take with him. He was out the door in fifteen minutes.

By the time he found Jamie standing next to her car waiting for him he was pretty clear headed. She got in beside him and gave him the address.

Ali turned into the parking lot of the strip mall and drove toward the tangle of police cars and emergency vehicles at the end near the seawall. He parked next to an empty paramedic rescue truck and followed Jamie toward the knot of people on the dock. They were gathered around a black body bag lying on the pavement. Ali recognized Lt. Davis in the group and pushed his was to him through the crowd. Ali tugged at Davis sleeve and jerked his head away from the crowd, indicating Davis should follow him away to a more private place. Davis fell in behind him and Ali walked about twenty paces and stopped, glancing around to make sure no one, especially the press who were beginning to arrive, was in earshot.

"What's the story?" Ali asked as Jamie joined them. Davis frowned at him and Ali wondered if Davis could smell alcohol on his breath, he doubted it. He had sucked on a breath mint on the ride to the scene just in case.

"Looks like one of your missing couple just turned up." Davis said, nodding toward the body bag. "Passerby spotted him floating and called it in. Dive team is on the way to check for evidence in the water. It looks by my estimation that he was shot in the back of the head with the same big damn gun."

"Which one is it?" Ali asked.

"I dunno. The face is pretty much blown away. Blond hair, obviously male, he was naked so it wasn't hard to tell." Davis answered. He turned to Jamie and asked her to excuse them for a minute and she walked back to the group on the dock. He turned back to Ali.

"Are you okay for this or do I need to reassign this case?" Davis asked.

"Fine, why?" Ali replied.

"Ali, I'm a supervisor not an idiot. I am a cop and I haven't forgotten everything I knew before I got promoted. I've let the drinking go 'cause I'm your friend and I know what you've been going through and it has never affected your work, but I can tell what kind of night you've had so don't bullshit me okay?" Davis said softly.

"It won't affect my job this time either. It won't be a problem." Ali replied, looking at the ground.

"It better not. After this case is done we need to talk about it but for now stay away from the reporters and the bosses, deal?" Davis said.

"Yeah boss. No problem." Ali answered. They turned and returned to the dock together.

Jamie was squatting next the body bag on the ground. She had rubber gloves on and silently handed a pair to Ali.

"You might want to do that downwind." One of the uniformed cops said. Ali could already smell the stench through the rubber bag before Jamie unzipped the bag causing the group to take a few steps away in unison. Jamie pulled the slit in the body bag open and the stench of decaying flesh roiled up. A few of the uniformed cops that didn't need to see suddenly decided to head for the crime scene tape line to hold the onlookers back.

The body was frozen in a grotesque position. The arms were bent at the elbows, the lower arms sticking straight up. The naked skin was stark white and wrinkled, spotted with blue bruises on the torso. The belly was bloated and there were empty holes where the eyes should be. The face was little more than a jagged gaping hole making it hard to distinguish what damage the bullet had done and what the fish and crabs had helped with. There were a few teeth clinging to the top and bottom gums. Ali could see what looked like small circular burns on the chest and neck, probably done with a cigarette.

"Great way to start the morning," a voice behind Ali said. He turned and greeted the medical examiner. They shook hands and the medical examiner leaned over the body. He pulled on rubber surgical gloves and reached down, pulling the mouth open on the corpse.

"Well, we got some teeth left which is good. Looks like he was tortured," the ME pointed at the bruises and cigarette burns. "Lemme see what time of death looks like."

The ME opened his briefcase and removed a long pointed rod with a temperature gauge on the end. He inserted it into the corpse's torso and the stench got worse. He left the rod there for a few seconds then withdrew it. He looked at the temperature gauge and grunted. The ME then walked to the seawall and dropped a thermometer on a long white string into the water of the canal. He reeled it back in a few minutes later and examined it. He made some calculations on a note pad and walked back where Ali and Stevens were standing.

"Preliminary guess is that he's been in the water around twenty hours but I'll know more after the post," the ME told them. He motioned to two men in short sleeve dress shirts and ties guarding a stretcher close by.

"You guys need to see anymore?" The ME asked.

"No thanks. We'll come by the morgue for the post. Put a rush on this one doc if it's who we think it is, his partner is still being held somewhere and we need to try to find him before he ends up fish bait like this guy." Ali answered. They watched as the two attendants zipped the body bag closed, hoisted it onto the stretcher and wheeled it toward a white van in the parking lot. Ali could hear camera shutters clicking as the newspaper photographers snapped shots for tomorrow's edition. Ali scanned the crowd for Davis and spotted him standing in front of a phalanx of television cameras, answering the reporter's questions. He also spotted Rodney James of CAD in the front of the crowd and took Jamie by the elbow, guiding her away from the crowd and toward their car.

"Let's get some breakfast and away from this shit." Ali said in a low voice.

After breakfast in a small diner, Ali dropped Jamie at the federal courthouse downtown and drove back to the homicide office. He settled down to his computer and logged in to the Building departments website. He located the contractor who built the addition to Brand's house and printed out a copy of the building permit. Ali spent an hour writing an affidavit for a search warrant. He decided not to wait for Jamie, who was still waiting to testify in a court case. He figured she would be busy there the rest of the day. Ali called the Medical Examiners Office and was told it was very busy there and the autopsy would be put off a couple of hours.

Ali had been waiting for thirty minutes to see the homicide DA. He hated to wait but attorneys worked on a different time clock. Ali walked to the reception desk and asked the bespectacled receptionist how much longer he would have to wait. She gave him a frosty smile and said it would be a few minutes she had said the same thirty minutes ago. He returned to the overstuffed pink leather couch and dropped into it, aggravated. He settled back into the couch watching the parade in the hallway.

Attorneys in expensive suits passed, intermingled with attorneys is cheaper suits. The cheap suits were the public defenders and prosecutors who didn't make the big money with expensive clients. Ali knew that even he was better paid than they were. Most were recent graduates of law school who were cutting their teeth in court until they could leave for some fancy private practice. The parade included lots of pretty women, attorneys, secretaries and court reporters. Ali watched them all amusing himself trying to guess what they did and if they were for the prosecution or the defense. The courthouse was a constant flow of humanity. He watched a young black man pass wearing the huge baggy pants so popular with the teens and young adults. They were gathered at the crotch where he gripped them tightly to keep them from falling to the floor. He wondered why these kids wore those pants since the only thing they were good for was to slow these kids down when they ran from the police. Cops loved these pants because it made it easier to chase down these kids on foot. Ali couldn't understand dressing that way to appear in court. It definitely didn't impress the judge or jury.

"Detective Castillo?" The receptionist motioned from her desk. "You can go in now."

Ali hoisted himself from the couch and waited to be buzzed through the security door trying to could remember the time when there were no security doors.

"Detective Castillo, sorry to keep you waiting," the state attorney apologized, beckoning Ali to a chair. "Now what can I do for you?"

"I'm working on the gay murders and I need a search warrant to enter a suspect's residence. There is a possibility a missing man is being held there and I'd like to get to him before he's next." Ali opened his file folder and handed the prosecutor his paperwork who nodded and began to read the papers. Ali waited for what seemed like forever until finally, the prosecutor looked up from the file.

"This is all you have?" He asked.

"The suspect, Brand had last contact with the victim's. He has a new addition to his residence which could be where the other victim is being held. I think exigent circumstances apply here."

"Sorry. I can't take this to a judge and even hope to get a warrant. You have next to nothing. The judge would laugh me out of his office." the prosecutor dropped the file on the desk.

"And what if the other victim is in there and we don't get to him in time? We just pulled the body of his partner out of the Intracoastal. He appears to have been shot with the same gun as the other gay victims. His blood will be on our hands." Ali said quietly.

"You know as well as I do that the fourth amendment to the constitution doesn't allow fishing expeditions which is exactly what you're asking to do. Sorry. I am surprised that you would even bring me this, you usually are better than this. Get me something I can use and I'll get you a search warrant," the prosecutor answered, picking up another file and beginning to read it. Ali figured he was dismissed so he rose and left the office.

Ali entered the medical examiners office and was led through large double doors into the autopsy room. It was airtight to keep the smell of death from reaching the lobby and the family members waiting there. The room was filled with shiny medical equipment. Large stainless steel tables were set in a row down the length of the room. A chemical smell permeated the room intermingled with the smell of rotting human flesh. In the center of the row of tables, the medical examiner was bent over the body of Daniel Carnes. He was dressed in surgical scrubs and had a mask with two canisters over his mouth and nose to protect him from the smell and any bacteria. Jamie Stevens stood next to him, a similar mask over her face. An attendant handed Ali a mask and gloves and he was thankful for the mask. Jamie looked up at him as he approached the table. Standing nearby was a crime scene tech from the crime lab.

"Hey, I got done in court so I figured I'd meet you here," She said to him. Ali nodded. He was glad to see her and wasn't sure what to think about that feeling.

"What's the verdict, doc?" Ali asked having to talk loud to be heard through the mask.

"Just got started." The medical examiner answered glancing at him over his mask. He was digging in the chest cavity which was gaped open and held in place with large steel hooks. "No fluid in the lungs so he didn't drown, which of course we knew by the hole in his head." The ME began to probe in what was left of the mouth.

"Well, this is interesting, looks like there is a broken tooth here. Doesn't look like

the kind of damage done by a bullet either, more consistent with a punch to the face. There is bruising around the side of the head that also doesn't look like it was caused by the gunshot. That would be consistent with the cigarette burns on the torso and the bruises there. It looks like he suffered a pretty bad beating before he was shot."

The ME picked up a pair of forceps and began to probe around the few remaining teeth. He extracted and tiny piece of flesh and examined it under a large magnifying glass on a stand next to the autopsy table. After a minute he dropped it into a test tube held by the attendant.

"Looks like we have some skin from the person who beat him," the ME said. "Get that to DNA analysis and have them compare it to the victim please."

"How do you know it's not from the mouth?" Jamie asked. "That bullet must have pushed a lot of stuff around."

"That piece has hair follicle attached. The skin of the hand is thicker and has wrinkles and sweat glands, probably from the back of the hand. It was jammed into the broken tooth. The puncher left us a present," the ME replied. "Unfortunately the bullet went through and wasn't recovered so ballistics match will be difficult. Judging from the face, the victim was shot in the back of the head leaving a small hole in the back of the head, massive damage to the face from the gasses entering the skull and pushing out the front."

The ME and the attendant rolled the victim over. The ME measured the bullet hole in the back of the head with a ruler and then shaved the area with a disposable razor. He examined the area closely and measured it again.

"No speckling to speak of, bruising around the rim of the wound, gunpowder residue is consistent, blowback damage to the tissue around the rim of the wound. This is a contact wound. The gun was right against the skull," the ME said, straightening up and glancing at Jamie and Ali. He and the attendant rolled the body over onto its back. He checked the ruler and held it so the attendant could see it. The attendant made some notes and calculations on a notepad and held it for the ME to see. The ME nodded.

"Looks like a forty-five. Is that consistent with the others?" He asked, glancing at Ali who nodded. The ME then began to check the rest of the body, stopping at the knees.

"Hmm, this is nice. There is some bruising on the knees. Looks like a square pattern, maybe four by four in size, probably made by kneeling on a tile floor." He rolled the body on its side and examined the buttocks, "Same with the buttocks and upper thighs."

The ME took some scrapings from under the fingernails and placed it onto two microscope slides. He handed it to the crime scene tech who immediately left the room.

The ME continued the examination. He checked the entire body from top to bottom.

Finally he straightened up and faced Ali and Jamie.

"Here's what I find so far. The victim was restrained by the ankles and wrists probably by handcuffs as indicated by the bruises, they have no lines of striations consistent with rope. He was severely beaten before he was shot. The cause of death is one gunshot wound, large caliber probably a forty-five to the back of the head. He's been in the water around twenty hours so he was kept somewhere awhile before death. Now we need to get prints to make a positive ID since there's not enough left of the face for anyone to recognize him and no distinguishing marks to ID by."

The ME retrieved a large needle filled with clear liquid from a metal tray. He inserted the needle into each fingertip in turn, injecting saline into the finger to smooth out the wrinkles caused by submersion in the canal. He then rolled each finger tip with black ink and rolled them onto small 3 by 5 cards. He handed these to the attendant.

"That's the major post for now. Blood gas and toxicology will take a few days," the ME said, pulling a plastic sheet over the body. Ali let out a small breath. He hated autopsies. He always struggled to try not to imagine Maria laying there, her chest opened like a sleeping bag.

The crime scene tech returned to the autopsy room and handed Ali a handwritten form. Ali glanced down at it.

"The stuff under the fingernails appears to be a rough gritty substance probably grout from an unsealed tile floor. Its light gray but I'll have the make and brand in a few hours," the tech said turning away and leaving before Ali could answer.

"Thanks doc," Ali said and led Jamie from the autopsy room.

Ali led the way to the car. Grout from a tile floor? He thought back to the addition to Brands house and wondered if the room had tile floors. He retrieved the computer paper from his pocket and decided was time to find the building contractor who put on that addition.

Ali held the door to the building for Jamie to enter then followed her inside. The lobby had two leather couches crouched against the walls which were adorned with poster sized photos of homes and buildings. A short glass table squatted between them. A twenties something brunette with large glasses was seated behind a tall counter.

"Can I help you?" The receptionist asked. Ali held up his badge.

"We need to talk to Mr. Graham," he said. The receptionist frowned.

"Can I ask what the reference is?" She asked.

"Sorry it's confidential. We need to talk to your boss, now." Ali answered. He was developing a serious headache and was in no mood to be diplomatic.

"I'm sorry but Mr. Graham is out on a jobsite, if you leave your card I will have him call you when he returns," the receptionist replied a bit miffed at Ali's attitude.

"I'm sorry but we need to talk to him immediately. We will need the address where he is at this moment." Jamie interjected, smiling sweetly. She could see Ali was going to turn this woman off and it was going to be difficult to get any cooperation.

The receptionist wrote down the address and handed the paper to Jamie with a flick of her hand.

"Are you gonna piss everybody off today or is there a select few?" Jamie asked him once they were outside. "I just want to know if I'm on the list."

"Sorry. I've got an angry headache." Ali answered.

Jamie rummaged around in the fanny pack she wore around her waist. She handed him a bottle of aspirin.

"This should help." Jamie smiled gently at him wondering how drunk he had gotten last night. Well, it was really not her business. She wished she could do something to help. Damn there's that motherly instinct again, she thought. She wondered why this man stirred so many varied feelings in her. Damn!

Ali stopped at a convenience store and bought soda to take the aspirin. He also hoped that putting some sugar in his stomach would help him feel better. It only helped a little. His stomach was still sore and he felt like someone had beaten the stuffing out of him.

Ali turned into the chain link fence and drove slowly through rows of buildings in differing stages of completion. The ground was dirt since the parking lot would be the last stage of completing the condominium complex. Ali hoped he didn't drive over a nail and blow a tire. He did not need to be out in the sun changing a tire in this sun, he was sure he would bleed to death through his eyes, which by the way felt like they had a pound of fine sand in them. Many of the building were nothing but four walls of gray concrete block. The roofs were simple wooden frames.

Ali followed the dirt track around the complex to the rear. The area was festooned with flat concrete pads, sticks of metal rods reaching out of them. Ali drove toward a white single wide trailer at the end of the track. Two dusty pickup trucks were parked in front of the trailer, both with metal tools boxes in the beds. Ali and Jamie walked toward the trailer, clouds of dust exploding at their every step. Ali could hear the small air conditioner protruding from the side of the trailer, humming over the din of hammers and shouting around them.

Jamie led the way up a set of metal frame stairs and knocked on the trailer door which made a hollow tinny sound. She faintly heard a male voice holler to come in. Jamie opened the door and was met with a blast of cold air, a refreshing change from the dust and heat outside.

Two men were huddled over a makeshift wooden table in the center of the room scrutinizing a large diagram. Huge blueprints were pinned to the walls, their unsecured edges rising and falling in the breeze of the air conditioner. One man was large and deeply tanned dressed in a dirty t-shirt, dusty jeans and tans work boots faded white with dried concrete caked to the soles. A tool belt, darkened with sweat clung to his waist, decorated with a hammer and numerous other construction tools. He had large hands that looked like old leather; large calluses were visible as darkened rings. The dust on his face was streaked with lines of dried sweat. The other man was much shorter and not as muscular with short cropped graying hair and a matching mustache, reading glasses struggled to stay perched on the end of his nose. He wore a peach color polo shirt, khaki color pants with pleats and tan leather boat shoes. He also had calloused hands, roughened from physical labor. He straightened and faced them when they entered.

"Can I help you?" he asked pulling the glasses from his nose and letting them drop to hang from the strap around his neck.

"We're looking for Clyde Graham," Ali replied, glancing at the larger man.

"I'm Clyde Graham and who might you two be?" The small man asked. Ali was a little surprised. Graham was not what he pictured a construction worker to be. Ali introduced himself and Jamie.

"This large dirty man next to me is Walter Billings, my foreman." Graham said nodding toward his companion.

"I would shake your hand but you probably would never get the dirt off," Billings said with a large smile.

"I guess I'm not what you expected to find, eh detective?" Graham chuckled. "It's okay I get that all the time. I do the brains work mostly now and let Walt do the heavy lifting but there was a time in the not so distant past that I spent every waking minute just as dirty as Walt. Now what can I do for you?"

"We're conducting an investigation, the basis of which I am not at liberty to discuss at this time and we need your assistance." Ali replied.

"One of my people in trouble?" Graham asked.

"No sir. It concerns an addition you did to a residence." Jamie answered.

"Okay, shoot." Graham said.

Ali handed him the printout from the city website. Graham retrieved his glasses from around his neck and stuck them on the end of his nose. He scrutinized the printout.

"Oh yeah this one," Graham handed the paper to Billings. "Remember this guy?"

"That pain in the ass," Billings frowned, glancing at the printout.

"Excuse my language ma'am." He said, looking at Jamie who smiled and told him not to worry about it.

"What can you tell me about this?" Ali asked.

"Kind of a strange job, he wanted a bare room. No closets no shelving just bare walls and floor with a drain." Graham said.

"Drain?"

"Yeah a drain. We piped a drain in the middle of the floor and connected it to the piping for the swimming pool so it would drain from the pool overflow then out to the street." Billings joined in the conversation. "The client said it was a workout room of some type or other and he wanted to be able to wash down the floors to keep the germs down and wash the sweat off the equipment. Had us put in some metal rings in the floor and walls so he could attach pulleys for working out."

"How was he gonna wash down the walls and floors?" Jamie asked.

"My tile guy did the walls four feet up and the floors." Graham answered.

"Tile walls and floors?" Ali asked, getting excited at what he was hearing. "What size tile?"

"Four by four, if I remember. Four inch by four inch tiles." Graham replied.

"What type and color and grout?" Ali asked. Graham shrugged the held up his index finger indicating they should wait. He crossed the room, extracting his cell phone from his belt as he went. He dialed a number and had a short conversation with someone. He returned, clipping the cell phone to his belt.

"My tile guy," Graham said pointing to the phone, "Stormy ocean mist."

Ali and Jamie had confused looks on their faces.

"The grout. Stormy ocean mist was the color and they were four by fours." Graham said, solving the confusion.

"Oh. What color is stormy ocean mist?" Ali asked.

"Light gray." Billings interjected.

"Do you have the manufacturer's name?" Ali asked. Graham wrote it on a strip of paper and handed it to Jamie.

"Anything else you need?" Graham asked. "Just let me know."

"Thank you Mr. Graham, Mr. Billings you have been of invaluable help." Jamie and Ali shook hands with Graham. Billings started to extend his hand then stopped pulling it back. They all laughed.

The heat and dust slammed into them when they stepped outside and Jamie fought the urge to cover her mouth and run for the car. Ali turned the car's air conditioner on full blast and they sat until the car cooled enough to be bearable. Ali could not remember when it was this hot this early in the year. He thought back to his childhood and was positive it was never this hot. It seemed to him it got hotter every summer but when he was a kid he spent most of his time in cutoff jeans and shirtless not in a coat and tie. The weather channel did say the temperatures were three or four degrees hotter every year. Probably the damn ozone depletion or something like that.

Ali dialed the crime lab on his cell phone. A tech answered on the fourth ring.

"Hey Ali, I was just going to call you," the tech said. "I got your grout samples identified."

"Stormy ocean mist." Ali said and gave the name of the manufacturer.

"How the hell did you know that?" The tech asked incredulously.

"Just got it from the manufacturer. I need that report ASAP. We're on our way in can you have it ready in twenty minutes?" Ali asked.

"Already done. It's sitting on my desk it'll be waiting for you," the tech answered. Ali hung up the phone and glanced at his watch.

"We'll probably have to wake up a judge by the time we get the affidavit finished for a warrant." Ali said, glancing at Jamie.

"When we get to the office you start typing, I'll go to the lab and get the paperwork. Hopefully we can get a warrant without the autopsy report and a statement from Graham." Jamie replied.

"I've got the city building department paperwork and we should have enough to get the warrant. We can gather all of the other stuff after we get Martins out alive, hopefully."

Ali parked behind the police station. It was change of shift for road patrol and the parking lot was filled with uniformed officers heading for their cars. Some carried briefcases and some carried shotguns pointed at the sky. The squawking of police radios created a cacophony of metallic voices. Marked police cars were backing out of parking spaces and there was a line of cars at the gas pumps. One car, its roof lights blazing and the siren screaming raced out of the parking lot apparently getting an urgent call for help.

Ali and Jamie dodged between two cars in the gas line. Jamie entered the station door first and sidestepped two officers coming out. She turned left headed for the crime lab. Ali turned right and took the stairs two at a time, not wanting to wait for the elevator. He arrived at the third floor landing breathing hard and headed for his desk spinning his chair around and plopping into it. He was pumped up. Lt. Davis hurried to Ali's desk.

"What's up?" Davis asked, looking over Ali's shoulder at the computer on the desk as Ali typed furiously.

"We got enough for a warrant, I hope." Ali answered not looking up.

"Brand's house?"

"Yep. We got grout under Carnes fingernails and Brand had an addition added to the house with the same grout and tile patterns on the body. They match the pattern on Carnes legs and buttocks." Ali replied over his shoulder, continuing to type. He finished filling in the boxes on the affidavit form and switched screens to the application page. Jamie hustled into the room with a thin stack of papers in her hand and stopped at Ali's desk. She dropped them on the corner of the desk and Davis stepped to the side to let her stand next to Ali.

"The crime lab got the preliminary autopsy report faxed to them to save us time," Jamie said, "I got it too. What can I do?"

"Get on the phone, call the State Attorney and get us an ASA and a judge." Ali pointed at Jamie's desk. She sat down and snatched the phone off the hook.

"I'll get us a federal prosecutor and judge if I have to." Jamie said, dialing the phone with the receiver tucked on her shoulder.

"Make sure you take SWAT and be careful," Davis said patting Ali's shoulder. "I'll get the SWAT commander alerted and get them ready."

Ali nodded as Davis headed for his office.

Ali paced around the room. The walls were dark wood paneled and in the middle of the conference room stood a large rectangular table of dark mahogany. On a credenza in the corner squatted a colorful vase with a Native American design containing a fern which looked like it hadn't been watered in weeks, its leaves drooping toward the tabletop. The judges black robes hung on a coat tree next to the credenza.

Jamie sat at the table next to a young, pretty dark haired Assistant State Attorney wearing a dark blue dress and black high heels. Ali wondered how she could wear those shoes and stand on her feet all day in a courtroom. The judge sat across from them. He was a short squat man with small blue eyes and collar length shocking white hair slicked back on his head. His skin was wrinkled and his hands were festooned with dark liver spots and blue veins crisscrossing under the skin. He was wearing an electric blue silk shirt and a red and gray striped silk tie. He read the papers he held slowly and carefully. It took so long Ali decided he must have read them three times. Finally he grunted and picked up the gold pen off of the desk and began to sign the papers. When he finished he handed them to the State Attorney. He glanced up at Ali.

"Good luck detective. Try not to kill this suspect I'd like to see him in my courtroom so I can whack his gonads off personally," the judge smiled gently. Ali nodded. He liked this judge. The judge's family was one of the pioneer families in South Florida and Ali knew him as a tough but fair judge. He was the longest sitting judge in the county and even had a street named after him. Ali was impressed with that.

CHAPTER 16

Cassie Burnham set her daughter carefully in the stroller and tugged on the little pink lace bonnet to make sure it was on the babies head properly. She wheeled the stroller to the condominium door and retrieved her purse from the teak table just inside it then scanned the apartment and smiled. She loved this place. She had a view of the downtown and could see the ocean from the picture window on the east side of the sitting room. It wasn't as nice as her parent's condo in the Hamptons but it was close. In three or four years they would have made enough profit on this place to buy something better. Her husband had paid two point five million preconstruction prices for it and she was glad she had insisted he buy it.

Cassie pushed the stroller down the carpeted hallway to the elevator. The muzak in the elevator was Mozart. God, how she hated Mozart, one would think with what they paid for this place they could find some Chopan or something more suitable, but the older residents liked it. Some day real soon she would get herself elected to the condo board and then she would get some things changed. She would get those old foagies out and get some of the young and upcoming residents, like that gorgeous young heart surgeon and his wife down the hall, into power positions.

The elevator door swished open and Cassie waved at the security guard seated behind the big desk, her heels clicking on the white marble floor of the lobby. When she got close to her Porsche SUV she pushed the alarm remote button and heard the alarm on her car chirp. She started to open the passenger side door to put the baby in her car seat when she noticed the blue BMW parked on the other side of her car. That's strange, she thought, I've never seen that car in the garage before.

The windows of the BMW were halfway open and she approached carefully, peeking over the windowsill when she got close enough. Cassie recoiled at the sight and smell of the filthy creature snoring in the backseat. Dear god, she thought, wasn't it bad enough that these people had to infest the streets with their disgusting filth but here in her parking garage it was simply unacceptable. She remembered once having to walk past one of these scum on the sidewalk when she was shopping with her friend Jessica. She had flagged down a passing police car and demanded the cops removed the trash. After all, her daughter shouldn't have to grow up seeing that. Jessica had said something about them being people too and Cassie should use the situation to teach her children about tolerance for others. But then Jessica wasn't brought up properly, her husband had earned his money in the stock market. Cassie's family was old money and knew the value and responsibility of being important in local society.

Cassie backed away and pulled her cell phone from her two thousand dollar leather purse as she pushed the stroller back to the garage entrance.

Billy Joe stretched and rolled to his side. He wondered for a minute where he was and then remembered his good fortune. He took a deep breath of the leather smell and sighed. God he loved this car. He thought to himself how he would like to find a place to hide this car and maybe he could live in it forever. Naw, someone would take it away from him. Sasquatch would beat him to a pulp then piss on his dead corpse for a chance to live in this car. He decided he better get moving before somebody saw him. He sat up and glanced out the back window and saw the police car parked two cars away. Shit! Suddenly Billy Joe heard a loud male voice yelling at him from the driver's side of the car to put his fucking hands up. He raised his hands slowly and turned his head to look into the barrel of the automatic the cop had pointed at his head. The cop told him to slowly get out of the car with his hands visible and Billy Joe did as he was told. He laid on the ground with his hands out just like he was told and instantly the cop was kneeling in the middle of his shoulders, yanking his hands behind his back and snapping the handcuffs on. Billy Joe was rapidly searched and yanked to his feet. The handcuffs bit into his wrists and he let out a yelp. He was hustled to a police car and shoved into the back seat, the door slamming behind him. A minute later, almost like an afterthought, the cop yanked open the door and read him his rights from a small white card. Billy Joe looked up into the cop's sweaty face and said, "I found that car" but the door had already been slammed in his face cutting him off.

Billy Joe could hear the yelling before the door to the booking area even opened. The cop gripped his upper arm and aimed him through the door into the booking area. It was just like Billy Joe remembered it. The place stank of urine and vomit and sweat even though the air conditioner kept the air recycling. A large counter ran the length of the back of the room. Plexiglas covered the space between the top of the counter and the ceiling. Small round holes in the Plexiglas allowed Billy Joe to hear the questions the detention officer yelled through the holes in the glass. To Billy Joe's right, at the end of the room, was a mesh cage. Inside was a huge black man, who was screaming incoherently and slamming his body against the mesh and the walls. He was shirtless and his upper torso gleamed with sweat, making him look like black glass. To Billy Joe's left were small holding cells with large steel barred doors. In one room was a digital camera on a stand and a computer with a flat screen on top where the fingerprints were taken.

"What am I arrested for?" Billy Joe hollered to the officer behind the glass.

"Auto theft and suspicion of murder," the officer hollered back

"What? Murder? I didn't kill nobody. I was sleeping in a car. What is this bullshit?" Billy Joe yelled incredulously.

"The detectives will talk to you in a little while. Go with the officer to be processed," was the answer.

Billy Joe followed another officer into the processing room. The officer was wearing rubber gloves and handed his an alcohol wipe in a cellophane package.

"Clean your hands with this and then step up to the computer," the officer said, wrinkling his nose at the smell emanating from Billy Joe's filthy clothes. He cleaned his hands carefully and tossed the alcohol wipe into a plastic trash can in the corner. He was fingerprinted and photographed then led to a room with a shower.

"Wash thoroughly then throw those clothes into this," The officer said, handing him a towel, soap and a black trash bag. Billy Joe took his time; he hadn't had a hot shower in weeks. He soaped himself and watched as the filthy soap and water washed down the drain in the center of the floor. When he finished he dried himself thoroughly and dressed in the orange jumpsuit the officer handed him. The word PRISONER was stenciled across the back in silver reflective lettering. He joined four other men dressed in similar jumpsuits in a holding cell. Billy Joe glanced around and realized there was no place to sit so he lowered himself to the bare concrete floor and curled up, pressing his back against the wall as he had learned to do his first time in jail. One had to always protect himself in these places. Now all he could do was wait.

CHAPTER 17

Ali's cell phone rang as he and Jamie exited the courthouse. Ali glanced at the number and flipped it open.

"Castillo."

"Hey, they found Carnes and Martins car. In a parking garage," Lt. Davis said in his ear.

"Where?" Ali asked.

"Downtown. There was somebody in it," Davis told him.

"Who?" Ali asked.

"Some homeless guy. He was sleeping in it, said he found it." Davis answered.

"Okay. We got the warrant. We're on our way in now to meet with SWAT." Ali said.

"Okay we're here. The commandos are saddled up and ready," Davis answered. Ali flipped the phone closed. He turned to Jamie and told her the news. When she started asking questions he told her what Davis had said.

"Now remember, this guy may have a forty-five so let's don't anybody get shot. I would prefer we take this guy alive but if we can't, we can't. We are primarily concerned with finding this guy, he's the captive victim," Ali said to the group of men in front of him, handing out copies of Martin's picture.

The group was dressed in black combat pants and black t-shirts. They wore heavy bulletproof vest with POLICE in white letters across the front and back. Around their waists were black nylon belts with low slung holsters. Most of them had small deadly looking submachine guns slung across their chests. They had very stern tense looks on their faces.

Ali stepped away from the white plastic display board behind him as the SWAT commander stepped to the board. The SWAT commander drew a diagram on the board and handed out diagrams of Brand's house to each of the teams. The commander briefed each of them on their assignments. When he was finished they all trooped down the stairs to the parking lot gathering around a nondescript white van. Ali watched as the team members strapped on black ballistic helmets and checked their radios. He opened the trunk of his car and removed his suit coat and tie, withdrew a blue bulletproof vest from the trunk and slipped it over his head, attaching the Velcro straps around his waist and chest. Jamie walked to her car and returned wearing a black vest with FBI stenciled across the front. Ali and Jamie got into Ali's car and followed the white van.

Ali stopped behind the van three houses away from Brand's house. The side door of the van slid open and the black clad cops poured from the van quietly, instantly falling into a single file line. The officer in front carried a long, heavy black cylinder with a hand grip on each side. They slipped quickly to Brand's front door and stopped.

Ali was breathing hard and his heart was thumping in his chest. The cop in front swung the cylinder against the door as the SWAT commander yelled "Police search warrant," the door slammed inward and the SWAT team poured into the house, still yelling the announcement. Ali and Jamie stopped just inside the front door, guns at the ready as the SWAT team cops disappeared into different areas of the house, their yells echoing off the walls.

Seconds later they could hear voices yelling from all over the house that everything was clear.

The SWAT commander approached from somewhere deep in the house, pulling his helmet off of his head, the cop behind him was on his radio requesting the paramedics. The commander beckoned to Ali.

"Ali, you better see this. Back here," the commander said.

Ali and Jamie followed him into the back of the house. There was a door open to a room and as Ali approached the room he could see tile floors and walls. He saw a naked figure seated against the wall, its arms chained to the wall over its head. Ali and Jamie stepped into the room and looked down at Jonah Martins.

His skin was gray and his eyes were dark rimmed and sunken into their sockets. His head was resting on his chest. He reminded Ali of pictures he had seen of Jewish prisoners at Auschwitz. It had only been a few days but his ribs protruded from his chest, the skin loose and hanging. His breathing was labored and raspy.

"Jesus," Jamie said behind Ali. Ali's brain immediately started ticking off what needed to be done.

"Sarge, make sure all of your people are wearing gloves, I don't want anything contaminated." Ali said. The SWAT commander nodded and left the room. Ali could hear him giving commands to his men. Ali could faintly hear the siren of the rescue truck as it approached. He knelt beside Martins and whispered, "You're gonna be all right Jonah. You're safe now."

Ali could hear a voice from in front of the house telling the paramedics to be careful and wear gloves. Two fire department paramedics entered the room. One held a portable defibrillator the other had a red and white plastic box. They stopped just inside the door and stared for a second.

"Holy fuck," the younger paramedic whispered.

They immediately knelt beside Martins. Each of them held one of Martins wrists as a SWAT member cut the chains holding his arms with bolt cutters. The paramedics gently lowered Martin's hands to his lap. The older paramedic pinched the skin on the back of Martin's hand and lifted. When he let go the skin stayed in the same position.

"Some serious dehydration here, get an IV started right now," the older paramedic said to his partner.

"Is he gonna live?" Ali leaned over and asked quietly into the older paramedic's ear. The paramedic just shrugged.

"Gonna be a battle, dehydration, starvation, exposure, hard to tell but looks like some bruising, probably been beaten too," The younger paramedic sighed, looking up at Ali and Jamie.

The paramedics finished their work and loaded Martins onto a stretcher then wheeled him toward the front of the house.

"I'll ride with him," Jamie said, pulling off her bulletproof vest and handing it to Ali, "You stay here and handle the scene?"

Ali nodded sadly at her departing back. He walked to the porch and stood under the eaves watching one of the SWAT team members unwinding a yellow crime scene tape around the perimeter of the front yard. Uniformed cops had arrived and were relieving the SWAT team, who were huddled around their van, removing their vests and packing their gear away. Ali heard a shrill voice demanding answers. He looked toward the voice and saw an elderly woman standing at the edge of the yellow tape waving her finger in the face of a uniformed cop. Ali approached and asked what the problem was.

"I want to know who that was you just took out of here in that ambulance," The old woman demanded. She was trying to sidestep the cop who blocked her way.

"Who might you be?" Ali asked.

"I live next door. I know the city commissioner for this area and if I don't get some answers I'll be on the phone with him before you can sneeze," she demanded.

"Do you know the man who lives here?" Ali asked quietly, trying to defuse the situation but bristling at the threat. Nosy neighbors were a pain in the ass for cops. Everybody thought they were important and had a right to know everything. Threatening to call somebody important really pissed cops off.

"James? Of course I know James, very nice man. He carries my trash down on trash day. I just called him on his cell phone and he says he doesn't know what is going on here," the old lady snapped.

"You called him? Where is he, did he say." Ali asked. Christ, if Brand knew they were here already he was sure to disappear. This old lady had really screwed things up now.

"He didn't say and I have no idea. Now, I want some answers detective," She said.

"I am not at liberty to give any information at this time, so you call anyone you want," Ali snarled and spun away. He wanted to shout at her and tell her to go to hell and that she had really fucked up his investigation but he controlled himself. Normally he would interview the old lady and find out what she knew but he would have to wait until he calmed down. Right now he wanted to go to the hospital and see if Martins could talk. The best witness was a surviving victim. Hopefully he wouldn't need to talk to this woman later.

The crime scene investigators arrived and Ali left after telling them to call him with updates. He saw Davis' unmarked car drive up outside of the yellow crime scene tape. Davis and the Chief emerged from the car and approached him, three other detectives from the squad in tow.

"I brought some help since this looks like it will be a long night. Tell them what you want them to do; they can take some of the burden off of you." Davis said to Ali.

"Thanks I appreciate it. Somebody needs to get a statement from the neighbor next door. She has already called Brand and he's probably in the wind but we need a statement from her anyway.

Somebody can ride herd on the crime scene techs and keep me updated, I'm headed to the hospital, and Stevens rode with the victim." Ali answered. Davis left with the detectives, leading them toward the house. The police Chief placed his hand on Ali's shoulder.

"You okay Ali?" the Chief asked looking into his face.

"Yeah Chief thanks." Ali replied.

"You did good tonight. You saved one, that's what's important," the Chief smiled at him and Ali suddenly felt very weary. He glanced up and saw the television news vans lining up in the street. The Chief followed his gaze.

"Fuck them. They're my problem, give me an update then disappear and do what you need to do," the Chief said quietly. Ali gave him a quick synopsis then snuck toward his car as the Chief headed into the harsh glare of the news camera lights.

On the way to the hospital Ali called Jamie and got good news, Martins was alive. Davis called and reminded Ali about the car and Billy Joe being in custody. Ali replied he would be in to talk to Billy Joe after he went by the hospital.

Ali parked in the Emergency Room driveway next to an empty ambulance with the rear doors standing open. A large light over the doors shone down on the pavement.

The lobby was filled with people of all sizes and races. Some sat in the rows of chairs and some lounged on the floor. A little girl slept in her mother's lap. A young Spanish man sat holding an ice bag to his forehead. The television mounted in the corner near the ceiling had the local news on the screen but no sound. Ali was admitted through a second set of automatic doors by a security guard who sat at a podium reading a novel.

Ali followed the corridor around the corner into the triage area as nurses bustled past carrying assorted trays of medicine and medical equipment. In the center of the room was a large counter that ran all the way around the room. Around the sides of the room were curtained treatment areas, some with empty beds. Ali heard someone moaning behind one of the curtains as he passed. Jamie waved to him from across the room, standing next to a white curtain.

"How is he?" Ali asked, pushing the curtain aside to look at Martins lying on a bed.

"They're still looking at him, but he's not good. The doctor will fill us in when he's done with the exam," Jamie answered, glancing at Martins.

"I need you to stay here and keep me posted in case he says anything," Ali said, "I'm going to the station to talk to this guy driving their car. You okay for that?"

Jamie nodded. Ali placed his hand on her shoulder.

"Hang in there. You look really tired and it's gonna be a long night." Ali smiled gently.

"Not a problem, go." Jamie replied. Four uniformed cops approached down the hallway. They stopped and waited for instructions.

"Okay, two of you at the end of the hall, two more here. I don't want any reporters getting any closer than the end of this hall. Stay sharp and check every ID of every doctor and nurse, you never know how hard reporters will work to get a picture," Ali instructed the cops who nodded and took their posts.

Ali drove out of the parking lot and turned toward the police department. His cell phone rang and he pulled it from his belt, looking at the number on the display. He didn't recognize the number and frowned.

"Hello?" Ali said to the phone.

"Hello detective." James Brand said, causing Ali to slam on the brakes and nearly get rear-ended by a taxi riding too closely behind him.

"Brand?" Ali snarled into the receiver.

"Congratulations detective, you saved one of those pathetic assholes. I am impressed, you are better than I thought you were. You got the closest so far but unfortunately, this is as close as you'll ever get because I am gone and you'll never find me. Goodbye." Brand said and the phone went dead. Ali dropped the phone on the seat beside him. *I will get you, you son of a bitch*, Ali vowed.

CHAPTER 18

Bobby Joe Miller was shaken awake and blinked up at the guard towering over him. He glanced at the clock on the wall and realized it was one a.m. What the fuck were they doing waking him from the best sleep he had gotten in years?

"What's the problem? Leave me alone," Bobby Joe grumbled and rolled over. The guard grabbed his shoulder and yanked him to a sitting position.

"Get your ass up a detective wants to talk to you," the guard growled. Bobby Joe pushed himself to his feet and followed the guard.

Ali sat back in his chair and rubbed his face. He was drained, limbs feeling like they weighted a ton. His stomach was rumbling and he felt that if he closed his eyes he would fall asleep immediately. He realized his hands were shaking slightly. He looked up as Bobby Joe was escorted into the room.

"Have a seat Mr. Miller," Ali said to him, indicating a chair on the other side of the interview table. Bobby Joe settled into the chair.

"I'll get right to the point because I don't have a lot of time. I need to know what you know about that car you were found in." Ali leaned onto the table, resting his arms on the top.

"I found that car." Bobby Joe answered.

"Where and how?" Ali asked.

"What's in it for me?" Bobby Joe asked hoping to negotiate some perks from this detective. He had dealt with patrol cops many times but a detective intimidated him a little bit. He had never been in this kind of trouble.

"We'll see when you tell me what you know but I don't have time to fuck around. That car belonged to two men who were kidnapped and one of whom was brutally murdered. Right now you're my only suspect so don't fuck with me." Ali growled.

"Hey I didn't have nothing to do with that shit; I was just sleeping in it." Bobby Joe was scared now, sure he was fucked big time and would never see the street again.

"Tell me," Ali answered.

"I was asleep under the bridge where I usually am and I saw a guy park the car there."

"What bridge and give me the description of this guy." Ali said.

"I sleep under the Causeway Bridge, you know the 17th street bridge. I was almost asleep and I heard a car door slam so I looked and saw a guy washing his Beamer in the parking lot at the office building next door. I yelled at him and he hauled ass." Bobby Joe related.

"Did you see his face?" Ali asked.

"Yeah, he was a white guy, older maybe late fifties or early sixties. Well dressed."

"Can you give a sketch artist a hand in doing a sketch?" Ali hoped.

"I wasn't that close and I was kinda drunk, you know what it's like on the street. But I can identify him if I see him again." Bobby Joe replied.

"Can you identify a picture; maybe pick him out of a group of photos?"

"I think so but I ain't sure but I'll try." Bobby Joe smiled hopefully.

"Okay as of now you're a material witness, you're gonna stay with us for awhile, that okay with you?" Ali answered.

"Okay at least it's clean but you know I got a drinking trouble. I hope I don't get the DTs." Bobby Joe answered. Yeah I know the feeling, Ali thought. Ali opened the door and beckoned to the guard.

"Mr. Miller is a material witness, treat him accordingly," Ali told the guard. Bobby Joe followed the guard back to his cell.

Ali returned to the detective bureau and was met by Jamie Stevens coming in the door.

"He's gonna be in a coma for awhile." Jamie informed Ali. "They think he'll be okay but they need to keep him unconscious and hydrate him. He has numerous bruises and I'm sure was emotionally traumatized."

Ali looked into Jamie's eyes and could see they were red and bloodshot, drooping with exhaustion. He was sure his eyes looked the same. Lt. Davis entered and approached them as they sat at their desks. Ali glanced at his watch. It was four a.m.

"You two look like hell. There is nothing else to do now until the crime scene guys get done. Martins is under guard. I need you two fresh and ready to rock when the prints and things are done. We've got a BOLO out on Brand. Go home and sleep. Keep your phones on and I'll call you if anything breaks. That's not a request." Davis frowned down at them.

"He called me." Ali said quietly.

"Who called you?" Davis asked.

"Brand, on my cell, right after I left the scene. I don't know how he got the number."

"What did he say?" Jamie asked, leaning toward him.

"He congratulated me for finding Martins. Said I was better than he thought and that I got closer than any of the others."

"The others? That means he's done this other places, shit." Jamie breathed.

"Okay. That's it. We need to be rested. Go." Davis waved them toward the door.

Ali dropped Jamie at her apartment and headed home exhausted. He didn't remember how long it had been since he had slept. His head throbbed and he felt shaky. Ali's stomach was queasy and grumbled. He was familiar with the feeling. When he worked midnight shift in uniform it was not uncommon to work all night and spend the day in court, sometimes with no sleep for over twenty four hours this feeling had been a familiar friend. The problem was that at some point, no matter how tired one was it was nearly impossible to fall asleep. Ali hoped that would not be the case, he really needed to be fresh in a few hours.

Ali climbed the stairs to the detective squad room. He had actually gotten a few hours of sleep. The squad room was a bustle of activity. A tall, balding detective was dropping a stack of papers on Ali's desk as he approached. The detective had retired from Nashville Tennessee PD and had worked homicide there. He moved to Fort Lauderdale and decided he missed the job too much and hated retirement. Some cops were like that, couldn't wait to retire but found they missed the job and came back. Ali hoped he wouldn't be one of those.

"Got some information that came in for you," The former Tennessee cop said to Ali, pointing to the stack of papers. Ali thanked him and sat down at his desk, picking up the stack. One was a report from ATF on the owners of forty- five caliber revolvers.

There were over ten thousand of those guns in circulation at the present time, a dead end. The second report was a reply to Jamie's request of the FBI on similar type murders. There were five similar unsolved cases. Two in Alabama, one in South Carolina and the final two cases were from Atlanta. That must have been what Brand meant when he mentioned the others. Was Brand confessing or gloating? Ali intended to ask him someday.

Jamie entered the squad room and went directly to the coffee pot and poured herself a cup. She sipped carefully from the cup as she approached Ali's desk. He handed her the reports wordlessly and she sat down as she read. After a few minutes she glanced at Ali over the papers.

"Looks like Brand has been busy. Damn I hope we get to bag this guy. I would personally like to kick his ass." Jamie said.

"Is that any way for an FBI agent to talk? I thought the feds were college educated professionals who talked like accountants," Ali chuckled.

"I learned that from my dad. He was a real cop, remember?" Jamie smiled. They were interrupted by the arrival of the crime lab tech that approached, waving a file in the air.

"I've got presents for you," The tech said. He placed the file on Ali's desk with a flourish and stood there beaming at them. Ali picked up the file and waved the tech to a chair.

"So tell us Mr. Magic what have you found?" Ali asked. The tech smiled at the nickname.

"First, the prints in the house don't belong to James Brand," the tech said, quickly holding up his hand to stop the inevitable questions. He was enjoying this.

"The prints in the house belong to a Sander Vance. I ran them through AFIS and got a hit out of Montgomery Alabama. Sander Vance was arrested for disorderly intoxication in Montgomery. I called the records division at Montgomery PD and got a copy of the arrest report. He was arrested outside a gay bar. Report's in the file. I ran a nationwide search for Sander Vance including birth records.

He was born in Bryantville South Carolina. I also ran a nationwide search for James Brand. The real estate association in Illinois had his records on file. His picture is in the file also. So, Sander Vance took James Brand's identity and has been playing him ever since. James Brand has probably been dead for a long time, I suspect killed by this Sander Vance when he took over his life," the tech sat back, spent but gloating.

"You did good Magic, I'll take it from here." Ali rose and shook the tech's hand.

Ali retrieved the ATF report and scanned it. Thank god it was in alphabetical order. No Vance on the list. Jamie was sitting across from him, she had the phone tucked on her shoulder and beckoned to him. She placed her hand over the receiver.

"I'm getting the phone number for Bryantville South Carolina. Let's call and see what they can tell us. Maybe Vance is headed home." Jamie said. She placed the phone back to her ear and listened, writing on the pad in front of her. She thanked the operator and hung up the phone.

"Bryantville has no police department to speak of maybe ten cops, apparently it's too small of a town, but the sheriff's office there handles all of their crimes. You want to call or you want me to?"

"We'll do it together," Ali answered and picked up his extension as Jamie dialed the number.

"Bryant County sheriff's office," a female voice with a very southern accent answered the phone. Jamie introduced herself and explained why she was calling.

"Hang on ma'am. Lemme get the Sheriff for you," The woman said.

"Sheriff Thomas heah," A deep male voice with the same southern accent said, with some hesitation.

"Sheriff, we're sorry to bother you, I'm sure you're a busy man. My name is Jamie Stevens of the FBI and on the phone with us is Detective Castillo. We're investigating a homicide here in Fort

Lauderdale Florida and we need some information from you." Jamie said.

"Whatever I can do," the Sheriff answered.

"We need to now if you are familiar with a man named Sander Vance?" Jamie asked.

"Sander Vance," the Sheriff said, his voice trailing off as if reliving a memory. "Sure I know Sander Vance, haven't heard that name in ages though."

"What can you tell us about him?" Ali asked.

"Me and him went to school together, sad thing that boy's life. I never could understand him. Parents both dead, a murder suicide. My daddy was the Sheriff back then. I reckon we was about 13 or 14 at the time."

"What can you tell us about his parent's deaths?" Jamie asked slowly.

"Well, what I remember is his daddy killed his momma with a handgun then kilt himself with the same gun. Sander came home and found them dead. Don't think the boy was ever right after that," the Sheriff replied.

"Sheriff, can you find the file on that case?" Ali asked hopefully.

"Well, that might take some time."

"Does Vance have any family still in the area, any friends he has stayed in touch with?" Jamie asked.

"Got an old maid aunt still lives here; she raised him up after his folks died. Guess she must be in her eighties or better now."

"Thanks Sheriff. We'll be in touch soon." Ali said.

"Anything I can do for the FBI." He pronounced it effa bee aye.

Ali sat down at his computer and punched up the list of gun owners he had received from the ATF, scanning the list for the name Vance. No listing. Ali had figured it would not be there After all, the father had a different last name being that he was Vance's stepfather

It took Ali and Jamie almost two hours to convince her bosses of the necessity of going to South Carolina. She had to use her trump card by telling them Vance had intimated to other murders in other parts of the country, making it the FBI's jurisdiction if the murders crossed state lines. Lt. Davis was also difficult to convince. Jamie sealed the deal when she informed Davis the bill would be paid by the FBI but first they had to cover all of the bases and make sure Vance had left the area.

CHAPTER 19

Ruth Lefebre was leaving her house when Ali parked the unmarked car in her driveway. She frowned at them as they approached.

"Ms. Lefebre, we need a few minutes of your time," Ali said abruptly.

"What can I do for you?" Lefebre sniffed.

"James Brand. We found one of your former clients being held and tortured in his house. Did you know his real name wasn't Brand?" Ali confronted her quickly to keep her from having time to make up a story.

"Oh God, I never would have imagined James would do something like that and no I didn't know he wasn't James Brand. Who is he?" She asked the shock obvious in her face.

"His real name is Sander Vance and he's a serial killer," Ali replied. "Does he have any friends who would hide him or anyplace he would go?"

"Not that I know of, he seemed to be kind of a loner," She replied.

"If you hear from him or think of anything, call us," Jamie interjected. "And I think you'll need a new employee."

CHAPTER 20

Sander Vance drove aimlessly, trying to think. Where could he go where the cops wouldn't be able to find him? He racked his brain. Should he go back to Bryant County? They would probably find out his real name eventually. That would lead that bastard Castillo to Bryant County. That son of a bitch had ruined everything. I got half a mind to track him down and kill his ass, he thought. Well, I can't stay out in the open. By now the cops had his description out on their damn radios and would be looking for him. Then he had an idea.

CHAPTER 21

Ali eyed the little plane with fear. He wasn't sure he wanted to get in that damn thing but it was better than driving. Ali and Jamie had landed in the Columbia airport two hours ago. The FBI had made their travel arrangements. Ali would have preferred to drive from Columbia but this was the fastest way to Bryantville, which had an airport too small to land anything but this single engine death trap. Any other large airport in South Carolina would have been a day's drive from Bryantville.

Ali picked up his bag and followed Jamie across the tarmac to the plane. The air was heavy with jet exhaust and Ali was already feeling claustrophobic. He looked longingly at the large jets parked nearby. They seemed safer even though he hated to fly and had gripped the armrest the whole trip except to gulp the drink the flight attendant had kindly brought him. God he needed a drink now. Thank goodness he had been able to sweet talk the flight attendant into giving him half a dozen of those little bottles of booze the airlines were so famous for.

Maybe going to South Carolina was a bad idea. Ali wondered if it was too late to change their plans but they had come this far, two and a half hours in the air to Columbia and he knew he couldn't change his mind now. The cockpit of the plane was warm and cramped. Ali hated to be in cramped spaces. He sat next to

Jamie and prayed the flight would be quick, holding his breath as the plane raced down the runway and only exhaling when he felt the landing gear thump against the underbelly of the plane. Ali looked out the window at the forests of pine and oak trees passing below them. They were close enough to the ground that he saw a group of deer huddled in the shade of a big oak, but then the clouds obscured his view as they gained altitude. He sat back and closed his eyes and pretended to doze but his insides were quivering.

Ali opened his eyes when he felt the wheels skip on the runway. He pretended to yawn in hopes Jamie had not noticed how scared he was. They stepped out of the plane onto the tarmac and stood waiting by the belly of the plane for their luggage. A tall lanky deputy with a droopy mustache and long 1970's style sideburns approached them, dressed in a uniform of black pants with a gray stripe down the side of the leg and a gray baggy uniform shirt. His gun belt clung to his hips and gave the impression he had to keep his belt tight to keep it on his waist. He wore black cowboy boots that were shined to a bright luster. A gold sheriff's star flashed on his chest as he held his hand out a large, rough, calloused hand.

"Welcome to Bryantville. Jack Strand. The sheriff asked me to meet ya'll here and bring you to the office," the deputy said, shaking Ali's hand firmly. He hesitated when Jamie held out her hand then shook it carefully, as if he might crush it. They introduced themselves and followed the deputy toward the small airport terminal.

Strand parked in the back of a small brick building which housed the Bryant County Sheriffs Office.The north side of the building was surrounded by a ten foot chain link fence topped with razor wire. The windows on that side of the building had wire mesh embedded in the glass causing Ali to guess that must be the jail. The parking lot was expansive and dotted with oak and pine trees. A prisoner dressed in an orange jumpsuit was raking leaves along the edge of the parking lot while a uniformed deputy lounged in the shade watching, a shotgun cradled in his arms. There were a number of marked police cars parked in the lot. The roof of the building was topped with a large radio tower which appeared to be at least a hundred feet tall and a large hawk stood in the crossbars of the radio tower, scanning the parking lot.

The deputy led them through a metal door with a sign that read SHERIFF PERSONNEL ONLY mounted on it. They followed the deputy down a narrow hallway to a door marked SHERIFF PRIVATE. Somewhere in the bowels of the building, they could hear a police radio crackling. The deputy knocked on the door then swung it open.

The Sheriff's private office was large and three walls were paneled with wood. The fourth wall was glass and they could see deputies and civilian employees seated at desks through the windows. Apparently they had been escorted through a private entrance. The walls of the office were decorated with plaques and certificates. A large deer head was mounted behind the large mahogany desk. A college degree was prominent among the plaques along with pictures of a young man in a football uniform from the University Of South Carolina and pictures of the same young man in a Marine Corps uniform. Behind the desk sat a short stocky, muscular man with strawberry blond hair, cut in a flattop wearing the same gray uniform shirt and gold badge. He wore sharply pressed blue jeans with a large silver buckle with a gold sheriff's star in the middle. On his hip was a hand tooled leather holster containing a forty-five automatic, blue steel with pearl grips. He came around the desk and held out his hand. His arms were thick and his forearms were huge, like small tree trunks.

"Sheriff Bill Thomas. Glad to meet ya'll."

"Ali Castillo, Jamie Stevens," Ali replied, the sheriffs grip was like a vise.

"Please have a seat," the sheriff smiled, indicating chairs placed in front of his desk. "I got rooms for ya'll at the only hotel in town. It isn't much but it's clean. Here's the file on Sander Vance. I skimmed through it."

"Can you give us the condensed version?" Jamie asked.

"Sure thing ma'am. Sander Vance's stepfather, John Greene killed Sander's mama with a forty-five caliber Smith and Wesson revolver then apparently shot himself. Sander found the bodies. The state placed him with his aunt until he was eighteen. Sander stayed in the area for a short while then disappeared into the world. He got arrested a few times for minor things but nothing serious."

"You said his father used a forty-five?" Ali asked. "Our victim's were killed with a forty-five revolver. What happened to the gun his father used?"

"It was given to Sander after the coroner's inquest."

"The gun was given back?" Ali asked, incredulous.

"This is the deep south detective. Guns are a way of life here. Hunting is a big pastime and everybody around here has at least one gun. We don't dispose of a perfectly good gun here, unless it's used in a crime. The crime was solved, murder suicide. I know that where you're from the guns get melted down or thrown into the ocean, but not here," the sheriff said it like Ali should have known that.

"Why don't we get you settled in at the motel and you can review the file. Then we'll get into this further."

"Who handled the original case?" Jamie asked.

"My daddy was the sheriff then. His daddy was sheriff before him. You might say that being sheriff is sort of the family business." He pointed to the degree on the wall. "I realize you probably think of us as jerkwater cops but I have degree in criminal justice from the University of South Carolina. I am trying to bring this place up to the level of bigger sheriff's offices. I was also a marine, recon. And I played football in college, starting linebacker."

"We had no prejudgments of you or your department Sheriff, I was simply curious." Jamie soothed. The sheriff's frown relaxed.

"Would it be possible to talk to your father?" Al asked.

"Sure. I figured you would want to do that so I made sure I knew where he was today. Let's drop your stuff at the motel and we'll go see him."

Thomas led to the parking lot and headed for a black unmarked Ford, the trunk was festooned with radio antennas of varying sizes. Ali took the back seat and Jamie climbed into the front next to the Sheriff. He pointed the car down the main street of town while Ali scanned the file in his lap.

The motel was two blocks from the sheriff's station. The building was brown and the paint was peeling in numerous places. The building was L shaped with an empty pool in the middle and three old rotting chairs squatting on the deck around the edge of the pool. Tall weeds poked through cracks in the pool deck. It obviously had not been used in a very long time. The motel sign was once lighted with neon but some of the letters had burned out, leaving the sign to say ANTVILLE Motel.

Thomas parked in front of the office and waited while Ali and Jamie went inside to register. The office was sparse with a low table in front of a tired sofa. Two worn National Geographic magazines were spread on the table.

The woman behind the desk was over eighty years old wearing thick glasses and a tattered blue flannel shirt. Her hair was in disarray and piled on top of her head. Ali could see through a doorway behind the desk into a small sitting room. A black and white television sat on top of a rickety looking snack table that sagged under its weight. Apparently the clerk lived in the room behind the desk. Ali signed in and got keys to two rooms while Jamie produced her FBI credit card to pay for the rooms. The clerk held the credit card up to her nose and scrutinized it then mumbled something about the federal government.

The rooms were clean and neat. Ali dumped his suitcase on the single bed and locked the door.

Back in the car, Thomas apologized for the motel as he pulled back onto Main Street. Main Street was paved with brick and they passed through a neighborhood of homes, set back off the road, many of which were red brick fronted. They passed into the business district which consisted of a Food Lion supermarket and more brick buildings, the tallest of which was two stories then circled around a town square which had a tall statue wearing what appeared to be a confederate army uniform in the center.

"That statue is of Effron Bryant. He was a captain in the South Carolina Volunteers during the civil war. The town is named after him. Before the war it was called Grangers Mill. Bryant was the most famous confederate soldier from this area so they honored him by renaming the town." Sheriff Thomas said, catching Jamie's notice of the statue. Jamie wondered why so many small southern towns honored their heroes from the Civil War and not other wars. Maybe what they say is true, the war ain't over yet, she thought.

Along Main Street were five churches, the most prominent being the Baptist church in the center of town. We definitely are in the Bible belt, Jamie mused. They crossed over a set of railroad tracks and the buildings became more rundown and poor looking. Black men sat in the shade under a large tree playing cards on a piece of plywood propped on top of an old wire spool, the kind the electrical company used while a chicken raced around a dirt yard chased by a crowd of giggling black children. Every town, big or small has its ghetto Jamie decided. The last building on the outskirts of town was a ramshackle wooden building with a large sign in front that read FRESH BAIT. The road headed into the countryside.

They passed forests of pines, hickory and oak trees sporadically interrupted by homes, their yards cleared of trees. Horses or cows stood in some yards, grazing. The embankments along the road were red clay. Occasionally they passed fields of tobacco and cotton filled with bronze skinned workers bent forward, picking the crops. Mexicans, Ali thought, illegals probably. They were the only ones who would work in the fields for the kind of money farmers paid.

"Daddy's down at the river fishing. It's about a ten minute ride." Sheriff Thomas informed them.

"How well did you know Sander Vance?" Ali asked from the backseat.

"Not real well. He was kind of a strange kid, never had much to say. Stayed to himself mostly. The other kids picked on him sometime. I never did know his momma and stepdaddy but his real father was a cross country trucker, got killed in a wreck somewhere in the state. His momma remarried after that." Thomas answered.

"I was wondering why you haven't asked about our case." Jamie said.

"I figured you would tell me when the time was right, but I must admit I am a mite curious, especially with the FBI involved." Thomas replied.

"Now's as good a time as any I guess. Sander Vance is a suspect in a series of murders of gay men. Three were killed and a fourth was found in his house, held hostage and probably was going to be killed eventually. His life partner was killed." Ali told him. "Vance called me and told me there were others but he didn't elaborate. They were all killed with a forty-five revolver, we believe."

"You believe? How come you aren't sure? Didn't ballistics match?" Thomas asked.

"None of the slugs were recovered but there were no spent casings so we're pretty sure it was a revolver and the wounds are consistent with a forty-five size projectile." Jamie interjected.

"Gay men. Well, I can't say that surprises me much."

"Why is that?" Ali asked.

"Well, remember I told you the other kids teased Sander? A lot of it was because the other kids thought he was a little effeminate. Even accused him of being gay," Thomas replied.

"We believe he was possibly molested as a kid, the killings were a rage type of killing, and the bodies were mutilated." Jamie told him.

"Hmmm. Well I guess even little towns have their ugly secrets," Thomas said quietly. He slowed the car and turned onto a red clay road that wound through a canopy of trees. They drove for about five minutes and Thomas parked next to a new model silver pickup parked at the end of the road. An old beat up station wagon was parked next to the truck. Thomas exited the car and headed down a narrow footpath and Ali could hear water running ahead of them. They stepped out of the trees onto the bank of a river approximately forty feet across. The water was a muddy brown.

An older black couple was seated next to the river holding cane poles, their lines draping into the water to small red floats. They sat on overturned plastic buckets. The woman's skirt was a faded flower print and hung to the ground. She wore a large straw hat with the center missing.

Down the bank to their left, stood an older version of Sheriff Thomas, same strawberry blond hair with a lot of gray mixed in, cut in a flattop. He was dressed in faded blue jeans, a t-shirt and work boots, the stub of a long burned out cigar clenched between his teeth. The muscles of his thick forearms twisted and flexed as he cranked the handle of the fishing reel. The rod was bent toward the water and swayed back and forth as the fish on the line fought for its life. He bent and plucked a large bass out of the water by its gill plate then tucked the rod under his arm and removed the hook from the fish's mouth, dropping it back into the river with a splash. He glanced up at their approach.

"Hey, daddy. Looks like you're having a good day," Thomas greeted his father.

"Yessir, sho' am. You need to grab a pole. They're hungry today." His father smiled warmly.

"Caint. Got real criminals to catch," Sheriff Thomas laughed.

"Real criminals? Where you goin', Columbia?" His father joked.

"This here's Special Agent Jamie Stevens, FBI and Detective Castillo from South Florida. 'member I told you about them,"

Sheriff Thomas said, indicating toward them with his hand. The older Thomas nodded to them.

"No offense meant, I would shake your hand but then you'd smell like fish the rest of the day, I'm Bill Thomas senior," he said.

"That's okay. No offense taken," Ali answered. The elder Thomas set his rod down and sat on the rocks near the river bank.

"Junior tells me you're here about Sander Vance."

"Yes sir. We have some homicides we think he committed. He seems to have fled our area," Jamie said sitting next to Thomas senior.

"Homicides, as in more than one?" senior asked.

"Three. All gay men and we were able to rescue one he had imprisoned in his house. We don't know if that one will survive." Ali said. "We think there may have been more."

"Tsk, ain't that a shame, Sander Vance a possible serial killer, of gay men no less." Thomas senior shook his head. He pulled a Zippo lighter from his pocket, clicked it open and lit the stub of cigar. Pungent smoke circled his head as he puffed.

"He used a forty-five revolver daddy, just like the one killed his momma and stepdaddy," Sheriff Thomas said.

"Damn. Oh, excuse me miss," Thomas senior tipped his head in Jamie's direction. She smiled at him. The old southern gentlemen weren't supposed to curse in the presence of a lady in fact, some southern states still made it an arrestable offense to curse in the presence of women and children.

"What can you tell us about him," Ali asked.

"Well, lemme think. His real daddy Jack Vance was a long haul trucker got himself killed in a crash over near Charleston. His momma was named Janice and she met John Greene 'bout two years after Jack was killed. They got married a year later and moved into the house Janice owned. Greene weren't worth much. Did odd jobs and worked for awhile as a mechanic. Vance was hard man, tough on the boy, as was Greene. Guess his momma liked hard men, drank a lot and such. I always suspected he may have taken a hand to Janice and the boy but could never prove it. Green killed Janice, then himself with a pistol. Sander found the bodies. After that he moved in with Janice's sister until Sander came of age then he left the area. Haven't seen or heard from him since." Thomas senior stuck the cigar back in his mouth and puffed a few times.

"We think Sander may have been abused and possibly molested in his youth, possibly by an authority figure." Jamie said.

"Molested? You mean sexually? Naw, Green wouldn't never touch a male child. Now if he had a daughter, I wouldn't put it past him. Had a thing about queers, hated them with a passion. Wouldn't allow Sander to show a tear, ever. We did have an assistant scoutmaster that I always suspected was doing more than just taking the boys camping and showing them how to tie knots and such. He stayed round for about four years then left. Kind of a strange fellow, sort of a hippie type, wore his hair longer than folks like, stocky and thick kind of guy, had a scar on his lip from a cleft pallet when he was a kid. Had delicate hands and kinda limp wrists. Heard he went to Florida actually, don't know where. Sander was in his scout troop." Thomas senior picked at a hard callous on the palm of his hand with a fingernail.

"Do you think if Sander was on the run, you think he would come back to this area?" Ali asked.

"No, I doubt if that kid would ever show up here again. He hated this town. His aunt Diana still lives in town she might have an idea where he might go." Thomas senior replied.

Ali stood and brushed the seat of his pants.

"Well sir, we thank you for your insight. Good luck with your fishing," He said.

"Thank you and good luck to you too. Billy you take care of these folks and give them any help they need." He said to his son.

"Yeah daddy, no problem." Sheriff Thomas said. When they were out of earshot he turned to them, "I may be the sheriff and a college graduate and ex-marine but to him I'm still his little kid and he's the sheriff."

"You're always their kids, no matter how old you get," Jamie laughed.

As they drove back into town the sun was beginning to dip behind the trees. Thomas bent his head and looked through the windshield toward the setting sun.

"Gonna be dark pretty soon, too late to talk to the aunt today. You two are probably tired and hungry. What do you say we take this up in the morning?"

"Sounds fine," Ali agreed.

Thomas dropped them off at the motel. Ali asked the woman at the desk where the best place to eat was in town. She pointed across the street with her chin.

"Jimmy's is the best around," she said.

Jimmy's Bar-B-Que and Catfish House was fashioned like an old barn. One of those places where you could smell the bar-b-que for blocks. As Ali held the door for Jamie, he realized he was starving. A young teenage waitress led them to a table and placed menus in front of them. The tables in the place were long picnic tables with benches for seats. Jimmy's was filled with families with small children. The mothers wore plain dresses and half the men wore overalls and baseball caps with farm equipment logos on them. Ali and Jamie got a few suspicious looks as they picked their way to their table, apparently strangers were an oddity in this farm town. Ali ordered ribs and Jamie ordered the fried catfish and a beer. Ali decided to have a beer also, just one to be safe.

The waitress brought their food on large brown pottery plates. There were oval slices of garlic bread with lots of butter, baked beans in pottery crocks the size of coffee mugs and the beer was in pickle jars. They ate in silence.

"Well, what do you think about what the sheriff's father said?" Jamie asked when they were finished eating.

"Sounds like your profile was pretty close to right on," Ali answered.

"You think Vance would come back here to hide?" Jamie asked. Ali glanced around the restaurant.

"Well if he did, someone around here would notice. They don't seem to miss much."

"Small towns, everybody knows everybody's business." Jamie agreed. They finished their meal and Jamie paid with her credit card.

Ali was stretched out on the bed, drinking one of his airline bottles of gin and watching TV when Jamie knocked on the door. Ali stashed the bottle in a nightstand drawer before answering.

"Want some company?" she asked.

"Sure c'mon in," Ali stood aside to let her in. She was dressed in shorts and a t-shirt and he noticed she wasn't wearing a bra and her firm breasts pressed against the fabric of her shirt. She settled in the only armchair in the room and crossed her legs. Ali noticed how muscular yet feminine her legs were.

"Got another of those bottles stashed somewhere that you can share?" she asked, causing Ali to blush slightly. "I saw you get them from the stewardess. I'm a cop remember? I don't miss much."

"Apparently not," Ali replied, handing her one of the bottles. He handed her a bottle of ginger ale and a water glass then watched as she poured the gin into the glass and mix in the ginger ale, swirling the glass to mix the two. He was struck with a sudden longing and a twinge of guilt. He turned to the dresser and picked up the file on Sander Vance.

"Did you want to review this?" Ali asked.

He turned back and she was standing face to face with him. He could feel her breasts against his chest. They searched each others eyes for a long second. God, he wanted her but the guilt reared up again. He could feel Maria in the room but he couldn't move. He could feel her chest rise and fall against him with her breathing, her breath smelled of mouthwash, gin and ginger ale.

He was paralyzed, knowing he should pull away but couldn't, he could sense the longing between them.

She searched his eyes and knew what he was thinking. Slowly he leaned forward and their lips met, softly, hesitantly. He pressed his lips harder against hers and felt her sigh against him. Her lips were warm, soft and wet. He thought her heard Maria's voice telling him it was all right or maybe it was his own desire and not Maria at all. Jamie took a step back from him.

"We probably shouldn't do this," Ali said. He had trouble getting the words out he was breathing so deeply.

"Probably not," Jamie whispered, pulling her t-shirt over her head and letting her breasts fall free.

Ali opened his eyes and for a second could not figure out where he was then he remembered. He felt Jamie's body against him. She was still asleep, breathing deeply and evenly. Ali remembered the feel of her warm skin against him and the release he felt holding a woman again. Then he felt guilt. *What did I do?* He asked himself. There was an old saying that one does not shit where one eats and he had done just that. Workplace affairs never seemed to work. He felt as if he had betrayed Maria but at the same time he felt a deep peace and contentment.

He slipped carefully from the bed and stood naked, looking down at Jamie's naked back, partially uncovered. He wanted to hold her in his arms again and just stay there. He felt safe and sane when he held her. *God she was beautiful.*

Ali pulled on his jeans and t-shirt quietly and glanced at his watch and realizing that Sheriff Thomas would be there in an hour. He slipped his clothes back off and stepped into the shower letting the warm water cascade over him as he tried not to think.

Jamie woke to the faint sound of water running, rolled onto her back and glanced toward the closed bathroom door. She stretched her arms over her head and felt her muscles expand and then relax. She smiled to herself, recalling their lovemaking still able to feel Ali's strong hands on her skin, massaging and caressing her, making her breath catch in her throat. She realized she had been right about him. His actions were strong but gentle, bringing her to a crescendo she had not felt in a long time.

She remembered her first lover; a sometime boyfriend in college, a runner on the track team. He was tall and lean with shaggy hair down to his shoulders. Exactly the kind of guy her macho cop father would not have approved of. His lovemaking was hesitant and unsure and left her disappointed, to say the least. She had been with other men since then, always choosing strong, silent types like Ali and her father. *What would Freud have said about that?*

Jamie climbed reluctantly out of bed when she heard the shower shut off. Ali stepped from the bathroom and they were face to face in the tiny hallway. Jamie searched his eyes for some sign as to what he was feeling, afraid he would suffer from some guilt and she would be sure that her seduction was a big mistake and had destroyed anything they might have together. He looked deeply into her eyes and she was unable to read his look. She saw many emotions flash through them and then they softened. He slipped his arms around her waist and leaned down, kissing her deeply. She pressed against his chest and sighed. She also wanted to pull away because she was sure her morning breath was horrible but she couldn't.

"Morning," Ali said quietly.

"Morning,"

"You better get showered and dressed, Sheriff Thomas will be here soon," Ali smiled.

"Shit," Jamie yelped, pushing him away and ducking into the shower.

Jimmy's Bar-B-Que and Catfish House also served breakfast. There were thick slabs of bacon and Ali had eggs, sunny side up while Jamie ordered hers scrambled. Breakfast included a bowl of steaming grits with a puddle of butter floating on top. Ali mixed his grits with his fork to stir the butter in. Jamie pushed her bowl toward Ali.

"You don't want those?" Ali asked.

"Sorry, I don't do grits. Being from the north I'm a cream of wheat kind of girl."

Ali glanced over the top of his coffee cup as Sheriff Thomas picked his way to their table.

"Mornin' Sheriff," The teenage waitress greeted him as he sat at the table.

"Hey Ginny, how's yo' mama?" Thomas smiled at her.

"She's good. I'll tell her you was asking," the waitress answered. "Breakfast?"

"Just coffee thanks. My wife makes sure I don't leave the house without a full stomach." Thomas chuckled, patting his waist.

"Her mama and I went to high school together. So how are ya'll this mornin'? Sleep good? I know the beds in that motel aren't the most comfortable."

"Just fine," Ali replied, wondering how the Sheriff knew how comfortable the beds were in a local motel. He decided not to ask.

"I faxed the Vance file to your lab like you asked. You realize that when his folks was killed, the police didn't have any of the technology we have now like blood splatter knowledge, DNA and such. Can't blame daddy and the boys back then if they missed something." Thomas said defensively.

"I don't blame anybody Sheriff. I just think a new look with modern knowledge wouldn't hurt." Ali answered.

"Sorry I get a little touchy when daddy's judgment is questioned, no offense taken."

They finished their breakfast and Jamie led the way to the cash register to pay the bill. Ali had glanced at her when they rose from the table and saw the smile in her eyes but the rest of her face was expressionless. He hoped Thomas didn't catch the look and suspect something.

They made the drive in silence. After about twenty minutes, Thomas steered the car off the paved road onto dusty dirt track was lined with cypress and oak trees, their branches hanging over the track in a thick canopy. Ali could see a white house at the end of the track. Thomas pulled the car into a large open yard. The house was old and the paint was peeling from the outside, like the skin of a tourist in south Florida that had spent too much time in the sun. The front of the house was a large screened porch and Ali could see a woman sitting on the porch.

"Hello Miz Diana." Thomas hollered as they approached the porch.

"Hey now, if it ain't young Bill Thomas," a soft voice with a thick southern accent replied from the shade of the porch. "C'mon in here."

Thomas pulled the screen door open with a loud squeak.

"Damn that door. I gotta oil it one of these days."

The old woman sat in a large wicker rocking chair dressed in a faded print house dress with a yellow tinted apron draped over the front of her skinny legs and her nylon knee stockings bunched around the tops of scuffed square clunky shoes. Her white hair was pulled into a bun perched on the back of her head, small gold glasses hung on the end of her nose. The knuckles of her hands were large and disfigured from arthritis, her fingers bent and knarled. She held two knitting needles and a large pile of yarn cascaded down her lap to the floor and despite the affliction the knitting needles flew in her hands. Thomas introduced them and she pointed to chairs with a knitting needle.

"Now what in grace's name would the FBI and a detective from Florida want with an old bird like me?" The woman asked.

"It's about your nephew Sander," Thomas offered. Aunt Diana made a sucking sound with her lips.

"That chil', my lands he is a worry. What's he done now?"

"He is part of an investigation we're conducting," Jamie said, not wanting to give away too much. "What can you tell us about him?"

"Well, he was a quiet kid, kind of strange. Troubled I reckon you could say. After his momma and stepdaddy passed he came to live with me. He never said much about that tragedy. Sad thing, them dyin' like that. He was hard to manage but did good in school, very bright boy. Never had many friends, fact is, I can't think of any."

"What do you mean, strange?" Ali asked her.

"Well, did weird things. That gun his stepdaddy used, that the Sheriff give back to him was never far from him. He would sit in his room sometimes, holding it and clicking the trigger. I had a cat, an old calico, stupid cat but gave me some comfort. I found it dead with its neck wrung in the yard one day. Sander denied knowing anything about it, but I have no doubt he done it," the old woman looked off into the distance, remembering.

"Did he have any girlfriends?" Jamie asked.

"No, like I said he stayed to himself most times."

"Have you heard from him or do you know where he might be now?" Ali questioned.

"No, I haven't heard from him in years."

"Well, ma'am if you think of anything or hear from Sander would you call and let Sheriff Thomas know?" Jamie asked.

"Sho' will. Billy I made some fresh cornbread this morning, take some with you." Diana offered.

"No ma'am thanks, gotta watch my girlish figure," Thomas chuckled patting his stomach for the second time this morning.

CHAPTER 22

M ichael Riley packed his briefcase and left his office. The drive to the bank was a short five minutes but the wait to get into Bascomb's safe deposit box was much longer. Riley sat in a large stuffed chair and scanned the lobby. The elderly security guard by the front door kept watching him, his uniform hung baggy on his narrow bony shoulders. Riley figured him for a retired cop who was either bored with retirement or needed to supplement his pension income. He had been very suspicious while checking Riley's briefcase for weapons and maybe bombs.

Finally, the bank manager approached from the secured area where the safety deposit boxes were kept. She was an attractive black woman with skin the color of coffee with lots of cream. She appeared to have recovered from Riley's exasperation from having to show his Power Of Attorney and copy of Bascomb's will showing he was really the executor of Bascomb's estate and had legal access to Bascomb's box. The bank manager stopped next to Riley's chair and smiled pleasantly.

"Mr. Riley would you follow me, please?" the manager asked. Riley struggled to get up from the big chair and straightened his suit jacket, retrieved his briefcase from the floor next to the chair and followed obediently. Inside the vault, the manager slid the box from a row in the wall and placed it on a table. The table and a chair were the only furniture in the room.

"Just buzz when you're done," The manager said, pointing to a red button on the wall then she was gone. Riley settled into the chair and unlocked the box with a small key from his pocket.

The box was stuffed with envelopes and papers. Riley sorted through them, opening and reading their contents. Most of the papers were insurance policies and some letters to friends and relatives. Riley always felt a little creepy sorting through the remnants of a person's life, especially their homes. He had spent the previous day in Bascomb's house, sorting through its contents and deciding what would go to the estate and what would be sold at an estate auction. The house of a dead person always felt like a silent monument to that person. Riley always felt like the furniture was watching him, accusing him of being an intruder who was necessary but unwelcome. Riley shrugged off the thought.

In the bottom of the box was a thick, stuffed envelope with Riley's name printed on it in pencil. He carefully slipped his letter opener into the flap and zipped it open glancing at the note inside, written in Bascomb's careful hand.

Michael,

If you are reading this, I must be dead. I am sorry to put you through this old friend but you are the only one I can trust with my affairs. Besides, you are the only honest lawyer I know. The contents of this envelope have caused me great heartache and consternation. I have been unable to decide what to do with it, so being a coward I did nothing but now I trust you will do the right thing.

Friends always.

Riley glanced at the papers and his breath caught in his throat. *Damn. There was only one thing to do with this,* he thought. He carefully packed the contents of the deposit box into his briefcase and slipped the thick envelope into his coat pocket. He pressed the red button to be released from the room. Once he was back in the lobby he glanced nervously around, suddenly feeling like everybody was watching him. Riley exited the bank into the sunshine and fought the urge to run to his car and lock himself safely inside. Once he was safely in his Mercedes he retrieved his cell phone from his pocket and dialed quickly, reading the number from the business card he held in his shaking hand.

CHAPTER 23

Ali sat in the back seat and stared out the window, watching the farms and fields pass in front of his eyes but he could not see them. He was lost in thought, trying to decide what to do about Jamie. He wanted desperately to continue with her and he wanted to be with her again. But there was that damn guilt again. Was he violating his promise to Maria? Did he not have the right to be happy and move on with his life? But he made a promise to Maria to always love her. Could he have a life with Jamie and still love Maria even though she was gone. What did Jamie really want from him and his life? Was last night just a one time thing? He didn't think so. Shit, he really needed a drink. But he promised Davis he would try to stay focused and off the booze, like he could just turn it off and on like a faucet. His stomach churned and he felt the saliva building up in his mouth. He felt shaky. *Dammit I am an alcoholic, I need it too much. I really need to get my shit together. I've gotta get back in the gym and get back in shape. Maybe Antonio can help me get straight. Antonio, how the fuck did I get to here? I should have never stopped training.*

He thought about Antonio and how he had taken a chubby awkward kid and made him strong and graceful and fast. Ali remembered the first time he walked into the boxing gym with his father. He was terrified. The gym was loud and intimidating, all that activity, something Ali had never seen. The smell of sweat, old leather, liniment and many others Ali could not identify at the time. The smack of leather gloves against old leather bags, the grunts of exertion, the swish of jump ropes whistling through the air and slapping against the ground. Ali absorbed it all in an instant. Then he met Antonio, who ran the gym and trained the fighters.

Antonio was small in stature but huge in the eyes of his charges. His hair was thinning on top and his gray mustache was perfectly trimmed, almost looking like it was painted on. He always wore sleeveless, stained old t-shirts; his muscular but sinewy arms looked too long for his body. He was everywhere at once, flying around the gym, screaming, yelling encouraging and watching every fighter like a hawk. When he shook Ali's hand for the first time, Ali thought his hand had been crushed. The magic happened in the first ten minutes and changed Ali forever. Antonio had strapped on a pair of old boxing gloves on Ali's wrists and stepped back, 'les see what choo got pequeno' Antonio said. Ali could not raise his arms because of the weight of the gloves. He stood there feeling like the gloves were going to pull his arms from their sockets and they would crash to the ground. He felt so stupid. Antonio chuckled and said 'maybe we need smaller gloves.' He pulled the gloves from Ali's wrists without untying the strings, proving they were too large. Ali learned to love the smells and sounds of the gym and spent all of his free time there. And the sparring, oh how he loved to spar. He was not afraid to take on anybody and had been knocked to his butt many times but he bounced back up and jumped right back into the fray. Antonio used to tell him he had a huge heart. Right now Ali felt as if he had no heart, somewhere, sometime it had been ripped from his chest and he wasn't really sure when. Maybe Antonio could help him find his heart again.

Ali realized he had not heard from the crime lab yet about the reports Thomas had faxed to them. He pulled his cell phone from his belt and looked at the tiny screen. It was blank.

"You won't get service up here unless you got the local cell provider, too far from most cell towers," Sheriff Thomas said, watching him in the rear view mirror. "You can use the phone at the office." Ali nodded, wondering how long Thomas had been watching him. He glanced at the back of Jamie's head, wondering what she was feeling and thinking.

At the Sheriff's Office, Thomas directed him toward his private office saying he could use his private phone. As Ali headed down the hall he heard an irate woman's voice yelling from the area of the front desk. She was yelling about a goat eating her petunias for the last time. Ali sat behind Thomas' desk and dialed the number for Lieutenant Davis direct line. It rang for a long time until Davis' voice barked on the other end.

"Davis."

"Hey boss, its Ali."

"Did you find anything?" Davis demanded.

"We met with the former sheriff and the aunt, nothing. Vance must be still in South Florida or in the wind, he could be anywhere. I had the Sheriff fax some reports to the lab but haven't heard anything yet."

"Well, you need to get back here ASAP. The lab called about those reports, Martins is conscious and everybody is crawling up my ass for results. And Bascomb's attorney has been calling you, says it's urgent."

"We'll be back in the morning. Can you connect me to the lab?"

"Yeah hang on and hurry up and get back here, the shit's hitting the fan!"

"See you in the morning boss," Ali said to a standby signal, Davis had already switched the phone.

"Crime lab," The tech's voice came on the line.

"Hey it's Castillo. Did you get those reports we faxed?" Ali asked.

"Yes my dear I did and as usual I dropped everything I was doing to review them and you know I would only do it for you," the tech replied with a sweet voice.

"And?"

"And it looks like somebody was wrong. I compared the size of the wound and the blood splatter. The wound pattern shows that the gun was six inches from the father's head when it discharged. Nobody would hold a gun that far from the head to shoot themselves. The blood splatter on the wall was too narrow for the gun to have been against the head also. My conclusion, now mind you it was from some pretty grainy old crime scene photos, is the father did not shoot himself, someone else did."

"Thanks I owe you," Ali thanked her.

"Yes you do, again and one of these days I'm gonna collect."

Ali headed back to the front desk area. The goat complainant was gone. Thomas was leaning against a desk listening to Jamie talk. As Ali approached, he could not help but feel a twinge, looking at her. Jamie turned to face him as he approached.

"I called our lab on those other homicides we think Vance did. The wounds are consistent and the profile fits. They are confident Vance was the killer in all of them," Jamie informed him.

"Our lab says that Vance's father was killed by someone else, not a suicide. I figure Vance did that one too, sorry Sheriff," Ali apologized to Thomas.

"Better technology, more science no problem," Thomas shrugged. "I guess ya'll will be headed home in the morning unless there is something more you can do up here."

"I can't think of anything," Ali turned to Jamie, "Martins is awake and Bascomb's attorney has been driving Davis crazy, says he has something urgent to talk to us about."

"I wonder what that's about," Jamie answered. Ali glanced at his watch. It was nearly three o'clock.

"Guess we'll head home in the morning, too late to get to Columbia and catch a flight today."

"Well, I reckon I'll run ya'll back to the motel," Thomas said, pushing away from the desk.

Thomas dropped them at their motel telling them he would have a deputy pick them up in the morning and drive them to the airport. They shook hands.

"Sheriff, thanks for all your help. Sorry we took up so much of your valuable time and pulled you away from other matters," Ali said, gripping Thomas' hand.

"Hell, I enjoyed meeting both of you. It was interesting to see how other cops work and I learned a few things. Now, don't you worry, if Vance shows his face in these parts I'll personally lock him up for ya," Thomas touched his brow as if tipping an imaginary hat.

"Agent Stevens it has been my distinct pleasure." Thomas said. Jamie blushed slightly.

"The pleasure has been mine, Sheriff. If you need anything from the FBI you call me personally,"

Thomas waved to them as he slid behind the wheel of his car and backed out of the parking lot. An uncomfortable silent hung in the air between them. Ali was not sure what to do now.

"I think we need to talk," Jamie said, heading to her motel room door. Ali followed silently.

Jamie poured soda into two plastic cups, added ice and handed one to Ali. She kicked off her shoes and sat in one of the fake leather chairs in front of the window. Ali sat across from her and sipped his soda.

"Where do we go from here?" Jamie asked.

"I don't know," Ali answered quietly. This seemed a bit abrupt to him, like he was in a strategy meeting.

"I need to know what you want to do but first I need to tell you a few things." Jamie said, studying his face. "I have been attracted to you from the beginning. You do something to me that I haven't felt for a long time. I have had my heart broken in the past and I don't want to do that to you, I care deeply about you, which I know sounds funny since we haven't known each other that long. But if you decide you can't or don't want to have a relationship I will understand and won't cry and beg and make it difficult on you. I know or at least I have an idea what you're going through. I know about your wife, I know it's been two years and I know how hard it can be to start again, but I think you are special and I want to see where this leads. But I don't want to pressure you if that's not what you want." She finished and waited, trying to read his face for her answer.

"I do have strong feelings for you and last night was really special but you need to know some things too. I was asleep when Maria died. I had just worked a call out and had been up for twenty four hours straight so I went home and went to bed. I was asleep before she left that day and I didn't even kiss her goodbye. I feel really guilty about that. I feel that if I had been awake I could have prevented what happened. I know it sounds dumb because I wouldn't have been in the car anyway, but that is how I feel. We had something magical and I never thought I would find that so it was really a surprise to me to feel that much love and I miss that desperately. I want it again too but I feel as if I am betraying Maria by starting over again, like I should mourn for her the rest of my life. So I started to drink and I'm not sure I can stop. I feel so old and tired and out of shape and useless and lots of other things too. I need to find myself and get back up again. When I was boxing I would get knocked down and get right back up but this time I can't seem to get back up and I hate myself for that." Tears began to stream down his face.

"I want to be with you and I can love you just as you are. If you want to try I'll be there for you," She rose and put her arms around his shoulders. She kissed the back of his neck. He nodded. He rose and held her tightly against him.

"I want to try," He whispered to her.

"Maybe we can find you again, together."

The flight back to Columbia was uneventful. The small plane cruised smoothly through wispy clouds and landed gently in the big airport. Ali and Jamie had a light lunch in one of the many restaurants in the airport and boarded the large jet for the return trip.

The flight to Fort Lauderdale was another matter entirely. As soon as the plane crossed the Florida border it encountered a large thunderstorm which was the leading edge of a cold front. The plane bucked and rolled, sometimes seeming to drop ten feet at a time. The pilot turned on the fasten seat belt sign and made a point of reiterating the need to stay in ones seat over the loudspeaker. Ali was terrified but tried not to show it. He gripped the armrests so tightly he was afraid he would rip them from their fasteners. He rested his head back against the seat and closed his eyes. His heart was banging in his chest and he was warm and sweating. The bulkheads of the passenger cabin seemed to shrink rapidly. He glanced at the magazine pouch of the rear of the seat in front of him and wondered if there was a barf bag tucked in there with the in-flight magazine and the laminated card that demonstrated how to use the oxygen masks if they dropped from above. He prayed his heart would stop if the plane started to drop from the sky so he would not have to endure the long wait for it to hit the earth. Jamie reached for his hand on the armrest but couldn't pry it loose so she placed her hand over his and held it firmly. She seemed calm. Ali figured that being a federal agent she had spent more than her share of time on airplanes and was not scared. He was wrong. Her heart was racing also but she was able to hide it.

When the airplane finally touched down, Ali fought the urge to run screaming from the cabin, like a high school cheerleader who just caught her quarterback boyfriend making out under the bleachers with the ugliest girl in school. He gathered his carry-on bag from the overhead storage bin and walked on shaking legs from the plane. His stomach was doing flips and he felt as if he had just gone ten rounds in a world championship fight.

Ali and Jamie stepped from the terminal into a warm, windy, cloudy day, the kind of South Florida day that preceded the arrival of a cold front. Ali wanted to find a place to lie down until the world stopped tilting but instead he drove toward the office. Halfway there his cell phone rang. It was Lieutenant Davis wanting to know if they had landed yet. He informed Ali that his office was crawling with FBI brass and he needed to see them *'right fucking now,'*

CHAPTER 24

Lieutenant Davis was seated behind his desk when they arrived, his face red with anger. Across from him sat two men in the dark suits of the FBI standard uniform. The senior agent rose when they entered the office and held out his hand. He was tall and thin with dark hair, graying at the temples and looked to Ali like a lawyer not a cop. Ali could imagine him standing in a courtroom eloquently presenting his case to the jury.

"Senior Special Agent Thomas Robinson," the man introduced himself. "This is Agent Cruz." Robinson waved his hand at his companion who rose and shook Ali's hand. *A politician and his lap dog,* Ali thought to himself.

"I'll get right to the point Detective," Robinson said. "Since you have discovered that this case crosses jurisdictional boundaries, the FBI is going to take this case."

"Meaning no disrespect, I don't think so." Ali flared. "This is my case and I'm going to finish it." *Typical, he thought, now that the case is almost finished, the feds think they can waltz in and take it sot they can take the credit for all of our hard work.*

"Now Detective, there is no need for animosity. We have the resources to take this case to the next level." Robinson replied tersely.

186 - Alex J. McDonald

"Excuse me sir," Jamie said with honey in her voice, "The crimes in the other jurisdictions are still speculative at best. Detective Castillo has enough evidence and probable cause to arrest Vance and prosecute him. There is plenty of time to gather evidence and prosecute the other cases, but right now I think the Bureau's best course of action would be to allow Castillo to complete the case and if possible arrest Vance. Once he is in custody, we can take our time to build airtight cases in the other states. Besides, interagency squabbling would make everyone look bad and perhaps harm successful prosecutions."

Damn she's good, Ali marveled. She sounded just like a bureaucrat.

Robinson sat and considered this for a long moment.

"Perhaps you are right Agent Stevens. Very well, we'll let you have your case and when the time is right, we'll dovetail all of the cases together," Robinson decided. He rose and Cruz followed suit. Robinson shook hands all around. "We'll be in touch."

Robinson breezed from the office with Cruz in tow, like a conquering king

"What a putz," Jamie smiled after they had left. "Robinson is an arrogant ass but he is a good administrator. He wouldn't make a hair on a street agents butt however." Davis and Ali both chuckled at that. "Besides, I already called the Assistant Director in D.C. last night and made sure Robinson would not get this case."

"What?" Ali asked her.

"Yeah I know how these things work and I expected the local office to try to move in, so I preempted his strike. The Assistant Director and my father were old friends." Jamie smiled. Ali wanted to hug her.

"Okay let's get back to it," Davis said, shuffling through the papers on his desk. He extracted a pink phone message slip and handed it to Ali. "Bascomb's attorney has been calling frantically, here's his number."

Ali stopped at another detective's desk on his way to his own.

"Did you get anything on the BOLO for Vance?" He asked the detective at the desk.

"No luck yet," The detective replied, "But I checked stolen tag reports for cars the same make, model and year as Vance's. There was a tag stolen yesterday that may be it, I added it to the BOLO."

"Good work, thanks."

Riley answered the phone on the second ring and Ali figured he must have been sitting by the phone waiting for his call.

"Detective, thank God you're back. I must see you right away." Riley said, breathlessly.

"What is this in reference to?" Ali asked.

"I can't discuss this on the phone. I can be at your office in thirty minutes." Riley answered.

"Fine, I'll be here." Ali hung up.

Ali worked on his investigative reports while waiting for Riley to arrive. He had to document everything that had happened in South Carolina.

Riley arrived exactly thirty minutes later with a brown envelope tucked under his arm.

"I have something for you I think may be relevant. Is there somewhere private we can talk?" Riley asked. Ali led him to a private interview room, beckoning for Jamie to join them. When they were alone in the interview room with the door closed, Riley placed the envelope on the table in front of Ali. When Ali did not open it, Riley grabbed it and removed a stack of papers. He handed them to Ali impatiently. Ali scanned the first few pages.

"I'm sorry Mr. Riley, but what am I looking at?" Ali asked.

"As I told you, Mr. Bascomb was an investment banker. One of his biggest clients was CAD, Coalition Against Discrimination? He did some of their investments from membership dues." Jamie was examining some of the papers Riley had placed on the table.

"Six months ago, Bascomb found some discrepancies. He started to investigate and found that someone had been diverting funds to an offshore account, in other words, embezzling funds from CAD." Riley pointed to a printout with numbers and figures neatly in columns.

"Who?" Ali asked.

"Abramowitz, their attorney. This is the proof," Riley stepped back from the table and sat down across from them. "Do you think this could be why he was killed?"

"I can't say for sure Mr. Riley but this is very helpful. I'm sorry but I'm not real good with numbers can you explain this all to me?" Ali asked. Riley nodded.

"It's really very simple and ingenious. CAD invests money in different funds and companies to expand their money base. It's used for different expenses, legal needs, media advertising and of course Rodney James gets a salary paid from the funds. Abramowitz invests that money for CAD. He invests with companies that are shells. He invests the money offshore, non-American companies and puts the interest, about ten percent, back into the funds for CAD. That is a decent return on the money for any investment. But, on paper it appears that CAD still has the initial investment but that's a farce, the only thing they have is the ten percent interest. The original money that was invested goes into offshore accounts belonging to Abramowitz under different names in places like the Netherlands, Belgium and other countries that do not have banking treaties with the US. No one notices the loss because Abramowitz handles the money and the documentation." Riley finished and sat back, waiting to see if his explanation had gotten through to this simple cop.

"I have to ask you not to discuss this with anyone and I mean anyone, not friends, family, press, anyone until we have time to figure out how this relates to Bascomb's death. Understand?" Ali looked straight into Riley's eyes to make sure he understood. Riley nodded.

"Don't worry detective. If this has any bearing on my friend's death, I won't give any help to a defense claim when it goes to court." He rose and shook their hands then hurried from the room.

"Son-of-a-bitch! Abramowitz?" Ali asked, looking at Jamie. He was still exhausted from the plane ride and still a bit queasy. Jamie was reading the papers carefully. Ali admired her profile. He remembered that night in the hotel, wanted to feel her skin against him again, her breath on his neck, her soft moans. His heart quickened and he felt a sudden calm. Jamie glanced up and caught him looking. She smiled and Ali wondered if she was reading his thoughts.

"This would be a good motive. Bascomb's killing was different from the others. Remember we wondered if there was a different motivation? This could be it." Jamie speculated.

"Question is, did Vance kill Bascomb or did Abramowitz do it himself?" Ali answered.

"We need to find out."

CHAPTER 25

Bobby Joe Miller stepped from the shower, water running off of his skinny naked frame, thankful Castillo had decided to hold him. It kept him from the streets and he was clean and fed but he longed for a cold beer or some scotch or anything else alcoholic he could scrounge up. The first three days had been hard. He had suffered through withdrawal, curled up in his cell, soaked with sweat and shaking uncontrollably, vomiting until every inch of his body throbbed with pain. The medication the jail nurse had given him had helped some but not enough. The visions had been the worst. He had imagined his ex-wife and kids, armed with long bladed curved knives stripping his skin from him as he screamed, covered in blood. Then he awoke and realized it was only a nightmare. Sometimes the visions came when he was wide awake, suddenly without warning, causing him to curl up in a corner, screaming for help.

At least now he was a material witness and took private showers, no longer having to worry about another inmate sneaking up behind and throwing him down in the shower, sodomizing him while he thrashed in the water and soap suds while his screams were ignored. Yessir, this deal wasn't too bad at all.

Bobby Joe dried himself with the rough white towel and struggled into his jail overalls. He slid his feet into the rubber sandals the jail provided and stepped from the shower room. The door opened and a jail officer stuck his head.

"Hurry up Miller, somebody's waiting for you," the officer said, closing the door behind him.

Who the hell wanted to see him? Bobby Joe wondered. He didn't have an attorney yet.

Bobby Joe followed the jail officer to an interview room. When the door opened he found Ali and Jamie waiting for him.

"Hey, Detective Castillo, Agent Stevens, what brings you here?" Bobby Joe asked suspiciously. Ali flipped open a file folder in front of him and displayed six photographs.

"I need to know if you recognize anyone, Bobby Joe," Ali said grimly. Bobby Joe glanced at the photographs. *What should I do here? If I identify somebody, do I end up back on the streets? If I do recognize somebody and don't say so, I'll probably end up back on the streets because I'm no longer of any use. Shit. What's my best option here?* His mind raced with indecision.

"Well?" Jamie asked impatiently. Bobby Joe stalled, examining the photographs carefully, recognizing a face but not daring to say so. Ali wondered about his lack of reaction then he realized what the problem was.

"Bobby Joe let me explain how this will work. If you recognize somebody then you become very important to this case. You will be removed from the jail and placed into a hotel as a material witness. The auto theft charges go away and you get to stay in the hotel until the trial if necessary. That could take a very long time," Ali finished and leaned back. Bobby Joe glanced from Ali to Jamie and back to Ali.

"You swear?" He asked. Ali pointed at a mirror behind him.

"Bobby Joe, I'm required to inform you that there is a video camera behind that mirror. It is recording this entire interview, including what I just said, and I am now telling you, on videotape, that I promise that what I just told you is true and the promise will be honored."

Bobby Joe hesitated, hoping Ali was telling the truth, then with a shaking forefinger he pointed to picture number three. Irving Abramowitz. Ali exhaled softly.

"And for the record, raise your right hand," Ali said. Bobby Joe did what he was told. "Mister Miller, do you solemnly swear that your statement is true and accurate so help you God?" Ali asked.

"I do," Bobby Joe answered solemnly.

"Mister Miller, where do you recognize that person from?"

"I seen him park that BMW under the bridge, The BMW that I was arrested in."

"And there is no doubt in your mind that the person whose picture you pointed out parked that car under the bridge?" Ali asked.

"Absolutely no doubt."

CHAPTER 26

A li spent fifteen minutes trying to find a parking space in the hospital lot. He even stalked two different people, following them to their cars only to find that they were not leaving just getting something from their cars. Finally, he parked right in front of the entrance and flashed his badge to the security guard so as not to have the unmarked car towed away. He hated to take advantage of his badge but sometimes one had no choice. He and Jamie identified themselves to the nurse at the desk and the police officer on guard at Martens' door.

Martins lay in the bed, surrounded by space age looking machines, tubes running into numerous veins of his arms and legs. He was almost as white as the sheets he lay on and so thin Ali thought he looked like a skeleton. He had dark circles around both his eyes, making him look like a raccoon. His face was grotesquely swollen and bruised, the top of his head wrapped in gauze. A doctor in a lab coat stood next to the bed, writing on a metal clipboard as they entered. He glanced up and frowned at Ali and Jamie until Ali identified himself.

"How is he doing?" Jamie asked the doctor, walking around him to stand next to the head of the bed.

"Much better, his electrolytes have come up, he's better hydrated, that's a good sign and I think the bruises are looking better. His right wrist is broken, some internal damage that should heal in time but I think he'll pull through."

"We need to talk to him," Ali told the doctor.

"He's very weak so don't expect him to answer quickly it may take him a second to form the thought. I'll leave you alone but try not to push it too hard and not too long." The doctor turned and left, closing the door quietly behind him.

"Jonah can you hear me?" Jamie asked softly, leaning down to speak into Martins' ear. He opened his eyes slightly.

"I'm Special Agent Stevens FBI, this is detective Castillo. I'm sorry to have to do this right now but we need your help."

"It's okay," Martins rasped, barely audible.

"We need you to tell us everything that happened." Ali said from behind Jamie.

"Daniel and I were buying our dream house. We hired James Brand to find it for us," Martens statement was halting and slow. "We looked at a house and signed a contract to buy it. After we signed the contract we went to dinner with Brand and afterwards went to his house for a drink. The next thing I know we're chained up in a room and Daniel and I are being tortured," he began to sob softly. "It was horrible. I could hear Daniel being beaten then he would start on me. I heard Brand kill him. There was a loud explosion, a gun I think and then Daniel was gone. The next thing I know I'm here."

"Did you ever see Brand do any of this?" Jamie asked.

"We were kept blindfolded but I heard his voice while he laughed. He told me everything he was doing to Daniel. I know it was him. There was someone else too, one time right before the gunshot. A voice I didn't know."

"Another voice? You're sure?" Ali asked. Martens nodded.

"Could you identify that voice if you heard it again?" Ali asked. Martens nodded.

"I will never forget those two voices."

"Do you know Irving Abramowitz, the lawyer for CAD?" Jamie asked.

"No Daniel and I stayed to ourselves. We didn't go in for the gay organizations and the politics. Those people are fools and troublemakers. They just tend to piss off the straight people and create resentment towards gays."

Ali could see that Martins was beginning to fade, fighting to keep his eyes open. He reached into his pocket and removed a small tape recorder and placed it on the wheeled table next to Martins' bed.

"Jonah, I need you to listen to this tape, I know you're tired but let me know if you can identify any voice on this tape," Ali said gently. Martins nodded slightly. Ali hit the play button and Abramowitz' voice came through loud and clear. It was the tape of Abramowitz interview. Ali studied Martins' face and saw fear cross his features.

"That's him, that's the other voice," Martins whispered.

"You get some rest now. We'll talk more later and I'll need to get a statement from you at some point," Ali patted Martins shoulder but he was already asleep.

"Okay, if Vance killed Bascomb for Abramowitz how did they connect, how did Abramowitz know Vance and know that he would do the job. We assume that Bascomb was a hit, a contract as it were, but what is the connection?" Ali asked Jamie when they were back in the car.

"Real estate? Don't real estate transactions require a lawyer? Abramowitz is a lawyer, maybe that's the connection," Jamie mused out loud.

"Shit. That must be it," Ali growled, pulling a u-turn in traffic, nearly getting sideswiped by a pickup truck.

Chapter 27

Ruth Lefebre sipped her Margarita and watched her guests on the lawn. The party was going better than she had planned. Thank goodness the weather had not turned ugly and the rain had stayed away. The cool front, the first one of the year, had passed through yesterday, bringing with it the usual rain and Ruth had been frantic that the weather would not clear for this party. But the gods had smiled on her and the cool front did nothing more than break the heat and humidity and make the weather perfect for a garden party. The three-piece ensemble her friend had recommended was better than advertised. They played some light jazz along with Sinatra and the music wafted over the neighborhood. This party had been Ruth's way of damage control. Luckily James Brand had not been named as the killer publicly yet, but Ruth knew that as soon as he was, her name and the reputation of her business would suffer.

Ruth made her way through the guests, greeting this one, hugging and kissing that one, until she reached the mayor's side. She slipped her arm through his and pulled his arm against her breast. She knew his wife was in Aspen skiing and she also knew he was a notorious letch who had women friends, Ruth having been one of them in the past. She also knew he was a college friend of the newspaper editor and Ruth would need all of the friends in the media she could get. Among the group around the mayor were the local television station news director and two city council members. These were the people who would stand behind her and minimize the damage.

"How is the new house?" Ruth asked the news director's wife. Ruth had found them a great deal in a very fashionable part of the city.

"Oh I love it. Working in the garden is just what I needed to help with my arthritis," The wife gushed. Ruth had searched diligently for the right house. This one had an English style garden, walled in and very private. She also knew the wife liked to sunbathe nude and no one wanted to see that, especially the neighbors, the woman was over sixty years old after all. Ruth was careful to find a house without two story houses on either side so the neighbors couldn't look over the wall.

"I am so pleased," Ruth smiled sweetly. It paid to know her clients secrets and so many of them confided in their real estate agents, even more than their therapists.

"When are you going to let me find you the perfect house?" Ruth asked the mayor, tugging his arm against her. She made it a point to turn slightly sideways so he would be sure not to miss the feel of her breast against his arm, like he would ever miss that.

"When my wife returns from her trip maybe we'll consider it," The mayor replied, leering at her.

"You had better," Ruth laughed, slipping away from him and heading toward the bar to get another Margarita. She heard a commotion near the driveway and saw her valet trying to block Detective Castillo and Agent Stevens from entering the yard. Castillo was nose to nose with the valet and whispering to him. The valet suddenly stepped aside with a terrified look. Castillo spied Ruth in the crowd and stormed toward her. She considered running to the mayor's side but it was too late.

"Detective Castillo, what a pleasant surprise, you realize you are interrupting a party don't you?" A party you were not invited to?" Ruth sniffed at him.

"I don't really care right now," Ali growled. "We need to talk, now."

Ruth caught the mayor out of the corner of her eye. Good he was headed this way. Ruth eased toward him with Ali and Jamie in tow.

"Detective, do you know my good friend the mayor?" Ruth asked, stopping next to the mayor and turning defiantly toward Ali. She felt safe now. The mayor would protect her, she knew too many of his secrets, especially his sexual preferences.

"What is the problem Detective Castillo?" The mayor demanded.

"The problem Mister Mayor is that the serial killer I am after, as you are well aware, worked for your friend here and used her real estate business to find his victims," Ali snarled. He could see that comment had the desired effect. The mayor was silent, considering the political trap he was in. If he stood by Ruth, the gay community would crucify him in the next election and he did not want to alienate that constituency. On the other hand, Ruth could tell his wife secrets he would rather not have revealed. He decided his wife was the lesser of two evils; after all, she would only take half of everything he owned but being the mayor was the best thing that ever happened to him. Besides, the general public would accept some sexual dalliances on the part of their elected officials in fact they almost expected it.

"Perhaps you should talk to them," the mayor said to Ruth backing away. *You bastard*, Ruth thought, *I'm gonna burn your ass.*

Ali and Jamie followed Lefebre into the glass enclosed porch of the house. She whirled to face them and glared.

"You had no right to interrupt my party," Lefebre snapped, "There are some very important people in that garden, people who could ruin your career if I snapped my fingers."

"Your threats don't scare me; it looked to me like your high powered friends saw the wisdom of distancing themselves from you right now so I wouldn't count on a lot of help and I really don't care. I need to know some things and I can't wait because James Brand or Sander Vance, whichever you prefer to call him, is still out there and I want him. Would you like to go to the hospital and visit Jonah Martins and see what Vance did to him or maybe the morgue to see what is left of his other victims? Don't push me lady." Ali snapped back.

Lefebre turned from his wilting gaze and stared out the window at her party guests, wishing she could disappear into the crowd.

"What do you want to know?" She asked softly.

"I need to know if James Brand and Irving Abramowitz know each other and how," Ali replied.

"That's it? You made a fool out of me in front of my friends for that bullshit?" Lefebre turned to face him, a quizzical look on her face. Ali nodded grimly. "Yes they knew each other. Abramowitz handled the legal matters in real estate closings for many of our gay clients which Brand dealt with. They were comfortable with him since he was the attorney for CAD."

"Thank you," Ali led the way from the house leaving Lefebre to explain the visit to her other guests.

"Where do we go from here?" Ali asked glancing at Jamie seated next to him in the car.

"I think we need to drag that lawyer's ass in and squeeze the life out of him until he talks."

"Careful there, I thought the FBI was more subtle than us local cops, you're starting to sound like the rest of us," Ali chuckled. Jamie smiled, the fact that he laughed warmed her. She saw real hope for him now. She wanted to lean over the seat and kiss him but did not think it was the appropriate time. When they were working it should stay professional.

"I recently got some street cop in me," She couldn't resist the double entendre. Ali chuckled again and leered lasciviously at her.

Ali paced the squad room impatiently. He really wanted a drink and the tension was building up. His muscles were tense. He was slightly nauseous and his eyes burned. He glanced at Jamie, seated at a desk typing on a computer keyboard. She was watching him. She glanced around the squad room to make sure no one was looking and then smiled and winked at him, making him smile slightly. He realized he and Jamie hadn't eaten or slept for twenty-six hours, which explained how he felt. He realized his hands were shaking and rubbed them against his pants legs, trying to stop them. His headache seemed to be centered right behind his eyes. *Am I just tired or starting to go through withdrawal?* He wondered. He prayed for just tired.

Rodney James breezed into the squad room followed by Irving Abramowitz. Rodney James looked like he was miffed about being summoned to the police station.

"Well Detective. Congratulations for saving that poor man Martins," His voice dripped with sarcasm, "Too bad it was too late to save anyone else."

Ali fought the overwhelming urge to plant a right hook into his leering mouth.

"Nice to see you gentlemen, sorry for the urgent call, but we have some news. Since you seem to have a huge interest in this case, we decided to let you in on the news first and let you spin it to the media." Ali made a sweeping motion with his arm, indicating the door to an interrogation room. *I'm gonna enjoy this, you arrogant piece of shit.* Abramowitz stayed silent, he looked apprehensive as if he wasn't sure he was going to be able to leave this place a free man. Ali wanted to grab him by the neck and squeeze until his head popped off. He closed the door to the interrogation room softly as James and Abramowitz sat down.

"Agent Stevens, would you like to tell our guests what we have?" Ali asked, trying not to sneer.

"Certainly," Jamie said sweetly, playing off of Ali's enjoyment. She placed a large bulging file folder on the table and opened it. "Where shall I begin?"

"I'm glad you two are enjoying this, I am a busy man and you took me away from some important business," James sniffed, Ali wondered what his important business' name was and if he was of legal age.

"Mister Abramowitz has been stealing from you Rodney," Jamie said spinning a stack of papers around on the desktop and pushing them towards James. "Here is the proof."

"That's absurd," James snapped.

"Read the papers." Jamie smiled at him.

Ali stood at the door, blocking it to prevent Abramowitz from bolting as he watched the color rise in the back of Abramowitz' neck. Ali saw him begin to tense and got ready to grab him if necessary. Rodney James read carefully and Jamie watched his eyes widen and the color drain from his face. Finally, he turned the pages slowly stopping at every page. The room was deathly silent. Ali could hear the muffled noises from the squad room outside the door behind him. Time dragged as James read. Finally, James turned his head slowly toward Abramowitz.

"Is this true Irving?" Abramowitz sat perfectly still and stared at the wall across the table from him. He did not reply.

"That's not all. Mister Abramowitz knew one of the victims, Mr. Bascomb, who by the way compiled that proof, and he has been identified by a witness as the one who dumped Martins and Carnes' car under the bridge. He also knew the suspect through his real estate dealings." Jamie sat back and folded her arms.

"You bastard, I trusted you," James began to cry.

"Mr. Abramowitz, you are under arrest for embezzlement, and accessory to murder. Stand up," Ali said stepping toward him and pulling his handcuffs from the back of his belt. Abramowitz stood slowly as if he was in a trance. Ali handcuffed him and led him from the room, reading him his rights as they went.

"What do I do now? How can I get the money back for the coalition?" James asked after they were gone.

"You can't, the money is gone."

Rodney James wiped his eyes and nodded. He rose shakily and followed Jamie into the squad room. Jamie patted his arm gently and guided him toward the elevators. Ali joined her and they watched the elevator doors close behind him.

"Should we have warned him?" Ali asked.

"Naw, paybacks are a bitch," Jamie replied.

Lieutenant Davis had been outside informing a throng of reporters and television cameras about Abramowitz' arrest while Ali and Jamie were in the interrogation room. James was about to be ambushed by those reporters on the police station steps. Ali almost wished he could sneak outside and watch.

The ride to the county jail scared the crap out of Irving Abramowitz. He sat in the back of the sheriffs van, hands cuffed in front of him. The van rocked and swayed. A very intoxicated prisoner laid on the floor at Irving's feet, having defecated and vomited on himself, the smell and the closeness of the enclosed van made Irving lightheaded and nauseous. The ride seemed to take forever as the van made numerous stops to pick up more prisoners. At each stop a quick breath of fresh air swept through the van each time the door opened but each stop also added more bodies to the overflowing van, adding the smell of dirty feet and unwashed bodies to the stench and heat. Finally the van drove into the secured gate and the deputy opened the doors, ordering the occupants to form a single file line outside. Irving stood third in line and a large black crack dealer stood a little too close behind him, whispering in his ear something about sleeping well tonight. Irving feared his bladder would let go any second and everyone would know how terrified he was.

The booking area was not much better. The gray walls had unidentifiable stains on them and Irving saw one that he could only guess was dried blood. The noise was deafening. In one of the holding cells that lined the perimeter, a prisoner screamed a blood curdling scream non-stop and Irving felt a chill run up his spine. The smell in the booking area was not much better than the back of the hot stuffy van, except that now disinfectant and urine were mixed with the other stink. The acoustics were horrible and Irving had to strain to understand the orders of the deputy as he was fingerprinted and photographed. He was stripped naked and his suit was placed in a large clear plastic bag along with his shoes. He was allowed to keep his underwear over which he slipped the orange jail jumpsuit and rubber sandals were placed on the floor for him to slip his feet into. Irving hoped to have a heart attack and go the infirmary to escape this mayhem but no such luck.

Irving shuffled in line behind a small Mexican, who spoke no english, into a large cell which housed the prisoners before they went to court for a bond hearing. The cell was massive and two story. In the center were metal tables welded to the floors. The back of the cell had stairways leading to two man cells along the upper tier. Not that there was any room in those cells. The main floor held over seventy five prisoners, some slept on the floor along the walls while others lay on the metal tables. Other prisoners stood alone or in groups talking, one sat in the corner by himself with his knees pulled up to his chest, his arms wrapped around his knees, rocking and talking to himself. Irving shuffled to an empty space along the wall and sat down, his back against the wall for protection. He wondered how long he would have to endure this nightmare before he saw a judge and posted bond. He wasn't sure he would live through it.

CHAPTER 28

"**Y**ou two look like shit," Davis observed, glancing from Ali to Jamie as they lounged in chairs in his office, "Parker is walking the paperwork through the state attorney's office, I want you two to go get some sleep."

"What about Abramowitz?" Jamie asked, yawning uncontrollably.

"We'll let our friend Irving spend some time in county lockup, maybe he'll be interested in talking to us after that."

" Can't stop now, I don't want Abramowitz walking out of jail before we get a chance to talk to him," Ali answered, rubbing his eyes, which at this point felt like they were filled with hot coals.

"He won't be going anywhere for awhile, I called in a favor, he won't get to magistrate until the afternoon session. We're gonna stall the arraignment. I'm not asking Ali, I'm telling you to go crash for a while. I want you sharp when you talk to him. He's no fool and you're about to drop. We've got an alert out on Vance and he could be anywhere right now. I'll call you if anything breaks now get the hell out of here. Go."

Ali opened his eyes and looked around the unfamiliar room, confused. *Where the hell am I?* His right arm was numb. Jamie snored softly next to him, her head on his shoulder. He eased his arm from under her and sat up on the edge of the bed, realizing he was in her apartment.

The apartment was sparse in décor. There were none of the feminine touches he expected of her, but then this really wasn't her apartment, it was temporary housing provided by the FBI. A few blouses, skirts and slacks hung in the closet. Two empty suitcases were piled in the corner. He barely remembered the ride to her apartment and the debate as to where they should go. He decided they couldn't go to his place, it was too soon and there was too much of Maria still there, it just would not have been right. Jamie had agreed and they decided to come here. *Where is this going?* Ali wondered. *Is this a really big mistake? She's going to go back to Washington DC and I'll be alone again. I don't know if I can stand that.* He realized he did not want her to go, did not want to be without her. *Shit, I guess I'm in love with her but can I do this again?*

He padded quietly to the kitchen, closing the bedroom door behind him, trying not to wake Jamie. He poured himself a glass of orange juice from the refrigerator and sat down on the sofa, turning on the television, the volume barely audible. His head hurt and his stomach was sour. His hands were shaking again and saliva filled his throat, causing him to swallow hard to keep from running to the bathroom to vomit. He was covered with a thin film of sweat, his mouth tasted like old dirty socks.

You are a fool Ali, what would Jamie want with you? You are nothing but a pathetic, old broken down drunk. How the fuck did you let this happen? I didn't let it happen, it just did. She needed you for a while but now she's going back to DC and you're gonna drink yourself to death and that will be that. You pretty much deserve nothing less. Look at you, you used to be somebody, the toughest fighter in the ring but you've lost this round. I have not lost goddammit, I'm gonna get better, I gotta get back into the game. Prove it. Let's see if you are tough enough to beat this, tough guy.

Ali realized Irving Abramowitz' picture was on the screen behind the news anchor's head. He leaned forward and listened to the story of Abramowitz' arrest, the picture switched to video of Abramowitz shuffling into the county jail in handcuffs, mingled among the other prisoners. The sight made Ali smile. The picture switched again, this time to video of a harried Rodney James scurrying down the police station steps trying to avoid the cameras and the reporter's questions. *Take that asshole,* Ali thought.

The bedroom door opened and Jamie staggered out yawning sleepily.

"What time is it?" She asked, bending down to kiss him. He turned his head slightly so she wouldn't smell his horrible breath. When she stood up, her breasts swayed under her t-shirt, causing him to catch his breath.

"One pm. We slept for six hours. How do you feel?" He answered, glancing at his watch.

"Like I could sleep for twenty more," She replied, sitting down next to him, resting her head against his chest. "Rodney doesn't look happy." She was looking at the television.

"Yeah, I almost feel sorry for him."

"Yeah right," she answered, sarcastically. Ali slipped his arm around her shoulders, kissing her on the forehead.

"Let's go to talk to Irving."

CHAPTER 29

Sander Vance admired himself in the mirror. His recently shaven head was white, like the belly of a catfish, but the mustache was filling in nicely. His newly pierced ear was still sore but was getting better. No one would recognize him now. Soon he would be able to head for Aruba with impunity. His new fake ID was perfect. He had been lucky to find that Cuban guy in Miami. He recalled driving down the seedy streets of the poor section of Little Havana, terrified that he would be spotted before he could put the full plan into action. But he hadn't been spotted. Aruba sounded like a perfect place to hide. Sun, sand, those fruity drinks with the little color umbrellas, a tropical paradise and no extradition treaty with the United States. He just had to wait a little longer until the cops got bored and he would be home free.

Sander sat at the sidewalk café and ordered a big breakfast, realizing he was ravenous. He had been cooped up too long and was enjoying the hot sun on his back. He sipped his coffee and admired the bikini-clad brunette who strolled by. He wondered if he could hook up down here. Yes, he could find a man here easily but he was ready for a woman to please him, it had been too long. He decided he could stay here and it would be like Aruba but if the cops found him, he would be screwed.

He watched the tourists strolling by on the busy street. Families with kids, overweight pasty white parents holding their kids hands as if they were afraid some scum would lunge out of the bushes and snatch them away, devouring them in some sewer under the street. He noticed a couple coming toward him. The husband wore a tank top, a skimpy black racing suit, black socks and sandals The tops of his arms were colorless and white but tan from the elbows down. His wife was dressed in a multi-color one-piece bathing suit that struggled to stretch over the rolls of fat. Her thick legs were cris-crossed with blue veins. On her head she wore a large straw hat and a large canvas bag, the size of a briefcase, hung from her shoulder. Sander caught a whiff of coconut oil when they passed. He wished he had brought his gun with him; these two should be shot for crimes against fashion and good taste. A police car cruised slowly down the street and Vance tensed but the cop looked right at him and continued on. Vance smiled to himself. Idiots! Cops were such fools, here he was right out in the open and they didn't notice him except for that bastard Castillo. Sander wished he could get him in his sights, that fucker had ruined everything. He fantasized again about putting the barrel of his gun against Castillo's head and watching his brains explode out the back of his head. He recalled the night he was stopped by the trooper in Virginia.

The cop had written him a ticket, never knowing there was a dead man in the trunk. Vance had laughed to himself the whole time, wanting to scream at the cop that he was a moron and that there was a body in the trunk. But he resisted the urge, signed the ticket and went on his way.

Vance strolled down the sidewalk past an open air bar, Jimmy Buffett music wafted out of the bar onto the street, a couple of middle-aged dancers swayed to the music. The familiar smell of stale beer and cigarette smoke floated past him. Vance headed back to his hiding place, suddenly feeling exposed and vulnerable. He knew that Martins had identified him. He should have killed that sniveling bastard when he killed his lover. That was a screw up. It brought him out in the open for Castillo to notice and what about Abramowitz? Vance saw him on the news last night, walking into the jail. He should have killed him too. *That shithead won't last a day in jail without spilling his guts. I need to head for Aruba soon, maybe tomorrow.* He doubted the cops would find him before he was able to sneak away but Castillo had come too close.

CHAPTER 30

Irving Abramowitz shuffled into the interview room, the shackles around his ankles threatening to trip him at every step. His hands were handcuffed in front of him, giving him some ray of hope that if he fell, he would be able to catch himself before he crashed face first to the floor, breaking his nose and knocking out all of his teeth. The Kool-Aid and bologna sandwich he had been served for lunch churned in his stomach. If he got out of this mess, he was going to file a class action lawsuit against the Sheriff on behalf of all the inmates that had to eat that crap.

I will get out of this, I'm a great lawyer and they have no case. I'll convince Rodney to drop the charges and I'll be free. I can tear their witness to shreds in court and their accessory case will go up in a puff of smoke. Just watch me.

It had been a long night. The other inmates apparently didn't need to sleep and the guards really gave them no chance. Every fifteen minutes some deputy holding a clipboard had entered the cell and bellowed the name of a prisoner who was next to be booked or be moved to another part of the jail. Irving had lined up with the rest of the inmates for arraignment but was told by the guard that he was not on the list. Abramowitz had argued in his best lawyer voice that there was a mistake but the guard just shrugged and told him to sit down and shut up. Abramowitz told the guard in no uncertain terms that he would be added to the lawsuit. Now he was exhausted and had to face Castillo and Stevens. *Fuck them they're not gonna beat me.*

"Good afternoon, Irving," Ali smiled at him as he sat down in the hard metal chair. Abramowitz didn't reply.

"Well I guess your stay here wasn't too unpleasant, still an arrogant prick I see," Ali said, still no reaction. "Irving, we can help you with this. We really want Sander Vance or James Brand if you prefer. You helped him dispose of the car and I suspect at least one of the bodies. We also think you hired him to kill Bascomb, or did you do that one yourself?"

Abramowitz stared at the ceiling behind Ali's head, silent.

"I guess you think Rodney James is gonna feel sorry for you and not press charges. Well, he signed affidavits this morning to prosecute you and I'm quoting him, to the fullest extent of the law." Ali waited for a reply. He decided to not tell him that Martins had identified his voice; that would be a surprise for later. Ali rose and tapped on the door for the guard to take Irving back to his cell.

"Suit yourself."

CHAPTER 31

Sander Vance pushed past the crowd in Sloppy Joe's bar, pausing to admire pictures of Ernest Hemmingway on the walls. He had read some Hemmingway and admired his writing and his life. He particularly liked The Old Man And The Sea, the way the old man had overcome adversity and discovered the true meaning of his life. Vance felt the same way about his own actions. How he had discovered the true meaning of his own life and his calling. He had considered taking the tour of Hemmingway's house but he hated cats. He always felt as if they knew his secrets and were watching him like little, evil elves that could read his thoughts and would expose him given the chance. They were too sneaky for his liking.

Vance stood in the open doorway and watched a couple pass the front of the bar. The woman had long blond hair in a ponytail that reached middle of her back. She was wearing tight white shorts and sandals. The man with her was muscular in a lean kind of way and had dark, wavy hair. He wore surfer trunks and a tank top. The woman turned toward Vance and he noticed the Adam's apple and the bulge in the front of the tight shorts. He was immediately angry, wishing he had his pistol. It would have given him great pleasure in killing those two.

Vance slid onto a wooden stool at the polished bar and ordered a beer. The bottle was cold and perspiring when the bartender plopped it down on the bar in front of him. He placed the bottle to his lips and drank deeply, letting the cold liquid slide down his throat.

Vance scanned the crowd in the bar. His eyes fell on a young woman in the corner, sitting alone. She was sunburned and appeared out of her element. Perfect. A tourist, vulnerable and hopefully willing to embark on a fling, then go back to Minnesota or Wisconsin or whatever cow town she came from. She wore a skimpy bathing suit top that revealed her large, corn-fed breasts and a flowered sarong skirt, the kind that were for sale in every tourist shop in South Florida.

Vance approached her table and gave her his best friendly smile, which never failed to dazzle whoever he bestowed it upon. He wished he still had his hair; he was so much better looking with hair. He hoped the sunburned top of his freshly shaven head would give her the impression that he also was a tourist looking for a good time with no strings attached.

"May I join you?" Vance asked, sitting beside her without waiting for an answer.

"Sure, please do," The young woman replied, smiling back at him.

"You look a little lonesome. I take it you're not from around here?" Vance leaned toward her, his southern accent becoming smooth and gentle.

"Nope, does it show?"

"Only if you know what to look for," Vance leaned back, taking a sip from his beer.

"And are you from around here?" She asked.

"South Carolina. I'm just here on my boat taking in the sights and I must say, the sights got a lot better when I saw you," Vance raised one eyebrow.

"Well thank you. I'm Jackie," she smiled widely, a little flushed, and held out her hand.

"Richard," Vance answered, shaking her hand. Vance signaled to the waitress for more drinks. "Is this your first time in Florida?"

"Yes, I have wanted to come here for years so I finally saved enough money to make the trek," She glanced around as if afraid someone would hear her.

"Well, welcome to the south, I hope your stay is very satisfying," he leered at her, hoping she caught the double meaning. She did. She returned the little leer.

"It's gotten better in the last few minutes."

"So where are you from, and what do you do there?" he asked.

"Muncie Indiana, I am an administrator at an elementary school. I used to teach but now I find the administration side more gratifying."

"That's an admirable profession, I think teachers are underappreciated and underpaid," he smiled a large smile, hoping she caught his meaning that he would like to appreciate her until she was exhausted and spent. He remembered his first grade teacher.

She was a grandmotherly woman who wore her snow-white hair gathered by a hair comb on top of her head. She always had handkerchief tucked under her watchband. She also had a ruler in the other hand, and was not afraid to utilize it swiftly on the back of the head of any child who dared to disrupt her class.

"So you have a boat here?" Jackie asked.

"Docked right down the street, would you like a tour?" Vance waved his hand toward the docks.

"Sure, I love boats," she answered, already rising from her chair catching him by surprise. She staggered sideways and Vance caught her arm to steady her. This was going to be easier than he thought. He led her to docks and helped her cross the gangway without falling off into the green water below. Once inside the salon, she dropped onto a leather couch and sighed.

"This is a very nice boat."

"Thank you very much, would you like a drink," he asked, looking down at her.

"Any more booze and I will be asleep, besides, I want something else," she grinned drunkenly, reaching up and unzipping his pants.

Vance lay on his side, curled into a fetal position and listened to Jackie snoring deeply next to him. The sickening smell of alcohol emanated from her. She disgusted him. He couldn't understand himself, why did he do this every time? During sex he was ravenous and energetic, but never felt anything. Afterwards, he was disgusted with his partner and himself. He fought the urge to pick her up, carry her outside and toss her over the side. Well, at least he wouldn't have to see her again, once he got her ass out of here, that is. She stirred beside him and moaned. Vance figured her head must be pounding like a kettle drum. She pushed herself upright and turned to look down at him. She sighed and laid on him trying to give him a kiss. He tried not to let her but she forced his mouth open and stuck her tongue in his mouth. He wanted to shove her off, fighting not to vomit.

"Good morning to you too," he smiled at her.

"Mmmmm," She cooed and rested her head on his chest. He rose up, causing her to roll off of him. She groaned.

"I'm hungry, you want some dinner?" Vance asked, rising from the bed and trying to put some distance between them.

"I can't I'm meeting some friends at the hotel for dinner. Shit, what time is it?" she sat bolt upright, frantically searching for her watch then realizing it was on her wrist.

Relief swept over him. She was not gonna be one of those clingy bitches that wanted to move in and play house after one quick roll in the sack. His need was satisfied and he wouldn't have to throw her out, reliving the fun of the crying, screaming woman who called him a bastard and a user and stormed out only to go crying to her girlfriends about what a big mistake she had made.

"I don't usually do this kind of thing," she said as she gathered her clothes from around the room. Her breasts swayed as she tried to wiggle her bikini top back on.

"What kind of thing? Getting drunk in the middle of the day, or having sex with perfect strangers?" he asked.

"Both. I must have been rebelling against my catholic upbringing."

Great, she was catholic. Vance imagined her confessing to her priest when she got back to farm town, having to say a hundred Hail Mary's.

"Do you have any regrets?" he laughed.

"Not yet. But I'm sure it is only a matter of time," she answered, bending down to kiss him again. "Thanks for making my vacation complete, you were magnificent."

"You're welcome, see ya'" he called to her departing back.

As soon as she was gone he walked around the room and collected his clothes, folding them neatly and placing them on the dresser, making sure that all of the edges were lined up and everything in the room was in its place. He hated disorder and chaos. He knew he had survived this long without being noticed by the cops by being careful.

Vance dressed in shorts and a T-shirt. Suddenly anger welled up in him. The bitch had used him. She only wanted sex with him to fulfill her fantasy. His heart pounded in his chest. Women thought they were the only ones used by men for sex? Well, what just happened then? As usual the satisfaction was gone and anger and self-loathing remained. Everybody always used him. The scoutmaster, his mother, she used him to get a husband to support her, the men he had sex with, they used him for their own gratification, they didn't care about his pleasure.

"Son of a bitch!" he screamed, throwing a beer bottle against the teak wall causing it to explode into bits that showered the room and Vance with glass and beer. He wanted to chase after her and blow her brains out. He fought to control himself. Calm down, he thought, slow down the breathing, and let it pass his inner voice told him. Besides, just think how proud she'll be when she finds out whom she just slept with. When her friends who she is bragging to right now, find out she slept with a killer who had sex with men, she'll really be the laughing stock. She will spend the rest of her life worrying if AIDS would be the gift that keeps on giving and if she had gotten it from him. Enjoy it now bitch, he laughed to himself.

Vance was calm now; he was always able to calm himself down. He made a sandwich, grabbed the newspaper and went out onto the aft deck, and settling into a canvas chair, munching on his sandwich as he read the paper. He sensed someone approaching the boat and looked up to see a young man standing on the pier opposite the aft deck.

"Can I help you?" Vance called to the man.

"Oh....sorry, I was looking for my friend but I guess I have the wrong boat," the young man stuttered. He looked shocked to see him and Vance was immediately suspicious. Was he really at the wrong boat or had he recognized him? Before he could ask further the young man turned and headed back down the pier. I need to get loaded up and get the hell out of here soon, Vance thought to himself. He really didn't want to leave yet, he liked it here but a sense of urgency took over and he knew he was taking a big chance by staying around. He tossed the newspaper into the chair next to him and gulped his beer.

CHAPTER 32

"What is going to happen to us?" Ali asked, sitting on the couch in Jamie's temporary apartment as she gathered her belongings and folded them. She had two suitcases on the floor, the tops flipped open. She was packing to leave.

"I don't know. I have to go back to DC. My job is there. I am working on a few things but I don't want to say anything so you don't get your hopes up, I just need some time," Jamie replied, stopping what she was doing and kneeling next to him.

"I don't want to leave you either, Ali, you have to know that."

"I do. I just don't know how it's going to be, losing someone again."

He felt horrible, physically. He realized his hands were shaking and felt like his skin was crawling across his muscle and bone. Was it grief or was he starting to go into withdrawal. He needed a drink so bad he wanted to scream. He needed to get it soon. He could quit later but now he needed to stay on an even keel.

The meeting earlier at the office had been a big letdown. There was nothing left to do and Ali knew it but he didn't want to let go. Lt. Davis had asked if there was anywhere left to search, any leads to Vance's whereabouts. Ali had to admit there was nothing left. The warrants had been signed and an alert was out for Vance but this guy was such a ghost, he had stayed so uninvolved in day to day life, no friends, didn't hang out anywhere, there was no obvious place left to look. The search warrant at Abramowitz' house had been futile. They found personal papers and financial statements-which were turned over to the forensic accountant the FBI provided- they were trying to add federal bank fraud charges on Abramowitz-but nothing that mentioned Vance. Ali had wandered around the house, impressed with the place. The floors were marble in the rear sitting room which opened onto the back patio and the pool. A large, Greek looking statue of a naked woman stood at the back of the pool holding a gourd on her shoulder. Water jetted from the gourd into the pool. In the bottom of the pool, in color tile, was the figure of a large Marlin.

The bedrooms were huge, almost the size of Ali's entire apartment. The floors were covered in thick red carpet and a large poster bed was the centerpiece of each room. Paintings, which Ali figured were very expensive, covered the walls. There was a Van Gogh, Ali wasn't sure if it was an original or a copy on the wall of one room. The wall in the master bedroom was covered with a photograph, poster size, of Abramowitz standing on the deck of a fifty-foot Sunseeker boat. The background in the picture looked like one of the docks in the Bahamas. The boat was sleek and looked fast even for its size. When they were finished, Ali sealed the house with red evidence tape.

Ali rose from the couch. He needed to go home for a while and think. He pulled Jamie to him and hugged her tightly saying, "I need to go to my place for awhile, but I'll be back to help you finish up." He left before she could protest.

The sun blazed through the windshield as Ali drove, making his headache worse. The shakes were getting worse and Ali wasn't sure he would make it to his place, but he did somehow. He unlocked the door and stepped inside.

Ali moved quickly to the kitchen cupboard and snatched it open, removing one of the little airline bottles he had stashed there. He wrenched the top off and drank deeply, the gin burned his tongue and throat, making him gag but he drank anyway. He immediately felt a buzzing in his head, the room spun for an instant then warmth started in his stomach and spread through his body, making him sigh and sink into a dining room chair. He rose and got another bottle, this time he poured it into a glass and added ice and Sprite. He sipped it slowly trying not to think, trying not to accept the new loss of Jamie leaving. Was he that needy? Didn't he have the ability to live on his own? He decided he was pretty weak and sad if he couldn't deal with this. But then he had dealt with a lot since Maria left him. He had been raised in the church, his parents insisted on it, and they always told him there was a heaven. The bible said that one would be reunited with loved ones after death. Ali wanted to believe it, needed to believe it, it had been the only thing that had sustained him the last two years but he wasn't sure. Was there really anything after death or was it just darkness, without consciousness or awareness or thought? Would he really see her again in heaven or was it just a story the priest told you to try to ease the pain of losing a loved one? He had thought he sensed Maria's presence at times but he wondered if it was just his hope and he was creating the thoughts himself. Was she really watching over him like the priest said or was it just wishful thinking, he really wished there was a way to know for sure. Well, there was, but he was not ready to take that route. Weeks ago he was more than ready but then this case came along and Jamie came with it, giving him hope again, but now he wasn't sure there was any hope. That's the booze talking, he decided.

He finished his drink and lay down on the couch, still unable to sleep in the bed. He thought he had come a long way the last few weeks but now he guessed he had not come that far. The shakes had stopped, thank god, and the warmth in his stomach remained.

He tried to shut off his racing mind, the case raced through his thoughts, Sander Vance rose like a specter of unfinished business, Jamie leaving, Maria being gone, his drinking, all of it charged into his thoughts pushing each other out the way, vying to be in the forefront. Finally, he dozed.

CHAPTER 33

Sander Vance smiled at the checkout girl in the grocery store. She had looked overwhelmed when he approached with three shopping carts filled with groceries and other sundries.

"Going on a trip?" she asked.

"Yep, headed for the islands probably, but I might just go out into the deep blue ocean and float for a month," He answered.

"Man that would be cool, I've always dreamed of doing that," the girl smiled back with a wistful look in her eyes. Vance was tempted to invite her but decided against it. She looked all of sixteen years old and that would cause a massive manhunt when her parents discovered their baby girl had been whisked away by some monster that was probably going to ravage her, turn her into a drug zombie and then sell her to pirates or kill her. Vance had enough trouble trying to get away before they caught him. Sure the cops, especially Castillo, wanted his ass but no one was really worried about catching a gay killer, but the absconder of an innocent young girl, well the public would scour heaven and earth to find him then. There would be posters on telephone poles and volunteers, who wouldn't leave their homes to find their own mothers, would come out of the woodwork to get a chance to be the hero who saved this poor little virgin. Vance decided the virgin part was probably long gone. Instead he paid for his groceries and aimed the shopping carts toward the rental van in the parking lot.

Vance parked near the dock and loaded the groceries onto a dolly provided by the marina. An older couple, tourists probably, wandered past and greeted him pleasantly. He smiled back and gave them a cheerful 'good day'. It gave him comfort that they greeted him, it meant they didn't recognize him from his picture being splashed all over the morning television news. He pushed the dolly down the pier, smiling and nodding to the other boat owners who busied themselves polishing the metal works or expensive wood trimmings on their boats. He felt almost giddy and fought the urge to dance and shout 'you don't know me, I'm invisible but you will know me someday'.

He hefted the grocery bags over the railing and stacked them on the aft deck, wheeling the dolly back to its parking space at the end of the pier when he was done. Vance was lifting a bag of groceries from the deck when he heard the KLOP KLOP of horse's hooves behind him on the dock and he froze. He slowly turned his head, afraid to look. A large gray and white horse, pulling a fancy coach was slowly plodding past the row of boats, the coach loaded with tourists. Vance breathed a sigh of relief. He remembered the damn pony his step- father had led home when he was ten years old. The poor thing was rail thin, its ribs protruding from its sides. He had tried to love it but ended up hating the thing because it was snake mean. His step-father told him it was his responsibility to feed it and muck out the stall but smell of horse shit made him gag and he was terrified every time he took food to its little stall. The pony would back into the corner of the stall, glaring at him with its beady little eyes; ears back against its head and showing its evil yellow teeth to him as he stood trembling in the opposite corner, struggling to hold the feed bucket in his scrawny arms. He did not dare to turn his back on it because it took great pleasure in biting him if he got a chance. The little beast finally started to fill out and fatten up. It even would let him ride it on occasion. The pony would stand still while he hefted the worn tattered old saddle onto its back and as soon as he hoisted himself onto its back, it would swing its head around and try to remove his kneecap with its teeth. He finally could not bear to go near it for fear he would lose a limb and after he did not feed it for two days, it was taken away and he never saw it again. He did remember his stepfather giving him a stinging slap on the side of his head when it was discovered that the pony was being neglected. His step-father had screamed at him that he was a 'useless piece of shit' who couldn't even care for a poor defenseless animal which Sander thought a little hypocritical since the only way the pony would stand still to be saddled was if his step-father had beaten it into submission first.

He busied himself putting the groceries away. He first placed them on the counter in rows, every row precisely straight and every can was placed in its proper group, fruit with fruit and vegetables with vegetables. When he placed them in the cupboard they were set so that every label was facing front and readable. He hated having to search through cans to find what he was looking for. This just made it easier. While he did this, he was thinking about Castillo. Was he coming for him? Had Martens survived to testify against him, the news had been mum about his condition, and what about Abramowitz? That coward would throw him to the wolves without a thought but the cops hadn't shown up yet and that meant Abramowitz hadn't talked yet. Maybe his self-preservation instinct was stronger than Vance thought. It was too bad Vance couldn't get to him, and kill him for not doing what he was supposed to, getting rid of the cars and making sure it was clean. His only job was to make sure there were no fingerprints or anything to link him to the victims and he could not even do that right. His stepfather had been right about one thing, never trust a lawyer to do anything right. When his real father was killed in that truck crash, the lawyer his mother found had taken almost half of the insurance money for himself. Of course, Sander was too young to know about that, he only discovered it later when he was old enough to inherit his mother's assets. He would have gotten that lawyer's ass but he could not find him, not that he did not try. He had searched every web site and every lawyer's directory but could not find the bastard. He probably wasn't even a real lawyer. Okay Sander, brighten up, he told himself, you will be gone tomorrow and they will never be able to touch you because you are too smart for them.

Vance finished stowing the groceries and checked the cupboard where he kept his gun and realized he did that a lot. For some reason he was afraid someone would steal it or that the cops had already been there and were waiting to grab him suddenly and violently. The thought instantly frightened him. He hefted the gun and searched the boat, the gun held in front of him, ready to fire at the first thing that looked out of place. The boat was empty. He breathed a sigh of relief and put the gun back in its hiding place. He needed to calm down. They won't find you, he told himself.

Vance opened the drawer where he kept his ammunition and removed a small wooden box. Inside were the empty shells he kept after every kill. They were arranged in a neat row, lying on a pad of cotton so they wouldn't roll. He lifted one from the cotton and held it to his nose and breathed deeply. He recalled the kill and smiled. He carefully returned it to its resting place and carefully returned the wooden box to the drawer.

He went into the salon and poured himself a scotch from a crystal goblet, settling onto the couch and turning on the television.

CHAPTER 34

Jamie put the rest of her slacks in her suitcase and stopped, plopped onto the bed and lay back onto the pillow. She wondered what she was doing. She could not stop wondering if she doing the right thing? Did Ali really want her to stay? He said he did but she had heard that once before. Damn, love was a confusing thing. She remembered the tears and the screaming from the last time.

She had come home early from a case and found her supposed fiancé in bed with another woman, some dancer he found in a bar. He had told her he loved her and wanted to spend the rest of his life with her and she was the only woman for him, blah, blah. Then he did this. She remembered how it felt when she walked into the room, as if she had been kicked in the chest, the air sucked out of her lungs in a whoosh. Her legs went weak and she feared she would fall on her face. Tears immediately rushed to her eyes and then rage exploded in her, she screamed at them, threw the first thing she could find, unfortunately it had been a pillow and not a large brick then she rushed out of the house and into her car, leaving a black patch in the driveway as she spun her tires backing into the street.

She had driven aimlessly, struggling to see through the tears that flooded her eyes and streamed down her face, not knowing where she was going or even aware she was driving. Common sense finally took over and she realized she was going to kill someone driving like this so she turned into the first parking lot she could find. She slammed the car to a stop and sobbed, pounding the steering wheel until her hands throbbed with pain. She was thankful that her gun was locked in the trunk or she might have killed them both.

She had cried and screamed until she was exhausted then sat, numb, staring out the windshield but not seeing anything. Then she went to a motel and got a room, ignoring the incessant ringing of her cell phone, the caller ID showing it was him calling. She never went back. Letting him have all of their possessions and the house, which was his anyway.

She came back to the present and Ali. She wanted to be with him, the feeling stronger than any she had ever known. The look in his eyes when he left told her he felt the same way, but the man had baggage. Could she handle all of that? She knew what she was facing. He had a drinking problem and she recognized its magnitude even if he didn't. He was going to have a terrible time quitting; she had seen it before in graduate school when she did a stint in the alcohol rehab facility. The physical pain, the terrible sweats and nightmares, she wondered if she was strong enough to handle it all and if she really loved him enough to face it with him. Jamie also wondered if Ali was willing to go through it. Life had beaten him up pretty bad. She decided it was worth a try and sat up. She dialed the long distance number and listened to it ring at the other end.

The ringing of the phone jolted Ali awake. He fumbled for it, finally found it and answered it with a sleepy mumble. The words floated through the fog and his eyes jerked open.

"What did you say?" he asked.

"I said we have a lead on Vance, meet me at the office, now!" Lt. Davis said brusquely.

"On my way, did you call Stevens?" he asked, jumping to his feet and then regretting it as the room swayed before his eyes.

"She's on her way in," Davis replied then the phone went dead.

David Abrams fidgeted in the interview room of the homicide office. He hoped he was doing the right thing. He was tired from the drive and wished he had eaten before coming here, his stomach growled with emptiness. The detective who had escorted him to this room had given him a diet soda but it did not help. He considered leaving, just tell them he was mistaken and walk out but the door opened and a large, somewhat groggy detective entered the room with an attractive woman, who had a very large automatic in a holster on her hip. Abrams immediately noticed the badges they wore were different shaped. He wondered who the woman was, the detective he recognized from the news.

"I'm detective Castillo, this is agent Stevens, FBI," the big detective said by way of introductions.

"David Abrams," He answered, reaching to shake their hands.

"Talk to me David," Ali said, sitting across the table from him, placing his arms on the table and leaning forward intently.

"My father is Irving Abramowitz," Abrams said, then noticed the confused look on the detective's face, "I changed my name and shortened it to distance myself from my father and his reputation. I'm gay and my father doesn't approve of me, we don't talk much."

"Your father is an activist for the gay community isn't he?" Stevens asked.

"My father is an activist for his own bank accounts, nothing more. He really doesn't care for gays but as he put it 'they have money, pay their bills and don't bitch much.' I came out to my parents when I was eighteen and he kicked me out of the house. See, that's what is so hypocritical about him, later he became the attorney for a gay activist organization, yet he kicks his own son out of the house for being gay. Nice, huh?"

"So why are you here, David?" Ali asked.

"I know where the guy you're looking for is. I saw him on the news," Abrams answered. "I saw on the news that my father was arrested and that you were looking for this guy Vance, so I got to thinking, there is no doubt that my father is involved more deeply in this than anyone realizes and my father is famous for protecting his own ass before anyone else's and he probably helped this guy disappear, so I checked out my hunch." Abrams finished.

"And?" Stevens asked.

"And I was right. See I live in Key West, there is a large gay community there and I fit in. My father keeps a boat there, not that I ever see him when he comes down to the Keys."

"What does the boat look like and where is it?" Ali asked, the excitement building in him.

"It's a fifty foot Sunseeker, white with blue trim, named *Legal Fees*, it is docked near the Turtle Kraals restaurant in a marina just east of there," Abrams answered.

"The boat he has a picture of in his house?" Ali asked.

"That's the one. He loves that damn boat." Abrams eyes welled up with tears, signifying that he believed his father loved that boat more than he loved his own son.

"How do you know Vance is there?"

"I saw him, spoke to him. I went to the dock and there he was big as life, sitting on the aft deck, sipping a drink as if he owned the damn thing. He's shaved his head and grew a mustache and got an earring but it's definitely him."

"Did he know who you were?"

"No, I gave him a story that I was looking for a friend's boat and had the wrong one. Sad isn't it, my father lets a serial killer on his boat and I've never set foot on it," Abrams glanced from Ali to Jamie with a sad look.

"Thank you David. Another detective will take a statement from you," Ali rose and rushed from the room. He waved to Davis outside the room and Davis beckoned a detective to take the statement. Ali headed for his desk saying to Jamie over his shoulder,

"I'll call Key West PD,"

"I'll call the local FBI office," Jamie said at the same time, grabbing the nearest phone.

Ali spoke to a Lieutenant in the Key West police department and told him the situation, making it very clear that they did not want Vance to know he was under surveillance. The Lieutenant assured him it would not be a problem. He hung up and looked at Jamie who was still on the phone. She held up an index finger indicating he should wait. She thanked the person on the other end and hung up.

"I got us a US Marshall Service jet to take us to Key West," She said to him, then noticing the apprehensive look on his face, remembered the flight to South Carolina and how he had almost ripped the armrest off the seat. "I know, but it's a long drive to Key West and it takes a lot less time by jet. I figured we were in a hurry,"

Ali nodded grimly. He walked to the door of Davis' office and stuck his head in.

"Key West PD has been alerted, they're going to put a surveillance team of Vance, and we're set on a jet to Key West, anything else."

"Go," Davis said, waving his hand in the air.

Ali drove fast to the airport, flashing light on top of the car and siren screaming. He dodged through afternoon traffic on I-95, swerving around cars and between semi-trucks. Traffic had cleared a little bit, the working crowd having made it home to their dinners already. He raced up the ramp to the US Marshall Service hangar where a small jet sat on the tarmac, engine already winding up. The jet sported the Logo of the Marshall Service down both sides. The smell of jet fuel and exhaust assailed Ali as he followed Jamie across the Tarmac to the jet. Heat shimmered and squirmed up from the asphalt around the jet and Ali's heart began to pound, but he wasn't sure if it was fear of flying or anticipation of confronting Vance. Ali glanced at his watch, six-fifteen; he prayed that Vance had not sailed yet. The jet began to roll as soon as the door was closed and locked. The pilot taxied into line behind a jumbo jet, which was fifth in line to take off. Ali tapped his foot nervously.

Suddenly, the jet's engine began to wind up to a high pitched scream and Ali was pushed back against the seat as it began to pick up speed, racing down the runway and leaping into the air. The jet seemed to be going straight up then banked hard to right. Ali glanced out the window and realized they were already at least two thousand feet up. He looked to the west and could see all the way to the west coast, or so it seemed. The sun was setting into the ocean to the west; a big, red ball surrounded by a multitude of colors, red, orange, violet and lavender and Ali was struck by the beauty of it. He looked down and could see the green ocean beneath them, dotted by tiny white boats. His cell phone vibrated in his pocket and he fumbled to dig it out. He glanced at the number and saw that it was the Key West police number.

"Castillo," Ali said into the phone.

"Castillo, Lt. Rodriguez, we have the boat under surveillance, it's still at the dock, I'll let you know if anything changes," the voice on the phone said.

"Okay we're airborne and should be there in a little while," Ali replied, breathing a sigh of relief. Vance was still in reach. Ali hung up the phone and turned to Jamie, seated next to him.

"The boat's still there."

"Good, we still got a shot at him," Jamie nodded.

It seemed like only minutes when the sound of the engine changed. It seemed to quiet and Ali got a little apprehensive as the nose of the jet started to drop and Ali wondered if they were crashing or landing. He glanced out the window and could see the dark coastline approaching and beyond the coast he could see the dark island and the lights of the houses and hotels.

Suddenly he felt the tires chirp onto the runway and the jet settled to the earth, taxiing quickly toward a hangar. The whine of the engine had just begun to wind down when the pilot exited the cockpit and walked down the aisle, unlocking the door and swinging it outward.

A uniformed Key West cop was waiting for them next to a dark blue unmarked car. He shook hands with them, informing them Lt. Rodriguez was waiting for them. The drive to the police station was a unique experience. The streets were narrow, with cars parked along both sides of the road in front of old houses of New England architecture. Most of them had walkways around the top floors, Widows Walks. Key West was originally inhabited as a fishing village; the walkways were called Widows Walks because the wives of the fishermen would stand on the walkways, scanning the ocean to see if their husbands were coming home.

The unmarked car raced through the streets nearly sideswiping the parked cars then coming to a screeching halt at the front doors of the police department. A large man with a dark complexion, dressed in blue jeans and black polo shirt was standing at the doorway. He opened the door as soon as the car stopped and Jamie and Ali climbed out. The large man held out his hand.

"Carlos Rodriquez, welcome to Key West."

Jamie and Ali shook his hand and followed him into the police station. He led them down a hallway and into a large conference room bustling with activity and filled with cops in various modes of dress. Some were in jeans and t-shirts and had long hair and beards or mustaches. Some were dressed in black SWAT gear. One man stood in the corner, wearing black BDU pants and a blue t-shirt with words FBI across the chest in large white letters. The front of the room displayed a large map of a marina. The FBI agent approached them, threading his way through the crowd.

"Andrew Carter," he said, holding out his hand.

"Jamie Stevens," Jamie said, then turned and indicated Ali, "Ali Castillo."

"All right, grab a seat, let's get started," Rodriquez announced from the front of the room, clapping his hands to get everyone's attention. There was a scramble in the room as everyone found a chair and settled into them. Rodriquez handed Jamie and Ali a packet of papers. The top sheet had a surveillance photo of a bald headed, mustachioed Sander Vance standing on the deck of a boat.

"When you called me I had my team go and shoot some pictures," Rodriquez explained to them. He straightened up and addressed the room.

"You all have your packets; the top picture is our target as he looks now. Everybody study and memorize the face, I don't want this guy to walk past one of you and you don't take him down." There was a loud chuckle from the crowd. They all knew it had happened before.

"This is the marina," Rodriquez said turning toward the map, "We have undercovers here, here and here," He touched the map in various places, "This one is dressed as a homeless guy complete with shopping cart filled with junk. This one is in a dinghy, acting like he is painting the hull of his boat; hopefully the target won't get suspicious about a guy painting his boat in the dark."

Another chuckle from the crowd. "There is a police boat at the mouth of the marina, far enough out not to be noticed. Now, Sgt. Jones will give the lowdown on SWAT."

A tall, very thin black man in SWAT gear walked to the map. He gave the SWAT team their assignments and positions. When he was finished, Rodriquez again took center stage.

"Detective Castillo and Agent Stevens have been primary on this case so I'll let them say a few words," Rodriquez stepped aside as Ali stepped forward.

"I want this guy alive if possible," Ali said to the group. "He is a serial killer and we assume he is still armed, with a forty-five revolver and possibly other weapons. This guy is very dangerous and isn't afraid to kill if he's cornered so be careful. After we have him contained, I'm gonna call him on his phone and try to talk him out but don't take any chances, I don't want any cops hurt." Ali finished and sat back down.

"Okay SWAT, do your thing and we'll be along directly," Rodriquez ended the briefing. There was a commotion in the room as the SWAT team gathered their gear and left.

After the crowd thinned out, Ali noticed a large heavy set man seated in the corner of the room. The first glance caused Ali to do a double take. He had long white hair and a beard that rested on his expansive chest. At first Ali thought he was imagining things, Ernest Hemmingway was supposed to be dead but here he was right in front of Ali's eyes. The man wore khaki shots and a t-shirt with the likeness of Hemmingway on the front. The man approached and held out his hand. Rodriquez chuckled at Ali's confusion.

"Castillo, this is Charles McGinnis. He is the dock master of the marina where Vance's boat is. He is also the winner of the last five Ernest Hemmingway look-a-like contest, that's a big thing here in Key West."

They shook hands as Ali examined McGinnis.

"I can see why he won. I've only seen pictures of Hemmingway but I thought he had come back from the dead."

"I hear that a lot," McGinnis smiled.

"McGinnis is going to be part of this operation. I asked him to contact the other boat owners at one-hour intervals and have them leave in their boats, in case there is any shooting. Bullets will go through fiberglass hulls like butter and we don't want any innocents hurt," Rodriquez said. Ali realized he would never have thought of that. "Having them leave at intervals will hopefully not look suspicious and tip our boy that something is going on."

"Sounds like you've done this before," Ali marveled.

"Once or twice. When you live on an island, boats are a big part of life." Rodriquez replied. "Unfortunately, not all of the boats have shoreline phones so we're gonna have to wait until Vance goes to sleep and SWAT will evacuate the stragglers then"

"Do we know if Vance is planning to leave soon?" Ali asked, turning to McGinnis.

"Not sure. He didn't file any float plan with me or the Coast Guard, but it's not mandatory. I did see him loading a shitload of groceries earlier, looks like he's either planning to leave or maybe just settling in for a long stay," McGinnis answered.

"One of our tactical problems is that the docks are so close together, the boats block each other and we can't get a clear line of fire on Vance's boat for the SWAT guys, so we had the boat next to him leave as soon as we verified he was there. The one on the other side is leaving shortly. We wanted to wait for full dark before SWAT moved into position," Rodriquez informed Ali and Jamie, then, as if right on cue, the portable radio Rodriquez held crackled to life.

"SWAT command to Rodriquez," the voice on the radio said.

"Rodriquez, go." Rodriquez answered; holding the radio up to is mouth.

"Teams are in position. The lights are on in the target; we can see shadows moving around inside but all of the shades are pulled so no clear visual."

"Okay. Hang tight and keep me updated," Rodriquez answered.

Special Agent Carter touched Jamie's arm and beckoned her to step aside with him.

"SAC Robinson has been bugging me for an update," Carter whispered into Jamie's ear. "He wants to be involved."

Jamie shook her head. She didn't know Carter and did not want to say something that would get back to Robinson.

"Your office has responsibility for the Keys area. He's from the Broward office. It's not his operation."

"Good, he's an asshole. Probably wants to be here and grab the limelight anyway. My SAC is on his way, he's a good guy and won't push his weight around." Carter answered, walking away. Jamie smiled at his back, glad to know where he and his boss stood.

Apparently, Robinson was well liked even down here in paradise. She rejoined Rodriquez and Ali.

"You guys must be starving. We can't do anything but wait. Let's go to the cafeteria and eat," Rodriquez said to the group and headed out of the room, not waiting for agreement. Ali wanted to get to the dock but Rodriquez was right, he was starving.

The group paraded down a long hallway and turned through a swinging door into a large cafeteria. There were long tables with chairs filling the room. At the end of a long table sat two uniformed officers, one male and one female. They leaned across the table toward each other talking quietly, intimately. Ali wondered if they were lovers.

The cafeteria had a cooking area, complete with a very dark Haitian woman in a white uniform, standing by a griddle. There were fryers for cooking French fries and pre-prepared salads rested on top of ice in metal trays. There were steam trays of cooked vegetables.

"Very nice," Ali said, admiring the cafeteria.

"Yep, everything's run on gas. They installed this place in case of hurricanes, so the cops can eat even if there is no power. Order what you like, it's on the house." Rodriquez answered, grabbing a salad from one of the metal trays.

CHAPTER 35

Special-Agent-In-Charge James Robinson drummed his manicured fingers on his desk. He was not in the habit of being in the office after 5 pm but it was the best way to have this meeting without too many people being aware of it. His shoulder was sore from his morning workout in the office gym. He disliked the workouts but had been faithful to it since appearances were everything. His uncle, the senator had taught him that. He always said that if one wants to move up the ladder you had to look better than the other guy in line for the position. So he watched his diet, exercised, got manicures and was very discriminating in the suits he wore. Of course, it was easy to be discriminating when you had enough money. He had inherited quite a large sum from his father and he made good use of it. His suits were more expensive than his competitors, who had to make due with the FBI salary. He knew there was some resentment from other agents in the office due to his impeccable appearance and obvious class. Some of the agents said he was not a real cop but a fashion plate. He could not understand that kind of small minded thinking, after all, he had grown up in the tough streets of New York. Okay, so it might have been Central Park west in a million dollar condo and not Brooklyn or the Bronx but it was still New York. It was not his fault that his father was the president of the second largest bank in the city. His father had never understood his desire to join the FBI.

He remembered the argument when he graduated from law school and announced he was applying to the bureau. His father had ranted on about how much had been spent on his education and now he was taking a lowly government job. He calmed down when Robinson assured him it was just a stepping stone to political office and he had no intention of making it a lifelong career and it would look good on a campaign resume.

The other thing his uncle, the senator, had taught him was that if one wanted to be noticed and therefore considered for better positions, one had to stay in the limelight and in the upper echelon's minds. That was the reason for this meeting. Stay out in front. He still resented being put in charge of a local FBI office and not in charge of the regional office in Miami, after all he had picked his cases carefully and kissed the right asses to rise quickly to the position he deserved. He believed he should have at least been an assistant director by now. Unfortunately, his uncle had let him down and died before he could he could use his influence to make that happen. But his time would come and he would be damned if he would let some local homicide detective and a lowly profile agent from the DC Beltway upstage him. A knock on his office door interrupted his musings.

"Come," Robinson bellowed. The door opened and Agent Cruz, Robinson's right hand man stepped into the office followed by the mayor, Michael Coletti.

"Ah Mr. Mayor please have a seat," Robinson said, indicating a chair with his index finger. The mayor sat, looking apprehensive and obviously wondering why he had been summoned.

"Relax sir, would you like some coffee or a soda?" Robinson said, his voice oozing with friendliness. The mayor shook his head. "I'm sure you are wondering what this is all about, so I'll get to the point. This case detective Castillo is working is a media bonanza. I know you called Washington and requested a profiler and that was a wise move on your part. I want you to get credit for your decision."

The mayor began to relax and settled back into his chair. He was always willing to listen to something that would benefit him.

"Good," Robinson said soothingly. "Here is what I'm thinking. My office has been kept in the background up until now, but I intend to change that. I have obtained federal warrants for attorney Abramowitz and also for this killer, what's his name, Vance. Now, you and I are going to do a news conference announcing these warrants. You get to take credit for calling us in, and that won't hurt your image any or your bid for the senate seat next year, which I know you are planning."

Coletti was surprised Robinson knew about that and wondered what else the FBI knew about him. He hoped they hadn't dug too deeply.

"I do my homework, Michael," Robinson gave him a knowing look. Coletti took it as a warning and as confirmation that the FBI had dug real deep and that frightened him. Robinson's uncle always told him to make sure you know everything about people you needed, one never knew when that knowledge would come in handy.

"Look Michael. You and I both are bureaucrats, as they say, and as such we have ambitions and that is a good thing. This is a win-win for both of us. My office gets some much needed credit and you get to look good to your constituents, which also can't hurt."

"I like the idea. Let's do it," Coletti smiled broadly.

"Good," Robinson said, reaching for his desk phone and buzzing Cruz. When he answered Robinson told him to inform the press they would be ready shortly. Robinson noticed the confused look on Coletti's face.

"I took the liberty of having the press here in the media room. I knew you would see the benefit for both of us."

Coletti was not happy. He knew he did not have time to spruce up to stand in front of the cameras having come straight from city hall after sitting in meetings all day. His shirt was wrinkled from sitting in his leather chair all those hours and his hair was no longer perfectly coiffed. He was going to look like the homely sister next to Robinson. He suspected Robinson had done it intentionally. He was right. Cruz entered the office.

"Would you escort the mayor down to the press conference, I will be there shortly," Robinson told Cruz, who nodded.

Coletti obediently followed him out.

Robinson spent fifteen minutes brushing his suit and making sure his hair was perfect. He selected a new file folder, with the seal of the FBI emblazoned on it, from his desk and placed the warrants in it. He checked himself in the full-length mirror in the corner and decided he was magnificent. When felt he had let them wait long enough, that his entrance would have the desired dramatic effect, he left the office and headed for the press room.

The press room was abuzz when he entered from the door behind the podium. Coletti was seated in a straight-backed chair on the dais. Robinson walked to the podium, slowly, the ultimate politician about to make a major announcement.

"Good evening, ladies and gentlemen. I have an announcement to make," Robinson said to the television lights then paused to let anticipation build. "The FBI has obtained warrants for Irving Abramowitz, who, as you know, is the attorney for the Coalition against Discrimination, and Sander Vance. Mr. Vance has been identified as the person responsible for the homicides of gay men in numerous states and here in south Florida. The warrants for Mr. Abramowitz are for international bank fraud and also civil rights violations as the victims were targeted for their sexual orientation, which constitutes a hate crime. Mr. Vance is charged with civil rights violations and federal murder charges with the federal hate crime enhancement."

"Mr. Robinson," every reporter in the room hollered his name and waved their hands, trying to be the first one recognized to ask their question.

"Yes," Robinson said, pointing to a pretty, young, female reporter in the second row. Robinson had seen her at other press conferences and lusted after her in his heart. He thought she wanted him also and he was just waiting for the right moment to get close to her. She thought he was a pompous scumbag.

"Isn't this case being investigated by the local police department?" the reporter asked.

"Yes, but the FBI was involved from the very beginning. Mayor Coletti was very wise in calling in the vast resources of the bureau at the beginning, proving he is very concerned for the safety of the citizens of this city. That is all the questions I can take right now, I have a lot of work to do on this case, but mayor Coletti has a few words to say. Mister Mayor." Robinson turned to Coletti who stood and approached the dais. As he passed, Robinson leaned toward him and whispered, "Short and sweet and don't fuck this up."

"The city and I would like to thank the local FBI office for their untiring assistance in this case. If not for Mr. Robinson and the agents of his office, I believe this vicious criminal might have never been identified. Thank you," The mayor turned from the bank of microphones before any more questions could be posed. He followed Robinson from the room and down the hallway. Robinson turned and held out his hand to Coletti.

"Well done, mister mayor. I think you are destined for great things and I will do anything I can to assist you." He turned and hurried off, leaving Coletti standing with Cruz, who directed him toward an exit.

The police chief was sitting on the couch in his living room watching the news with his wife, who was nursing her second martini of the evening. He suddenly sat upright when the image of Robinson and the mayor came on the screen. When the press conference finished on the television, the chief's immediate response was to yell, "BASTARDS!" scaring the crap out of her beloved Shiz Tzu which went from lying on its side, sleeping peacefully on the floor, to leaping straight up into the air, turning a complete somersault and disappearing into the kitchen without touching solid ground. A second later it stood trembling, eyes bugged out, peeking around the corner of the doorjamb, as the chief's wife glared at her husband, mopping the spilled martini off the front of her blouse.

CHAPTER  36

Lt. Davis passed through Marathon at seventy miles per hour. He saw the Monroe Sheriffs car too late and took his foot off the gas but the police car was already growing closer in his rearview mirror, lights flashing. Davis pulled to the roadside and placed his hands on the steering wheel as the young cop strolled to the window. Davis told him who he was and after telling the deputy he had a pistol in the car, he was allowed to show his ID and explain the situation. The young cop looked skeptical at first then accepted his explanation and waved him on. He kicked it back to seventy, knowing he had at least another hour drive even at this speed. Luckily traffic was light. He knew he should have jumped on the jet with Jamie and Ali. He had not even intended to go to the scene, he had total faith in Castillo to handle it with the local cops but the angry call from the chief had changed all of that. Davis had watched Robinson's news conference on the television in his office and just laughed at it. He figured anybody with any sense could see Robinson was just strutting. But the chief did not see it that way and ordered him to go. His back ached and his butt was numb, he had already put in a full day and then some and this drive was a long tedious exercise in futility. He knew he would never rise above the rank of lieutenant because he was not a politician and did not want to be. Captains and above had to be game players and he was not interested in any of that. He was content to be where he was.

Davis sipped cold coffee from the Styrofoam cup on his console and tried to concentrate on the road. He hoped Vance would be in custody by the time he got there and he could grab a hotel room, sleep a few hours and drive home with Castillo and Stevens.

Agent Carter was startled when his cell phone vibrated in his shirt pocket. He pulled it out, rose from the table, and walked out into the hallway before he answered it. He listened to the voice on the other end and nodded.

"Yessir, I understand I will be ready," Carter said to the voice on the other end and hung up. He walked back to the table and sat next to Jamie again. He leaned over to her and said quietly, "I need to talk to you."

"What is it?" Jamie asked.

"In private," Carter answered, jerking his head in the direction of the hallway, indicating she should follow him.

"Carter, quit being a company man and just say it. There are no secrets here," Jamie frowned at him.

The conversation at the table stopped as all heads turned toward Carter. He sighed.

"SAC Robinson just gave a news conference taking credit for this case and claiming his office was in charge all along. My boss figures he's going to be on his way down here as soon as he finds out Vance has been located. Castillo, your mayor was there also." Ali shook his head in disgust.

"Your lieutenant is apparently already enroute," Carter continued, "My boss intends to beat Robinson here. He wants Robinson kept out of the scene and since this area is the responsibility of my office, I'm in charge of keeping Robinson at bay until my boss gets here. Lt. Rodriquez, I may need your assistance in that regard."

"No sweat Carter. We've been keeping the bureaucrats out of our asses for years. Haven't you heard about the Conch Republic?"

Rodriquez chuckled, causing Carter to sag with relief. "This is an island. We can keep him in Islamorada for a week if you want."

That brought a chuckle from the table.

"SWAT One to Rodriquez," Rodriquez' radio crackled, interrupting the discussion.

"Go ahead." He answered.

"All positions are up and green. Lookout One reports movement on the boat. We can't see the target, all the blinds are down on the windows, but Lookout One can see someone's shadow moving inside. The neighbors left ten minutes ago so we have a clean shot at both sides of the boat if we need to take it. We're ready for you."

"Okay SWAT One, we're moving now," Rodriquez answered. He placed the radio on the table and looked around at the group, "Time to rock."

The group piled into unmarked cars and headed for the docks. Ali opened his window and could smell stale beer as they passed the bars on Duval Street. There was a light crowd wandering the sidewalks, stopping to gaze into the windows of the t-shirt and tourist shops. A few were standing in the open, brightly lit doorways. He hoped that Vance was unaware of the presence of the SWAT team. Ali wanted to have the upper hand in the beginning when he called him.

Rodriquez parked the car in a dimly lit parking lot within walking distance of the marina. Ali could smell salt water, rotting fish and boat fuel which told him they were close to the docks. They threaded their way through the parked cars to a large motor home parked behind a vacant building. The motor home had a large gold Sheriffs star on the side with the words Mobile Command Post. Two SWAT officers stood outside the side door with Sgt. Jones. Jones turned as they approached.

"Everything is quiet so far." Jones informed them. Rodriquez nodded and turned to Ali and Jamie.

"The Sheriffs office lets us use their command post for operations like this when we want high tech toys and want be close to the action. Welcome to the brain center." He opened the door and waved them in.

The inside of the motor home was lined on both walls with electronic listening equipment. At the far end was a white plastic drawing board with erasable markers lined along the bottom. There were padded swivel chairs lining both sides in front of the electronic equipment. It looked just like the one Ali's department had and made Ali wish he owned the company that made them for the police departments. He figured they must cost a pretty penny. Rodriquez motioned toward a telephone receiver mounted on one wall.

"There's the phone. Make the call whenever you are ready," he told Ali.

Ali sat in one of the swivel chairs and glanced at the sheriff's deputy who was seated next to him. The deputy was wearing headphones and adjusting the recording equipment in front of him on the wall. He gave Ali a thumbs up. Ali looked at the readout of his cell phone where he had stored Vance's number and dialed. His heart was thumping and he was nervous. He hoped Vance had his cell phone with him. He wondered why he didn't think of that sooner. Maybe Vance threw that phone away. If he did not answer they were screwed. Plan B was to use a loudspeaker and that was a hassle and not very reliable. The phone was ringing on the other end.

The phone rang ten times with no answer. Shit! Ali thought and hung up. Now what? He looked at the deputy and raised his eyebrows.

"What?" Rodriquez asked, standing over Ali's shoulder.

"No answer. I'm not even sure he still has that phone." Ali answered.

"Try it again. This number comes up on caller ID as the sheriff's office. Either he doesn't have the phone or he didn't dare answer it or maybe he is trying to figure out why the sheriff's office is calling," the deputy offered.

"Post one to Rodriquez," the portable radio in Rodriquez' hand squawked.

"Go," Rodriquez answered.

"Don't know what you guys just did but somebody peeked out through the curtains."

"That means he's there. I betcha he looked out the window to see if the cops were outside when he saw the number, try again," Rodriquez said to Ali. Ali dialed the number again.

"Hello?" Vance's voice answered the phone on the third ring.

"Hello Sander," Ali said, relief flooding him.

"Well, well, detective Castillo, so you found me. Good work," Vance's voice dripped with sarcasm.

"Yes Sander I did. I want you to know that you are surrounded by SWAT cops with big guns and nobody wants anyone hurt, so just come out with your hands up," Ali said evenly and without emotion.

"I don't think so. I think we'll stay in here for awhile, so thanks anyway."

"We? You have someone in there with you?" Ali asked, fighting to keep his voice from showing surprise.

"Guess you'll have to figure that out," Vance answered and hung up. Ali put the phone down and looked around at the group in front of him.

"Dammit," Rodriquez swore and grabbed his radio. He informed the SWAT team that Vance possibly had a hostage. Afterwards, he called the dispatch center and asked them to check for any missing person reports. When he was finished, he turned to Sgt. Jones.

"Now what?" Rodriquez asked Jones. Jones shrugged his shoulders.

"Now we need to find out if it's true. My guys can't see much from outside. It's impossible to get a listening device into the boat. If it was a building we could snake some cameras and listening devices in but there is no cover around that boat to work with. We can't get close enough to get eyes and ears in. That's the bad part of these things when they happen on water. We already considered killing the land power from the dock to put him in the dark but we decided we needed the background light from inside to see movement. That is still an option open to us but I don't like it much. We'll just have to get him to give us more info to work with. It's up to you guys to get what you can out of him to confirm it." Jones finished.

"It could also be a bluff," Jamie offered.

"Well we'll just have to get confirmation somehow." Ali answered. He dialed Vance's number again. There was no answer. He got up and walked out of the motor home. Jamie followed. Ali walked to the end of the vacant building and stood looking at the marina. He sensed Jamie standing behind him.

The marina was well lit and Ali admired the sleek boats floating next to their docks, he could hear the water lapping softly against their hulls. A pelican was perched on one of the pilings, its head resting on its chest, sleeping. It seemed so peaceful. Being near the water always seemed to calm him. He thought of his father and how much he loved the sea. Ali understood the feeling. It was hard to imagine that in this peaceful setting, evil was just a few hundred yards away in that boat. He prayed that there was no one in there with Vance, knowing Vance was not averse to killing when he felt the need.

"Well, Jamie, what do you think? You're the one with the degree."

"Hard to say, I think he's bluffing but who knows. I would hate to make the wrong decision and get a hostage killed. Let's just talk to him and see what we can get out of him."

"I hate being the one responsible for making that decision. I can do an investigation and arrest a killer but I don't feel like I'm qualified to do this negotiator stuff."

"He sought you out. He seems to have a connection to you somehow. I think he sees you as a worthy adversary and that frightens him. You are the only one that has come this close to him and I think he hates you for it and admires you at the same time. He's conflicted as to how he really feels about you but I do know he feels superior and feels like he has the upper hand on you right now, like he's in control of this situation and he's willing to exploit it as long as he can. We need to find a way to rattle him and get his emotions wound up but we have to be careful not to crank him up too much because he'll explode and kill the hostage if he has one."

"Well let's just see," Ali answered, angry now. He wanted to storm the boat and beat the crap out of Vance. He turned and strode rapidly back to the command post, stepped inside and grabbed a megaphone he had seen on a counter. He marched to the edge of the building then around it into the open and headed to the area of the docks. Jamie tried to grab his arm and stop him but she was too late.

"SWAT one, what is he doing?" Jones voice squawked on Rodriquez' radio. Rodriquez leaped from the command post and raced to Jamie's side at the corner of the building.

"What the hell is he doing?" Rodriquez breathlessly asked.

"I don't know," Jamie answered. She wanted to run out and grab Ali. She desperately hoped he was not trying to get shot, wondering if he was suicidal.

"Cover him," Rodriquez ordered through his radio.

Ali stopped at the end of dock and held the megaphone to his mouth. It made a loud squeaking sound when he pressed the talk button.

"VANCE! HERE I AM YOU CHICKEN SHIT. YOU ARE NOTHING BUT A COWARD AND I WILL COME FOR YOU!" Ali hollered through the megaphone. He stood next to a pylon supporting a dock light and waited. "C"MON TOUGH GUY, I OUTSMARTED YOU NOW COME OUT AND TAKE IT LIKE A MAN, IF YOU CAN," Ali yelled through the megaphone again. He saw a curtain move slightly and he stepped closer to the pylon. *Gotcha.*

Suddenly a loud roar and bright muzzle flash exploded from the porthole. The bullet zinged off a dock to Ali's right. He ducked and zigzagged in a trot back to the edge of the building.

"No shot, no shot," Rodriquez radio crackled.

"What the fuck are you doing?" Rodriquez demanded when Ali rejoined him.

"Getting his attention," Ali replied and walked back toward the command post. Jones was standing outside the command post, arms folded across his chest, an angry scowl on his face. He grabbed Ali's arm as he passed.

"Look asshole, that was stupid and you know it. Not only did you jeopardize yourself but if you had been hit one of my guys would have had to come drag your sorry ass out. I don't risk my guys unnecessarily. Don't do that again or I'll kick your ass myself, do you understand?" Jones hissed in Ali's ear.

"Sorry but it was necessary," Ali hissed back. The phone in the command post was ringing and Ali snatched it up.

"What?" Ali demanded to the phone.

"I'm gonna kill you, you son of a bitch!" Vance screamed at him. "Or better yet maybe I'll kill this bitch in here and throw her dead ass into the water, would you like that?"

"I doubt it. You do that and we're coming in and blow your ass away." Ali snapped back. Well, at least they knew the supposed hostage was a female. He hung up the phone, deciding to let Vance stew a little and think over what Ali had said. Jamie stood over him, glaring.

"I know why you did it but that was a dumb way to do it. I hope you did not crank him too high too soon." She said then sat on the counter next him. Rodriquez dropped into a chair across from him.

"So do I," Ali answered.

"That was too close," he muttered. Ali turned to him.

"Have your dispatch narrow their parameters to missing females."

Rodriquez nodded and walked out of the command post. There was a commotion outside and Jamie stepped to the door. Agent Carter was standing outside the command post talking to Rodriquez. With him was a short stocky man in his late fifties, wearing dark blue slacks and a white dress shirt with the sleeves rolled up to expose long forearms. He had a pistol on his hip and an FBI badge clipped to his belt. His tie was loosened around his neck. Jamie thought he looked like a harried accountant during income tax season. She stepped out of the command post and joined them.

"Agent Stevens, Special Agent In Charge Ian Doonan." Carter introduced them as they shook hands.

"Agent Stevens, nice to meet you, may I call you Jamie?" Doonan asked with a thick Bostonian accent.

"Absolutely, sir," Jamie replied.

"Please, Ian. I'm here to make sure you have what you need to resolve this issue, not take over. I know FBI protocol requires you to use my title but I like to be informal in these situations. Takes too long to say, 'excuse me, Special Agent in Charge Doonan' when bullets are flying" He gave her a warm smile. Agent Carter gave her a sly wink. Jamie immediately knew why Carter liked his boss so much. Bosses like him were rare gems.

Ali stepped to the door of the command post to see what the fuss was about. Doonan approached him and held out his hand.

"Detective Castillo, Ian Doonan, FBI."

Ali shook his hand but eyed him warily. *Great, the feds are here to take over,* he thought.

"Relax detective, I'm here to assist and observe not to take your case away from you," Doonan chuckled, reading his thoughts. Ali was suddenly embarrassed.

"Sorry," he muttered.

"Okay, now that the bullshit is out of the way, fill me in if you will," Doonan said, stepping up into the command post. Rodriquez explained the operation and showed Doonan where the SWAT team was positioned. He explained about the supposed hostage and how they planned to deal with the situation. As Rodriquez spoke, Doonan nodded.

"Looks like you have everything covered," Doonan said then turned to Ali, "Do you feel that you can handle negotiations with this guy?"

"I think I can handle it, with Jamie's help," Ali replied.

"If you don't think you can, I will be glad to call our negotiators to come in but I'll leave that decision to you. Fair enough?" Doonan asked. Ali nodded.

"Let me clear the air a little bit so we all understand each other. I know how local cops think of the FBI as accountants with badges. I was a cop in Boston for twenty years before I went to the feds. I worked patrol, undercover narcotics, detectives and was on the SWAT team there. My father insisted I go to law school. Unfortunately being a cop was in my blood so the logical route for a cop with a law degree was to go federal. I have worked stakeouts and have commanded the FBI SWAT team. I did undercover work all over the world. I have been wounded twice so I'm a cop first and a fed second. I know what it is you do and how you do it. I promise to stay out of your way unless you need me. Okay, that's the speech and it's over. Damn I wish I could have a beer, I'm parched. You got anything cold to drink around here, non-alcoholic?" Rodriquez smiled and led him to a refrigerator in the rear of the command post.

Ali drummed his fingers on the counter in front of the phone. He snatched the phone from its cradle and impatiently punched the number in again. He counted the rings at the other end. No answer. He dropped the phone back on its cradle and glanced around at the faces around the command post. Damn. Why wouldn't Vance answer? When the hell was he doing in there?

Sgt. Jones hoisted himself into the command post and looked at Ali quizzically.

"Anything?" Jones asked him.

Ali shook his head.

"If we can't get him talking, we may have to consider making entry. I hope it doesn't come to that. Problem is, he's got food, a place to sleep, AC, he's comfortable in there and he can last a long time. We can't wait that long." Jones finished, looking around command post. Doonan sat at the end of the table, sipping a soda and nodded slowly. Suddenly, Agent Carter stuck his head in to the command post.

"Ian, trouble's here." Carter said to Doonan who rose from his chair and hurried to the door. He stuck his head out the door then looked back in at Ali.

"Robinson," was all Doonan said. He stepped from the motor home and strode purposefully to the plain black car and met Robinson at the door. Doonan looked past the parked police cars and saw two television news live trucks pull in at the barricades. It appeared Robinson brought his own news reporters.

"What the hell are you doing Thomas?" Doonan asked Robinson, folding his arms across his chest and blocking Robinson's path.

"This is my case and I don't appreciate being kept out of the loop and kept from the scene," Robinson glared at Doonan.

"Your case? I think you are mistaken. This is Castillo and Stevens' case. We were trying to keep this from the media to prevent this circus and here you are, bringing it right on top us. How did you find out anyway?" Doonan asked.

"I have my sources," Robinson spat.

Doonan suspected the source was that pretty little Cuban reporter that Robinson was rumored to be banging behind his wife's back. Doonan heard the sound of a helicopter overhead and glanced up. He saw two helicopters arrive and hover over the scene. News Choppers. Shit! Robinson was really a pain in the ass.

"Robinson, the Keys are in my region not yours and you need to remember that. I am the SAC in charge here and I'm not gonna let you fuck this up." Doonan growled.

"Such language from a man in your position, I am appalled," Robinson smirked. Doonan decided to take him down a few notches.

"I seem to remember your uncle the senator died and you lost your juice, don't push me Thomas. I am an old street brawler and you are an Ivy League pussy that would not know a good arrest if it bit you on your ass. Stay out of the way." Doonan whirled and stomped back to the command post, leaving Robinson red-faced and speechless.

Cruz sidled up next to Robinson.

"He can't talk to you like that sir," Cruz tried to console his boss.

"Oh, shut the fuck up," Robinson snarled, brushing Cruz aside and heading toward the news cameras setting up next to their trucks.

Ali and Jamie stepped from the command post and stood with Doonan, watching Robinson who was straightening his tie and combing his hair in the glare of the camera lights, waiting for the reporter to give him the signal they were on the air. Ali glanced at his watch. Ten thirty, the news went live at eleven. Ali had to admire Robinsons timing.

Ali also noticed his hands were shaking slightly. Jamie turned toward Doonan.

"What are we gonna do about that asshole?" she asked him.

"Timing is everything, my dear girl" Doonan answered and winked at her. He removed his cell phone from his pocket and dialed, watching Robinson. He stepped away from them and spoke quietly on his phone a minute. Jamie heard him say 'hang on' to the person on the other end of the cell phone. He stepped next to Jamie and watched until Robinson was joined by a reporter who held a microphone to Robinson's face.

Doonan walked quickly to Robinson's side and held the phone up to him. Robinson took the phone and held it to his ear. Jamie and Ali could not hear what was said but they saw Robinson's face turn bright red. Ali could see him sputtering and his mouth was moving rapidly. He handed the phone back to Doonan and pushed past the reporter, who stood open-mouthed with the microphone still held up to Robinson's face. She quickly slashed her hand across her throat, signaling the cameraman to turn the camera off.

Doonan walked back to them with a huge grin. He stopped and turned to watch as Robinson and Cruz slammed their car doors. He gave a low chuckle and turned to Jamie.

"As I said, timing is everything, that, and being a close friend with the Assistant Director for the southern region, who doesn't like being called at home this time of night. We won't be bothered by him again." Doonan said as Robinson squealed his tires leaving the parking lot. He turned and climbed back into the command post, still chuckling.

"I guess we know whose is bigger, huh?" Jamie said to Ali.

CHAPTER 37

Sander Vance paced the length of the boat. He held his gun in his right hand and every few seconds he sighted down the barrel and pretended he was firing the gun, imagining he was shooting Castillo right in his fucking spic face. How could he have missed him, his ass was right there in his sights. The gun had never let him down, ever since the day he first picked it up and it spoke to him, telling him how to solve his troubles. He held it up in front of his face and studied it. It was the same gun, black, sleek and deadly. *C'mon Sander, think, you have outsmarted the cops so many times before. This cop was no different. No, that wasn't true. These cops were smarter than that idiot Sheriff Thomas. But still they were just cops. How the hell did he get in this fix? He was doing so well. That fucking Irving, it was all his doing, he had trapped him. Vance decided he should have never gotten involved with him, should have never agreed to kill Bascomb for him. He was the reason Vance got caught. He trapped him into killing Bascomb and now wasn't it ironic that he was trapped in Irving's boat? Never trust a lawyer.*

Vance wondered how Castillo had found him here. Did Irving tell them where he was? Has he confessed to everything? Probably so, he was weak and weaklings got you killed. Vance imagined him sniveling and begging for mercy, agreeing to give Vance up for his own freedom. That coward, Vance should have killed him too, him and Martins both. Break clean, that had been his rule and he had broken it and here he was trapped like a rat. He continued to pace, feeling like there were eyes watching his every move. Watching him? How could they watch him? Suddenly it struck him. The lights, they can see my shadow moving with the lights on, Shit! He scurried around, turning off all the lights. There now he was invisible again. Invisibility, that had been his secret. He fit right into the flow of people wherever he went and nobody noticed him. He had been free to wreak his vengeance without anyone noticing or suspecting him until Castillo and Abramowitz. He raised the gun again and pretended to shoot them both. Then he began to pace again. He tried to figure out how to become invisible again and walk right past these assholes. It did not seem possible.

The incessant ringing of the phone was really beginning to grate on him. He wished they would stop calling because he needed to think.

"Shut up," he hissed at the phone. He threw a pillow at it and missed and that enraged him further. He flopped onto the couch and covered his ears, rocking back and forth, the gun against his head, its cold metal against his temple. When he removed his hands the phone had stopped. He sighed and settled into the couch.

The hostage! That was his way out of this. He had to convince them he had a real hostage. Now how could he do that? They would have to see the hostage or at least think they saw the hostage. He glanced around the room, pondering. Then it hit him. He grabbed Abramowitz' cap, the one that had the words 'Captain' and gold braid around the brim and fondled it. He placed it on its edge inside the curtain in one of the windows. The he retrieved a towel from the bathroom and draped it over the edge. Its shadow would look like a woman's head with long hair. Then he turned a light on across from the hat so it would be a dark shadow against the curtains. Perfect. Now he would wait for them to call again.

Lt. Davis parked behind a news truck and approached a uniformed cop at the barricade. A crowd had formed, having heard about the commotion at the marina and had wandered down to see and be part of the action, most of them were more drunk than smart. A news reporter stood in the glare of the camera lights, microphone held to her face and talking to the camera. A very drunk tourist in a flowered shirt, staggered behind her, waving to the folks at home. Davis avoided the camera by skirting the crowd. The uniformed cop held up his hand to stop Davis from stepping past the barricade. Davis held up his badge.

"Lt. Davis, I'm Castillo's supervisor."

The cop stepped back and waved him through. Davis knocked on the side of the command post and Doonan's head appeared in the doorway.

"Who the hell are you?" Doonan demanded.

"Lt. Davis, Castillo's boss and you?" Davis demanded.

"Doonan, FBI, come on in," Doonan replied and disappeared into the command post. Davis stepped into the command post and was met by Castillo.

"Hey boss, what brings you here?" Castillo asked, clapping him on the shoulder.

"Robinson did a news conference and made the chief nervous, so he ordered me here and I wanted to give you this," Davis answered, handing him a sheaf of papers. Ali glanced at the papers.

"We finally got Abramowitz' phone records. There are a dozen calls to Vance's number," Davis nodded at the sheaf of papers. Ali introduced Davis and Doonan who shook hands.

"Don't worry about Robinson, that problem has been dealt with," Doonan told Davis.

"Severely," Jamie laughed.

Jones and Rodriquez entered the command post.

"Any contact?" Rodriquez asked Ali who shook his head. Rodriquez turned to Jones. "Well?"

"For all we know the bastard is asleep in there. It's time for plan B," Jones said grimly.

"Which is?" Jamie asked.

"McGinnis is going to kill all the lights and put my team in the dark. Then we move some floodlights up near the boat to keep him blind and awake. Some music too."

"What will that do?" Ali asked.

"That will keep him awake. The more tired we make him the more chance he will slip up," Doonan interjected, "If that's alright with you Ali?"

Ali nodded. As if on cue, the marina went instantly dark.

"Sniper One to command," Jones' radio said. He answered immediately.

"Sniper One, I have one light on in the boat, I can see a shadow in the window, looks like a woman's head with long hair."

"Damn, I guess he really does have a hostage in there," Jones sighed. He spoke into his microphone again and loud rap music began to blare down by the docks and the boat was flooded with the glare of floodlights.

An hour passed with no movement from the boat. Ali sat morosely in the corner of the command post. The shaking in his hands had spread to his legs. He began to sweat profusely and he scratched at his thigh. It felt like he had dozens of bugs crawling on it. Davis sat next to him and watched out of the corner of his eye. Suddenly, Davis stood.

"I'm starving, Ali let's go eat something." He jerked his head toward the door. Ali stood.

"Is that a problem?" Ali asked the cop with the headphones on.

"Nope. I slaved the equipment to your cell, if he calls you we'll still be online here," the cop answered.

Ali stepped out of the command post and followed Davis toward the barricades. The air outside was cool and felt good as it washed over Ali. He felt the sweat drying on him. Relief flooded over him, the inside of the motor home had begun to close in on him.

Ali and Davis skirted the main street and entered a small corner bar. Jimmy Buffet was singing on an old fashioned jukebox in the corner. There was one customer in the place, a younger version of McGinnis, seated at the bar. Second runner up in the Ernest look-alike contest, Ali decided. A tall blond bartender approached from the end of the bar. She wore skin tight, aqua color, satin shorts and a Key West t-shirt tied at the waist. The front had been cut down to her navel and revealed firm massive breasts. Davis wondered if they were real.

"You guys cops from that thing at the marina?" She asked, leaning on the bar to reveal even more of her chest.

"How could you tell?" Davis asked.

"You look like cops and I know all of the local cops," She gave them a knowing look. Ali wondered if she knew the local cops in a biblical sense. Davis nodded.

"We need some sandwiches and my friend here needs a Screwdriver," Davis informed her. Ali jerked his head toward Davis who stared straight down the bartender's blouse. She smiled and didn't seem to mind. After all, lots of women paid lots of money for that look and hers did not cost her a dime and she liked the looks. She pushed off the bar and walked away to get their orders.

"What's the deal?" Ali asked Davis.

"Ali I'm not blind, I was watching you in the command post. You're starting to go through withdrawal, the sweats, the itches and the shakes. I am not judging you, because you don't know this, I've been where you are. I have been sober for ten years now. I got sober before you started working in my squad. I kept it hidden pretty well but I got clean. What's the problem? Vodka is your drink right? Nobody can smell it on your breath, right?"

"Yeah, I guess," Ali answered, embarrassed but he also saw Davis in a new light.

"But when this is over, you are going to get help, deal?"

"Okay."

"No not okay. That shows lack of commitment and if you really are gonna get clean it's gonna take everything you got, understand?" Davis demanded.

Ali nodded.

They finished their sandwiches as Ali swallowed the last of his drink. He felt better, the shakes and the crawly feeling had stopped. Davis gathered up the bag of sandwiches and led Ali out of the bar after giving the bartender one more leer, which she returned by blowing him a kiss. As they approached the motor home, Davis handed Ali a stick of gum which he stuffed in his mouth.

Ali sat silently as the rest of the group ate their sandwiches. He was embarrassed. Did the others know? Was it obvious? He was aware that Jamie knew but did the others suspect. He replayed his actions in his mind and tried to figure out if he had said or done anything that gave him away. He could not find anything and no one had acted like they suspected. Ali knew his father would be very disappointed in him. Suddenly the phone rang, breaking his reverie.

"Turn that goddamn music off or I'm gonna kill this bitch," Vance screamed into Ali's ear.

"Easy Sander," Ali said soothingly, just like Jamie had told him to. "We needed to know if you were awake." Ali could barely hear him from the music blaring in the background.

"Well, now you know," Vance screamed again.

"Okay Sander, we'll turn it down," Ali said evenly, motioning to the tech. The music died down instantly. "Let's talk awhile, okay?"

"What about?" Vance asked.

"Well, let's talk about how we're gonna end this thing without anybody dying."

"That is easy. You have your Gestapo untie the boat and I ride out of here. When I'm in international waters, I turn the bitch over to you and I sail off into the sunset. How's that?"

"That is not gonna happen." Ali replied.

"How did you find me anyway, Castillo? Did my dear friend Irving squeal like a little bitch and tell you where I was?"

"No actually it was just your bad luck. His son lives here and came down to check the boat and recognized you from the news. But Irving is talking," Ali lied.

"I'll bet he is."

"Let's talk about you Sander."

"What about me?"

"Why did you do all of this?"

"WHY? Why the fuck do you think. Do you know what those bastards did to me?"

"Who? Gay men," Ali asked.

"Very good asshole, you should be a detective," Vance snarled.

"Gay men did not make you do this. Or let me rephrase that, how did gay men do this to you?"

"So, now somebody wants to hear my story? Where were you when I was turned?"

"Turned? I'm sorry I don't understand," Ali replied.

"I don't want to talk anymore," Vance said sadly.

"Sander don't hang up. Talk to me. Maybe I can help," Ali said as Jamie held up a legal pad. She had written the words compassion and empathy on it.

"Okay, yeah turned, by a scoutmaster when I was thirteen. Every time we would go on camping trips he would sneak into the tent and have sex with me. That's how I was turned."

"Sander. That didn't make you gay. You were molested."

"I AM NOT GAY!" Vance screamed. Jamie held up the pad again. She had written the word 'easy' in bold letters. Ali nodded.

"Sorry. I did not mean to assume anything."

"I have sex with women. But because of that bastard, I also have a craving for men but that does not make me gay!" His voice raised an octave.

"Sander, listen to me. You were molested. There is a difference between being a victim and being gay. Gay men don't molest little boys as a rule."

"You're full of shit," Vance replied and hung up. Ali dropped the phone on the desk as disappointment flooded him.

"You had him talking, do not let him control this. You gotta get him back on the phone," Jamie said emphatically, placing a hand on Ali's shoulder.

Vance stomped back and forth around the boat. His fists were clenched and he was shaking. Castillo did not know what he was talking about. That son of a bitch had turned him into this, hadn't he? Before that had happened he was disgusted by the thought of a man being with another man. His mother had quoted the bible verse about man should not lie with other men over and over and over. Even when it started he was disgusted with himself. But the sexual excitement had overcome him and he learned to accept it and even enjoy it and that made him a disgusting creature. He remembered how he had wondered if everyone knew just by looking at him. He had withdrawn from the other kids at school and around town. He could feel their eyes on him, seeing through him and they had to know. He felt dirty all the time and no matter how many showers he took he could never feel clean. The phone was ringing again. He snatched it up.

"WHAT?"

"Sander calm down. I want you to know we can help you," Ali said gently.

"Help me? Help me? How the hell are you gonna help me. I know what happens in prison. I'll be passed around from one scumbag to another and I'll just get worse. They are gonna know what I am and they'll enjoy it. The famous serial killer of gay men. I'll just be a piece of meat in there. Now YOU LET ME OUT OF HERE!" Vance cried. He reached down and turned the ignition key and pressed the start button. The engines of the boat roared to life.

Everyone in the command post jumped up at once. Ali turned to Jones.

"Can he drive out of here?" He demanded.

"He'll tear the cleats off that boat if he tries, it's still tied to the dock," Jones answered then spoke tersely into his radio. The patrol boat at the mouth of the inlet suddenly lifted its bow and raced into the marina, stopping in front of Abramowitz' boat, blocking its escape.

"Sander? Sander talk to me!" Ali yelled into the phone. The group in the command post stood frozen. No one moved, no one breathed. Gunshots roared inside the boat and the glass of a window exploded, then the phone went dead.

"Did he kill the hostage?" Jones demanded over the radio.

"Sniper one, I still have visual on the hostage's head. It didn't move, I think she's okay," Jones exhaled sharply.

"Did he shoot himself?" Ali demanded of Jones who just shrugged his shoulders. The roar of the engines died and the boat sat silent, exhaust smoke still drifting up from the water at the stern. Ali quickly dialed the phone. Ali heard Vance's voice answer tentatively in a small child's voice.

"Sander, what happened? Are you alright?"

"None of your business," Vance snapped back.

"Sander let's talk awhile, okay?" Ali tried to calm him.

"About what? You wanna know my life's story?"

"How about your parents? Did you kill your parents?" Ali asked.

"My father died in a truck accident; don't you do your homework? I thought you were smart."

"Sorry I meant your mother and stepfather," Ali corrected himself.

"My stepfather," Vance sighed, "Was an asshole. He was a brute and beat me and my mother when he was drunk or angry or bored. I shot him, yes; you should have seen the look on his face. The cowardly little boy finally stood up to him and he didn't believe it, even at the end. He made me angry and I could not take it anymore."

"What about your mom, didn't you love her?"

"Love her? She didn't protect me from him. She was weak and didn't stand up for us, your mom is supposed to stand up and protect you. Instead she stood by and let him do that to me. She used me to get a husband after my dad, who by the way was no big loss. She used me like everyone else. She would drink herself into a coma while my stepfather beat me for stupid shit like spilling a glass of milk. Who beats their kid for spilling milk? And he made me go to scouts when he knew I didn't want to."

"Did you tell him why you didn't go?" Ali questioned.

"Tell him? How the fuck do you tell someone what they did to me. He would have just called me a baby and beat the crap out of me again. He would have told me to fight back and would have blamed me for letting it happen."

"But it wasn't your fault."

"You think that would have mattered to him? He thought that what ever happened to you was your own fault. When he was drunk and whipping me he would tell me it was my fault for making him angry, then he would say it was his fault that his life was shit because he married a 'bitch with a useless kid.' That he wanted a real son not a piece of shit like me."

"Sander I need to know if the hostage is okay. My bosses in here want to know."

"I have nothing more to say right now," Vance answered then the phone went dead

There was very little activity in the command post. It had been three hours since the engines fired up. Ali tried the phone every thirty minutes and still there was no answer. He glanced at his watch. Three thirty am. Was Vance alive? Did he kill the hostage? No one wanted to ask the question out loud.

Doonan, Davis and Jamie stood outside the door of the command post in the dark, talking quietly. Doonan puffed on a big cigar, smoke billowing around his head. Jones and Rodriquez stood at the rear of the motor home, around a small collapsible table, with the squad leaders of the SWAT team, plotting an assault on the boat. The technician had not turned the rap music back on because it was getting on everyone's nerves. Suddenly the phone rang, causing everyone to jump.

"Hello," Ali snatched the phone to his ear.

"Castillo?" Vance was sobbing on the other end.

"I'm here Sander." Everyone crowded around the door listening to the conversation on the speaker phone.

"You're gonna help me? Get me counseling and things like that?"

"Absolutely, anything you need." Ali consoled him.

"Before I surrender I want to make a confession, I assume you are recording this?"

"We are," Ali replied.

"Good. I, Sander Vance do hereby confess to killing the men I am accused of killing. I have written out an outline of where the bodies are in different parts of the country. I also killed my mother and stepfather in Bryant County, South Carolina but I want to make it clear that I did not do it alone. Irving Abramowitz, Attorney at Law, hired me to kill Richard Bascomb because Bascomb was going to expose his dirty dealing and his thefts from CAD. He also assisted me in disposing of some of the bodies of my victims."

Jamie suddenly had a very bad feeling. She waved at Ali.

"Something's wrong. Keep him talking, interrupt him, this is wrong."

"Sander? Sander" Castillo said urgently.

"I also want to make it clear that Abramowitz was not the only one who knew about me and what I was doing. Rodney James of CAD also knew. If you check my phone records you will see that he called me numerous times. He knew what I was doing and instead of stopping me or going to the police, he encouraged me to continue. I met him in a bar and was going to kill him too but he convinced me not to and said he could make me famous. He insisted I leave the south Florida bodies in public places to garner sympathy for gays and to get publicity for his cause. He's a pig like all the rest. Why do you think my other victims were hidden after death and not those? Because of Rodney. That is all I have to say." Then the phone went dead.

"Get him back on the phone!" Jamie said urgently. "He's not giving up. Ali you have to call him back. NOW!"

"I have movement, looks like he's coming out," Sniper Ones voice crackled over Jones' radio. The group turned to look.

The door of the boat's salon swung open and Sander's voice echoed across the water.

"Don't shoot!"

His head and chest appeared from the doorway and he straightened up and stepped into view. He was naked, his skin a stark white in the glare of the floodlights. He staggered onto the aft deck and stood with his arms raised in the air. Ali was struck by how much he looked like a statue of Jesus on the cross. His hands were shiny, bright red gloves; rivulets of red ran down his forearms. Crimson blood flowed from the area of his crotch. In his right hand was his gun and in his left hand he hoisted his severed genitals over his head, blood dripping onto his head and rolling down his forehead.

"Sweet Jesus!' Doonan breathed.

Suddenly Vance dropped his right hand and the gun roared, flame shooting from the muzzle, bullets whanged off the motor home and everyone scrambled for cover, except Ali who stood frozen, shocked by the site. A loud shot rang out from across the marina and Vance's head exploded in a crimson spray as his body somersaulted backwards and landed on the deck with a hollow thud. Then there was silence.

Jones grabbed his submachine gun and sprinted for the boat yelling,

"Entry team move!"

A line of black clad SWAT team cops swarmed the dock, duck walking rapidly, machine guns raised to their shoulders, toward the boat. They swarmed over the deck and three disappeared into the salon. They emerged a second later and stood over Vance's body on the deck. Jones hopped off the boat and approached the group. His face was ashen gray.

"There was no hostage, just a hat with a towel on it to make it look like a woman's head. Fuck!" He brushed past them and walked toward the paramedic truck waiting behind the barricades.

Ali did not move. He fought to breathe; his chest felt like there was someone squeezing his ribs preventing him from expanding it. The paramedics pushed past him following Jones, trotting toward the boat. Ali glanced at Jamie. Her eyes were wide and she was pale. Suddenly he felt the air whoosh out of him and he could breathe again. He walked on wooden legs to the boat and stood looking at Vance over the gunwale of the boat. The SWAT teamed was crowded around the body, not speaking. Rodriquez broke the moment.

"Okay, everybody off the boat, it's a crime scene now. Get the crime scene people in here." Rodriquez ordered.

Everyone moved slowly as if they expected Vance to sit up and laugh at them. They filed off the boat as a uniformed cop began to unwind yellow crime scene tape around the end of the dock. Rodriquez put his hand on Ali's shoulder as he passed.

"Looks like your case is closed. We'll have to do a print comparison to be sure it's him but I really don't think there is any doubt," Rodriquez said quietly.

"Not yet," Ali replied shaking his head slowly. He walked back to the command post and picked up the sheaf of papers Davis had given him. He retrieved his notepad from his pocket and began to compare phone numbers and there it was. Rodney James number on Vance's phone record.

"In the end he was telling the truth," Ali said to Davis, holding up his pad and the list side by side. "Rodney James knew."

"I'll have him picked up and brought into the squad. We'll bury that self righteous asshole." Davis promised.

Davis, Jamie and Ali sat in the command post for three hours, waiting for the crime scene investigators to finish their work. Ali stepped out of the command post as the stretcher carrying Vance's body was wheeled to the coroner's van, zipped into a rubber bag. He stood aside to let the stretcher pass. He tried to catalog his feelings. He was sad and did not understand that. Vance was a killer and would have gladly killed Ali if he got the chance. Was it a letdown that the case ended this way? Ali had never felt sorry for any of his killers before when he placed them into jail or testified in court and heard them sentenced to the death penalty. Why this time? Was it that Vance had ended it himself and Ali did not get to arrest him? Did he feel like Vance had beaten him in the end? Maybe it was just the shock of seeing another human being mutilated like that and realizing that someone could actually do that to himself or maybe he believed Vance was really a victim. It might be that he was saddened by the loss of human life, tired of being witness to it. Every time he closed his eyes he saw Vance standing on the deck with his genitals in his hand. It made him shudder. He tried to push it from his mind but it refused to go, demanding to be seen and remembered. Ali knew this was one he would always remember.

Ali, Davis and Jamie stood next to Davis' unmarked car, talking to Doonan as Rodriquez approached, his cell phone to his ear.

Rodriquez thanked someone on the other end and snapped the phone shut as he stopped in front of Ali.

"Got confirmation, it was positively Vance. I guess it's really over," Rodriquez told them. Ali nodded and held out his hand to Rodriquez.

"Thanks for everything. We'll be in touch."

"Come down anytime, just let's not do this again," Rodriquez smiled, shaking Ali's hand warmly. He turned to Doonan.

"Ian, thank for your help also, especially with Robinson."

"Anytime, and that part I enjoyed immensely. If you need anything else from me just holler," Doonan smiled. "Well, I guess Rodriquez and I better go talk to the news vultures." He pointed toward the barricade with his chin.

The Key West police chief was standing in the glare of the camera lights, giving the news reporters their sound bite. Doonan shook hands all around then strode toward the reporters, Rodriquez trotted to catch up.

"Let's go home," Davis said, opening the car door and climbing into the driver's seat. Jamie and Ali piled in.

CHAPTER 38

During the drive back north, Ali sat in back seat and admired Jamie's profile in the front passenger seat. The sun was beginning to peak over the eastern horizon but traffic had not picked up yet and looking at her gave him a peaceful feeling and he dozed, exhausted. The emotional rollercoaster of the night had taken its toll on him.

He didn't know how long it had been before it happened but he suddenly began to shake and it woke him. He felt like bugs were squirming under his skin all over his body. He saw a large spider, the size of a small dog, on the seat rest in front of him and he woke screaming, soaked with sweat. He struck at the spider but it seemed like his hand did not quite reach because it didn't move. It glared at him with Sander Vance's eyes, accusing him, demanding he not fight back and be devoured.

"Ali, Ali it's okay easy," Jamie was leaning over the seat, clutching his knee shaking it. He looked at her with terrified eyes. He did not know who she was and tried to shake her hand off of him. Then things went black and he went into convulsions.

Davis screeched to a stop in front of the emergency room and sprinted into the entrance, hollering for a doctor. The convulsions had stopped when Ali was wheeled into the emergency room, semiconscious. He was rushed into a treatment room as Davis corralled the doctor at the front desk.

Ali was only semi-aware of the bustling around him. He did not feel the pinch the nurse promised him when she inserted the IV. He knew Jamie was hovering over him, whispering that he was going to okay. A bright light blinded him when the doctor looked into his eyes. Then he saw the spiders scurrying around the walls. They all had Vance's eyes. He fought against the restraints they had strapped to his arms and legs. Dammit, why were they holding him down? Didn't they know it made it easy for the spiders to crawl down the walls and swarm across his chest biting him and he was helpless to fight them? Then he vomited, over and over until he retched; empty, but still trying to empty his stomach. He remembered Davis pulling his gun and badge from his belt. He pleaded with him not to leave him defenseless against the spiders. He calmed and slept after the nurse hooked up the Valium IV.

Davis and Jamie sat in the padded chairs and listened to the doctor behind the desk.

"The treatment is extensive. He will be in detox for thirty days. No one can visit him and he can have no contact with the outside world, none. He's in for a pretty rough time but we'll keep him sedated in the beginning and hopefully we'll get him healthy. Understand that there is the possibility that he may relapse when he's released, it is not uncommon, that is going to depend on how badly he wants to stay clean. The detox for alcohol is pretty similar to the detox for cocaine and even heroin. He's a strong guy so he has a good chance of winning this fight if he wants to bad enough."

Davis nodded and picked up the pen lying on the desk. He scrutinized the stack of papers in front of him then signed on the lines the doctor pointed out. He hated doing this to Ali but felt he was not doing it to him but for him. The legal commitment papers were the only way since Ali had no family.

"You'll keep us informed?" Davis asked when he finished signing.

"Absolutely. We take special care of our patients, especially the cops. We understand it can be a disease related to the stress of the job and from what you've told me he has a lot of other stuff to deal with. Don't worry; we'll take good care of him."

The first five days were the worst. The pain was incredible, it seemed like every nerve ending in every inch of his body was on fire. Ali battled the restraints until he was exhausted, lying on the sweat soaked bed, his bedclothes stinking with perspiration. The one time they tried to remove the restraints to clean him, he punched a doctor but wasn't aware of it. He had urinated on himself and could smell the sweet sour smell of it even in his sleep. He was aware of the nurse changing the IV they kept plugged into his arm, except when he knocked it loose with his thrashing and began to crave a new IV. He never dreamed he would end up like this.

The dreams were horrifying. He saw Sander Vance standing on that deck only it wasn't Sander, it was him holding his own severed manhood. He dreamed of Maria, she was crying and begging him to help her. He dreamed of Jamie, seated in Maria's car, bloody and broken from the impact, her head split open exposing her brain that shone bright and wet in the flashing of the police lights. When he was awake he saw the spiders, they were everywhere, crawling on him, biting him. They had Sander Vance's face or Jonah Martin's face and even Jamie's face. He thrashed violently, trying to shake them off.

After five days the dreams stopped. His nerve endings only hurt once in a while and the vomiting and convulsions had stopped. He was greatly relieved when they finally removed the straps and he was able to take a shower. He stood in the hot water, scrubbing his skin until it was crimson red, trying to wash off his own stink.

His first solid food tried valiantly to lurch back up his throat but he fought it back down and succeeded. It felt good to have his stomach full even if it was only soup and crackers. After the meal he tried to walk like the doctor insisted but only made it halfway down the hall before he slumped against the hallway wall sweating. The nurse helped him back to his room. After a few days he was finally able to shuffle the length of the hallway and celebrated with red Jell-O for desert.

Once he was able to keep the restraints off permanently he went to counseling. The shrink was a white haired man with a hawkish nose. Ali fought the urge to reach over and push the glasses back up because they always seemed on the verge of falling off. He resisted the urge to talk at first, fearful of exposing himself and his inner fears and feelings to anyone but once he did he could not stop. He told the doctor about Jamie and Maria and his father and how he felt about not being able to do the physical things as well as he used to. The doctor listened attentively and offered the right words at the right times, sometimes soothing, sometimes scolding but always gently. Ali began to trust him and told him things he wouldn't even tell Antonio or Jamie.

Ali tried group therapy the third week but only once. He felt foolish telling his secrets to these strangers but did realize he was not alone. He was not the only one who had fought this battle and some had even won. He decided he was going to win, no matter what it took. But some of those people were so pathetic with their reasons for being drunks he wanted to laugh at them. Hell, none of them had reasons as good as his and he told the doctor he couldn't go back to group. The doctor told him that was arrogant and childish but he did not care. He refused to go back and the doctor was forced to acquiesce.

When he was alone with his thoughts he wondered about Jamie. Had she gone back to DC? Was there anything left for him out there? He had his job and that was something but he yearned to see Jamie's face, hold her in his arms. These thoughts did not bring the guilt they had before and the feeling he was cheating on Maria had begun to fade. The doctor was starting to convince him he had the right to live, but did he have anything waiting for him? He wished he wasn't cut off from the outside world. He was beginning to understand that feeling of being trapped Vance had talked about. He counted the days until he would be able to have visitors.

Thirty days had passed. Today was the day he was able to have visitors and Ali shuffled to the visiting room hoping beyond hope someone would be there. He fought the feeling of embarrassment he knew would come if anyone was there. Maybe no one would come and he would not have to face it.

He stepped into the visiting room and scanned it slowly. Then he saw her seated at the far side of the room and she rose from her chair when their eyes met. Ali fought the urge to run to her, relief flooded his body and he began to cry. She rushed to him and he wrapped her in his arms hugging her tight. The feel of her body against him was amazing. He could smell her hair and her shampoo, senses he had not used in a long time were working and he felt more alive than he had in years.

"Ali, you're crushing me," Jamie gasped, her face buried in his chest.

"Sorry." Ali whispered, relaxing his hold. He held her at arms length and looked into her eyes. He could see they were wet with tears. He wanted this moment to last forever. He had the urge to dance around the room.

"Why are you here? I assumed you went home to DC." Ali asked.

"Let's sit down," Jamie suggested leading him to a chair. She studied his face. He looked drawn and much thinner and there were dark circles under his eyes. His skin was a light gray but there was a light in his eyes she had not seen before. He looked tired but determined.

"First, I am home," Ali opened his mouth to ask a question but she raised her hand to stop him. "I transferred to the local field office, I needed a change anyway and I wanted to do field work, this case made that desire stronger."

"But that means you're working for Robinson, how could you stand that?"

"Not really, Special Agent in Charge Robinson has been reassigned to Puerto Rico. Seems Ian Doonan has lots of powerful friends and Robinson's attempt to grandstand our case pissed off the director, who is a man that one does not piss off. Oh, and since Robinson doesn't speak Spanish, Cruz went with him to, uh, translate I guess. I work for Doonan now. I'm still getting settled but it is great working for Doonan. Jonah Martins is out of the hospital and doing okay, I saw him the other day. He has a long road ahead but he'll be fine I think. Rodney James was indicted for being an accessory after the fact and CAD is dropping into the toilet rapidly, some of the members are trying to resurrect it under a new name. The publicity has been fierce and no one wants to be associated with the name CAD."

"What about Irving?" Ali asked hopefully.

"He's still being an arrogant fuck, denying everything. His lawyer is trying to use your situation to show the case was flawed, claiming that you and I set him up as a vendetta and claiming the investigation was poor because of your drinking. The US Attorney is working on that so don't worry, it will work out."

"Damn, I was afraid of that," Ali said crestfallen.

"Hey, it will be okay. The US Attorney is sharp, he'll prove the case, Irving is going to jail for a long time," Jamie soothed. "Besides, you are a hero. The news is singing your praises for catching the killer that no one else could catch. Of course, you had help, namely me. I saved the articles for you and taped the news programs."

"I feel like I have been gone for a year. A lot has happened in thirty days."

"Good things move quickly, Ali. Real change takes time," Jamie replied then regretted it, realizing how he might take that remark.

"Yeah that's what they have been telling me in here."

"I'm sorry, I didn't mean it that way," Jamie said, reaching out to take his hands in hers.

"I know, its okay. Listen, Jamie I do not know what the future holds for us. Hell, I don't even know what the future holds for me. I hope you didn't transfer here to be near me, because I don't know if that is healthy for you. I am not well and it's going to be an uphill battle all the way and I may not be strong enough to make it. I don't want you to waste your life on me, you have so much to give to someone and I am not sure I deserve it."

"I transferred because I wanted to do field work. Yeah, I did transfer here to be near you but I think that together we have enough strength to make it. Besides, I told you I wanted to try and intend to give it all I've got. My dad told me before he died that you never know what the future brings for any of us so you just gotta go with it. Besides, you aren't getting rid of me that easy, I got a lot invested in you," Jamie looked deeply into his eyes and smiled gently. "Anyway the papers would eat it up if I bailed on you now, we're celebrities, remember?" She slid out of her chair and knelt in front of him, wrapping her arms around his waist and held on tightly. He kissed the top of her head and decided he never wanted to let her go.

Ali parked his car in front of the gym and switched off the engine. He sat looking at the entrance and remembered the first time he had walked through that door. His father had his hand on Ali's shoulder and guided the reluctant boy who was shaking with fright. The inside of the gym had seemed so big and intimidating. The boxers seemed like gods to him and he never believed he could be one of them.

Ali pushed through the door into the gloom and slipped his sunglasses off. The smell inside brought back a flood of memories. There was a comfort to it, like slipping into that ragged old bathrobe you should have thrown away years ago but didn't because it was warm and comfortable and gave you a safe feeling. The grunt of two boxers trading punches in the ring drew him closer. He saw Antonio standing next to the ring, hollering at the boxers in a raspy voice. He was smaller than Ali remembered and God he looked so old. He leaned on a wooden cane that he pounded on the floor to emphasize his point. His hair was white and thin and looked like it had been dried with a blender, scattered all over his head. He turned as Ali approached and when their eyes met, Ali was flooded with a deep affection. He felt as if he was looking at his second father, which Antonio had been after Ali's father died. Antonio limped toward him on his cane.

"Well look who has decided to come home!" he hollered. *Home?* Ali thought. *Yeah that was how it felt.* Antonio threw his arms around him and hugged him.

"Well, mi hijo, so you decided to return, is about time," He said when he released the hug.

"Hello Papi." Ali answered beginning to choke with emotion.

"Have you returned for good?" Antonio asked, studying his face.

"I am too old to fight anymore. I just came to say hello."

"Mi hijo, you are never too old to fight. Life is a fight, didn't you learn anything here?"

"Okay, I'm too old to compete then." Ali laughed.

"You are not too old to teach are you?" Antonio asked. "You know I always called you my little volcano, because of the way you exploded on your opponents. Listen Ali, a mountain has many sides, all of which lead to the top. Now, you have reached the top and you can show others how to do the same. Now get in there and show these two bums how it's done," Antonio said, throwing a pair of gloves into his chest. He turned and limped back towards the ring, a big smile on his face that Ali couldn't see. Ali also could not see the happy tears in his eyes.

rinted in the United States
42359LV00003B/11/P